UNDER

By AJ Chalkley

First edition; Printed in 2011

The text in this book is copyrighted by the author and is sold subject to the condition that it shall not be used or copied, in part or in its entirety, by anyone without prior consent from the author. The cover illustrations are also copyrighted by the author and is intended for use, solely on the cover of UNDER by AJ Chalkley. Copying of the illustrations by any means is prohibited without prior consent from the Author.

ISBN #: 978-1-4709-6250-0

Copyright © 2011 AJ Chalkley
All rights reserved.

WWW.RANDOMWORLDPRODUCTIONS.CO.UK

Random World Productions is a trading name of A and JE Chalkley

For my darling wife

UNDER

CHAPTER 1

Hillcroft House

The evening was clear and fresh, the air; cool, the sea swelling gently in the summer breeze and the stars twinkling through the cloudless sky. The moon was shining brightly and casting a reflection like a thousand diamonds across the water. Waves were slowly rolling onto the beach and lapping against Jasmine's bare feet as she sat silently on the sand. Behind her, up in the chalet the party continued; with music blaring and the sounds of people trying to enjoy themselves. Benny Marlow was reciting his repertoire of bad jokes and acting the fool as usual, a combination that seemed to delight Mary Sullivan who was desperately attracted to him; everyone else just cringed whenever he spoke. Most people were probably drinking far too much and starting to do some rather embarrassing dancing.

Jasmine knew she would not enjoy the party, but decided to go anyway, only to leave after about half an hour to sit in solitude on the beach. She felt she needed time on her own to think and go over the morning's events.

The time since she had first heard the news had been a landslide of feelings for Jasmine. First, there was the sudden shock, followed by a period of disbelief, and now the harsh reality and all the burdening questions that came with it. The rest of the day had been so busy that this was the first time the young woman had been able to simply stop and think, away from other distractions.

The tide was coming in fast and the water was soon washing over Jasmine's lap; soaking her shorts and the bottom of her T-shirt. She had always loved the sea, and did not care about the waves breaking around her. Her mind was totally engrossed and wondering in a sea of her own thoughts and emotions; she almost felt like her mind had drifted away from her body and was thinking on its own.

Failing her degree was not quite what she had planned for the end of the term. It had all gone so well for the first two years but for no real reason, Jasmine had found herself less interested in working hard, and her grades had been slipping throughout the final year. She could not quite understand why; Geology had always been the thing she loved the most and had always excelled in whilst at school. Perhaps the workload had become too much for her, or she had been too busy working at the local supermarket to study properly. However, it was not worth thinking about now; she could not change her grade. It might be possible for her to retake her final year again, but this setback had made Jasmine lose all interest in study. She needed something new to focus her mind on; something that she could work hard at and do well in, without having to do any more exams.

Jasmine had always believed she would do something worthwhile with her life, although exactly what that would be, was still a mystery to the 22 year old.

Another hour passed without Jasmine even realising. The wind was beginning to pick up, although it still was not particularly cold, it blew Jasmine's long dark hair across her face. The tide had come in as far as it would, leaving Jasmine sitting only a couple of metres into the water that rose and fell by just a few centimetres as each wave rolled in. The water, gently flowing around her legs and feet, felt relaxing and Jasmine wanted to be as relaxed as possible as she tried to plan what to do next. There were numerous options, but the one that kept appearing in her thoughts was to find a decent job and a nice quiet, but cheap, place to live. It seemed easy enough to decide to find a job, but what type of job should she go for? Every question that was answered just created more; a never-ending circle of decisions.

Jasmine's mother had died when she was five years old, although the memories of her mother were still strong in her mind; seventeen years later. She had never known her father, or what had happened to him, her mother would only say that he had other things to do and went away to do them.

After her mother had died, the young Jasmine grew up in a number of different foster homes until she went to university. She had never had the urge to keep in touch with any of her foster parents. Perhaps if any of them had adopted her properly she would have been more inclined to stay in contact, but she knew that the foster parents she had, although wonderfully kind, were there to bring up orphaned children, not young adults. Jasmine felt very alone in the world. She had friends, but no one she could rely on totally, no one she could open up to and talk to about her problems.

It would be very difficult to find somewhere to live; she had very little in savings and a lot of debt from her student loan. Jasmine was worried about what to do next but she was not particularly sad. Perhaps it would take a while for everything to sink in properly; there was always time for her to think things over carefully. She did not have to make all of her decisions whilst sat in the sea on a cool summers evening.

The young woman's thoughts were suddenly disturbed as a voice came smashing through the tranquillity like a hammer through a mirror. 'Fish!' the voice said loudly. Jasmine was suddenly more aware of her surroundings and stood up, her shorts dripping with seawater. Again the voice spoke, 'You a fish?'

Turning around Jasmine saw a dark figure standing at the edge of the water and two more a little way behind. The moon was shining on their faces, but the thin layer of cloud that had blown across its face dimmed the light. In the half-light it took Jasmine a few seconds to realise that it was Benny Marlow standing there with a beaming smile, and the people a few steps behind were Mary Sullivan and Toby Brookly: some of her fellow students.

They had all met at a party in their first year of university;

Jasmine had begun by talking to Toby, who she liked the most. Toby had introduced her to Benny. Jasmine had never understood why the mild mannered Toby was such good friends with the rather loud and brash Benjamin Marlow.

'Huh?' was the only word that Jasmine could think of to say. She felt like she had only just woken up, still a little confused, not switched on, and very embarrassed.

'Thought you was tryin' a be a fish; out there in the water.' Benny spoke with the worst grammar Jasmine had ever heard and a coarse east London accent. Benny was studying mechanical engineering and was surprisingly good at it. He was very tall, slim and good looking, with bleached blonde hair neatly spiked on his head. His clothes, however, were not as tidy as his hair; he wore baggy jeans with chains dangling around his knees, and a dirty football shirt. Most people grew out of wearing clothes like that when they became adults but Benny was far from being a grown up.

'I was just thinking about things,' Jasmine said as she walked out the water and stood near Benny. 'Just thinking and sitting, it was nice and peaceful.'

'Sorry if we disturbed the moment for you but we was thinking of going up to The House for a while, make the party a little more, how shall we say; interesting!' Benny was talking about an old deserted house up on the hill from the beach.

"Hillcroft House" had been deserted for many years and was very run down. It was a favourite place for young people from nearby to go and party in, and try to scare each other with tales of ghosts and ghouls.

'The chalet is starting to get a bit boring now,' Benny continued. 'Although, my jokes were certainly livening things up a bit. I don't think anyone else has gone to the house so there won't be anyone there that will annoy us.'

Jasmine thought for a bit whilst trying to wring some the seawater out of her shorts. 'I'm not in the mood for a party, that's why I just came and sat on the beach rather than being up at the chalet. I might just go back to Durrey's.' She was referring to Durraton Hawthorne Hall, the hall of residence that most of the university students lived in on the university campus; a huge nineteenth century hotel that had been converted into rooms for students. Although it had been modernised it still had an old feel about it and Jasmine liked to sit at the top of one of the stairwells. At night, the eastern stairs were quiet, with most people either in their rooms sleeping or in the common room socialising.

'Oh, come on Jazz, a party is just what you need. There will only be the four of us; you, me, Mary and Toby. Just come for a little bit, it's on your way home anyway so when you want to leave you're halfway there already. What do you think? Please Jazz.'

'I don't know, I...'

'I'm not taking no for an answer Jasmine Louise Smith! You're coming with us whether you like it or not. You will have fun and enjoy yourself.' Benny smiled and placed a hand on Jasmine's shoulder. 'Go on Jazz, it won't be the same if you're not there. Three's a crowd but four is lots of fun, and all that stuff.'

That sounded more like Benny, Jasmine thought to herself. He wanted to have some time alone with Mary but Toby always tagged along, and Benny wanted someone to keep him company. Jasmine had always liked Toby although she felt that his quiet personality was suppressed by the extrovert Benny. Toby would probably be a lot more outgoing if he had never made friends with Benny, but they were friends and close friends at that.

Jasmine sighed and reluctantly agreed, 'I will only stay for a little while and then I am going. Understood?'

'Excellent! Toby's got the beer, I've got my best ghost stories planned, Mary's bringing her torch and some candles; we're sorted!' Benny beamed a huge smile and turned. They met up with Mary and Toby further up the beach and continued towards the footpath.

It was a good fifteen-minute walk to Hillcroft House, along a narrow footpath that followed the edge of the beach for most of the way, before turning up the hill into the woods. The house could not be seen from the beach as the dense wood that covered the hillside shrouded it; this all added to the atmosphere a bit, as there was not much of a view either; just a lonely deserted house and its party residents.

The path was littered with potholes and tree roots; but the four had frequently walked along it, even in darkness, on their way to the beach and university chalet. It was something that first year students had to get used to, walking along the beach path at night. At the beginning of each year, when students started to find their way to the beach, there were always numerous amounts of twisted ankles and grazes from falling over the obstacles that littered the path.

Benny and Toby had marched on ahead and left Jasmine to talk to Mary. Mary was a kind and sweet person but spoke mostly of her love for Benny, and did not shy away from giving plenty of details. Jasmine half listened with one ear and used the other to listen to the relaxing sound of the wind in the trees and the waves rolling up the sandy beach.

The breeze was beginning to dry Jasmine's shorts and T-shirt but she started to feel cold. She longed to be somewhere warm, tucked up in bed with a good book or sitting on the eastern stairs; but felt that maybe she needed to have a bit of fun. Her mind had thought enough on the beach, now she could unwind.

The house loomed at the students as they passed the last clump of trees. It was a very big house, only two proper storeys but with lots of rooms in the roof space, with dormer windows jutting out from the red tiled roof. Most of the windows, once clean with woodwork painted white were now either broken or missing altogether. One of the chimneys on the left side of the house was crumbling, another completely missing. There were small trees and bushes growing all the way round in what were once beautiful gardens. The door had been broken off its hinges and lay splintered on the ground outside like a drawbridge, surrounded by empty beer cans and other party leftovers.

There was a strange, eerie feeling that seemed to emanate from the house; everyone that saw it would gasp momentarily at its forgotten, ghostly appearance. Some people at the university would never go to Hillcroft house, especially in the dark because they thought it really was haunted. Jasmine on the other hand did not believe in such things and had visited the house many times.

The group fought their way through the bramble bushes to the 'drawbridge' door and entered the house through the opening that had been left by the door's removal. The four students all seemed strangely silent, as they entered, not sure, if they should be talking, or being quiet in respect to the old house that stood in a deathly silence.

The vast main hall of the house had a few broken and dirty chairs and a large sofa in it; although the sofa, partly burnt, at the back, had definitely seen better days. Strewn about the floor were bricks and planks of wood, and leant against a fireplace was an old oak table. Even with its disarray, it was the best room in the house to party, or sit and talk.

The house must have been beautiful before it fell into disarray, Jasmine thought to herself as they looked around the main hall. The wallpaper had once been bright yellow, the furniture highly polished and the carpets swept clean. It was a pity to see it now in such a poor state of repair. Students over the years had certainly abused the house; there was the odd patch of graffiti and dozens of empty beer cans strewn about the floor.

The four made themselves at home by lighting a few candles and brushing as much dirt off the chairs as possible before sitting down. The table, once moved and placed properly on the floor, made an excellent footrest as well as somewhere to place the candles. Benny was happy in the fact he could tell ghost stories to scare the others, although his stories were normally quite obscene and disgusting. Jasmine had never really fallen for ghost stories but Toby, and Mary especially, seemed to become quite scared and anxious at the unbelievable stories.

Jasmine did find herself starting to relax as the evening moved on and the stories slowly turned to idle chatter. She felt she should not keep worrying, and just take each moment as it came. There would be many hardships ahead, but for now, she was going to forget her troubles and enjoy herself.

Slowly the questions began to drift out of her mind, still unanswered, but now distant and not important. Her body had relaxed too, her muscles felt less tired and her skin felt warm and soothed in the gentle candlelight.

The few remaining hours of the evening were pleasantly sailing by, although outside the wind was beginning to pick up, and the house seemed to creak and groan with each gust as if answering the whoosh of air. The four inside did not care about the weather outside or the lateness of the hour, they were too busy having fun; chatting laughing and playing silly games.

'It's got to be hide 'n' seek time,' Benny announced as he finished his third bottle of beer. 'Who is going to seek first?'

'Oh no Benny, I'll get scared,' Mary replied putting her arms around both Benny and Toby, who were sat either side of her.

'That's the whole point. What do you think Jazz? Toby?'

'I'm game,' answered Toby.

'Alright, I'll play as long as no one goes upstairs; I think some of the floors are rotten up there,' Jasmine said as Benny gave her a cheeky nudge with his elbow.

Childish games seemed right at home when students had parties. At Durrey's people often played hide and seek, truth or dare, and spin the bottle. Games they all used to play when they were about fourteen. Now in their late teens or early twenties, they had again become popular.

'Right, we'll hide first, and Jazz; you can come and find us. Just cover your eyes and count to fifty.'

Jazz sat back in her chair and covered her eyes with one of her hands. '1, 2, 3, 4,' she counted quietly so she could try and hear what direction the footsteps were going. '24, 25, 26, 27,' Jasmine started to feel a little nervous, and peeked out briefly from behind her hand. Unsurprisingly there was no one else in the room; the others were off busily trying to squeeze themselves into cupboards or behind curtains so as not to be seen.

'36, 37, 38, 39.' Jasmine hoped it would not take too long to find them. It would probably be fun but would definitely be a little eerie walking around the dark house on her own. Jasmine thought that Benny or Toby might try to jump out on her at some point, and Mary would probably not hide very well so she would be found as soon as possible.

The sounds of the wind outside seemed so much louder

without the others in the room; every creak and groan seemed like it was just outside Jasmine's ears. A cold shiver ran up her spine as there was one particularly strong gust of wind that shook the windows. Undeterred, Jasmine continued to count.

'47, 48, 49, 50! Ready or not; here I come.' Jasmine opened her eyes and looked around the room deciding on the best route to take. There were two corridors leading off the main hall and an archway into another room. There was also the main stairs but she knew they would not have gone up there.

Moonlight was shining brightly through one of the windows in the corridor to the right so she decided to take that one. It seemed the most obvious choice to go as it was the best lit. Jasmine picked up one of the candles and walked into the corridor.

Treading very quietly, Jasmine moved down the corridor checking every nook and cranny for signs of life. A door partway down opened into a small bathroom, it was empty except for a broken basin, and for some unknown reason; a car's exhaust.

Moonlight shining through the broken windows and the gentle flicker of candlelight made it bright enough for Jasmine to see where she was going but also cast long dark shadows that hid some corners. Jasmine had to search these corners carefully with the candle trying not to let it blow out. Occasionally drips of hot wax would tumble onto her fingers and she had to pick it off when it cooled.

Jasmine carefully looked into every room down the corridor but found no one. At the far end of the corridor was a curtain, hanging from a broken rail. It was possible there was someone behind it. It was a long red curtain made from a heavy material that clearly showed something behind it. Jasmine carefully listened for any sounds; but there was none, and the wrinkles in the curtain did not move an inch. Was there someone behind the curtain? Jasmine would have to walk right up to the curtain and check.

Taking a few more steps towards the curtain there was a slight creaking and rattling beneath Jasmine's feet. She froze with shock for a few seconds before taking another step forward.

Jasmine's eyes were fixed on the curtain up ahead; it was less than three metres away now. The floorboards creaked again as she took another step, but much louder this time. A blood chilling horror suddenly struck Jasmine as she felt the floorboards beneath her move; they gave up supporting the weight on them and began breaking.

Desperately Jasmine tried to decide whether to quickly run or to carefully walk back to where she had come from and hopefully safer ground. It took less than a second to decide but it was too late, a huge section of floor gave up completely and fell, carrying the terrified Jasmine along with it. The sound of splintering wood and cracking timbers was deafening, matched only in loudness by Jasmine's screams. The air was filled with dust and fragments of wood as she fell into the black void below.

Jasmine did not know how far she fell but landed with a thud on the mangle of broken wood. The ground she had fallen on wasn't flat; it was a dark uneven slope and Jasmine found herself sliding into an even darker abyss; frantically trying to grab at something to stop her decent.

The slope ended abruptly and Jasmine fell vertically again. There was a tremendous rumble above and some rocks started to fall from the opening Jasmine had just fallen from. Luckily, she managed to roll out of the way before the entire roof of the slope caved in. There was an eerie yellow/green light emanating from somewhere, so Jasmine watched with fear as the rock and earth tumbled down with an almighty crash and thud.

Stunned and shocked by the experience, Jasmine sat on the floor clutching her knees to her chest. Tears began to roll down her dirt-covered cheeks. She cried out for help, but after the tremendous noise of the cave-in, there was only silence in return.

Jasmine sat unable to move for a long time before carefully feeling across her body for injuries. Remarkably, there was nothing seriously wrong. A few bruises that would be painful for a few days and grazed elbows and knees that were seeping with only the smallest amount of blood; were the only injuries she had suffered. Thankful for her survival she stood shakily, and started to look around the small chamber she was standing in. It looked like a cave or a mine; rough walls, dug out from solid rock. The faint light and dust-filled air made it very difficult for Jasmine to see, especially any details; everything was just a blur. The candle Jasmine had been carrying had gone out although she still clutched it tightly in her hand.

Frantically Jasmine tried to see if she could dig her way back up through the hole she had come down, and started to pull rocks and clumps of earth down from the mound and throw them behind her. It took several minutes of hard labour to decide it was impossible; there were some huge boulders filling the gap that she or even the strongest man in the world would not be able to shift without mechanical help.

Tears were again rolling down Jasmine's face as she started to look around some more. The ceiling was propped up in some places with old wooden beams. The floor was strewn with rubble from the cave-in, and at the far end were two small tunnels. Jasmine walked over to the two tunnels and noticed one was completely blocked off by another cave in, but the other was open and light. Jasmine's head was spinning partly from shock and partly from trying to understand what had just happened and where the light was coming from.

Jasmine felt a slight excitement building inside her as she walked down the tunnel. It was cut out of the rock but there were no wooden support beams like she had seen in the first cave. 'Could this be a way out?' She wondered.

The excitement Jasmine felt grew less as she found the tunnel led downwards instead of up. At times there would be junctions or small chambers, but all other tunnels had been blocked off or led so steeply up or down hill that Jasmine could not walk along them. The strange seemingly source-less light continued to shine throughout the tunnels, although slightly brighter in some places than in others. There were no light bulbs, candles or anything that could explain the glow.

Jasmine walked for about ten minutes through the long tunnel but finding no way out; or anything else in fact. There was no sign of this being a mine, except for the shape of the tunnels and the first few wooden roof supports. The tunnel was the size and shape Jasmine imagined mine tunnels to be, but there was no sign of machinery or tools.

Jasmine stopped at one particular tunnel junction, a meeting point of four tunnels in a crossroads. The exits to the left and right led almost vertically down and the exit ahead was completely dark, not even a faint point of light could be seen down the tunnel. It was as if there was a huge black curtain hanging over the entrance.

There was no choice except to walk down the dark tunnel. Shaking with nerves Jasmine edged her way into the tunnel, it was darker than she could have possibly imagined; all of her senses seemed dulled. The sound of her feet on the dusty ground seemed distant, the musty smell was harder to detect and of course, there was nothing that Jasmine could see.

Jasmine had only moved a few metres down the dark tunnel when she found the air in front of her resisting her movement. It seemed thick and elastic; trying to push her back the way she had come. It was a strange sensation that could not be explained; the young women had never experienced anything like this before.

There was nowhere to go back to; either she continued through the darkness, or go back and wait where she first fell through. Jasmine placed the candle she was still carrying in her pocket and carefully felt her way along the walls. This tunnel was narrower than the others were and Jasmine found she could touch both sides at the same time.

The darkness was tightening around Jasmine's chest making it harder to breathe and there was an unpleasant coldness on her skin that made her shiver with fear. Every footstep was a struggle and every breath painful, when would this darkness end? Jasmine longed to be in the light again and feel the air softly around her, not resisting her every movement.

Jasmine's heart was pounding in her chest; she was blinded by darkness and choking on the thick stale air. Even an attempt to cough seemed to be stifled.

The trip into the darkness seemed never to end, with every

step the darkness closed around her more. Jasmine wondered if she was breathing in toxic fumes. She knew mines, especially coalmines, could contain methane and other toxic gasses. In desperation, Jasmine held her arm across her mouth trying to breathe through her dusty sleeve. It did not help much; the air was still thick and painful to breathe.

Still the darkness continued; a dark void of nothingness; empty, cold and lifeless.

Exhausted and confused Jasmine pushed on, struggling against the thick stale air. Her mind was set on getting through, but she doubted if her body would keep going. This dark tunnel may never end; it may lead to nowhere or a dead end, in which case Jasmine would have to walk back again.

Her weary body carried her slowly onwards until she came to a point where the darkness seemed, for a moment, to have a tiny shard of light in it. Stopping dead, Jasmine wondered if her mind was playing tricks on her or if there really was a slight flicker of light. Had she really seen it? It seemed to have been there for only a fraction of a second before it was gone.

The flicker sprang to life again, brighter this time; a single strand of light right in front of her face.

Mesmerised by its brightness after the immense darkness; Jasmine watched as it flickered about in front of her. It was like a thin crack in the darkness, perhaps a barrier where light could break through the thick, dark air. If it was a barrier, Jasmine could see nothing of the other side through such a tiny gap that only showed itself for a brief second. Jasmine stepped forward and pushed hard to get through what seemed to be the thickest patch of dark air.

Almost immediately, Jasmine found herself in a small cave similar to the first cave she had fallen into. The air was suddenly soft and Jasmine could breathe easily. She slumped to the floor to rest her tired body, filling her lungs with fresh air. Had Jasmine been anywhere else she would have realised that the air she was now breathing was not particularly fresh, just a lot nicer in comparison to the dark tunnel.

It took Jasmine several minutes to recover from her ordeal

in the darkness but as she slowly felt better, she began to look around.

There were piles of dust and rubble on the floor, a high ceiling propped up by more wooden beams and a door!

'A door?' Jasmine said aloud in amazement. 'Surely mines don't have doors like that in them.' In this strange underground cavern, there was a door. It was huge, and made entirely of wood; its frame built into the rock. It was dark and dusty but Jasmine could see that it was covered with fine carvings of people and buildings. Every centimetre of the wood was carved; some carvings in relief, some cut into the wood. There was a pile of rubble in front of the door and large boulders to the left and right.

Jasmine stepped across the rubble gazing at the great door set deep in its frame. She gently traced her hand across the ornate carvings. They were incredibly intricate and detailed. Some parts; having been touched by a thousand hands over the years had been worn smooth, other parts of finer detail had suffered damage; by means no one alive would remember. This door had not been touched or perhaps even seen in a very long time.

Even in its ageing state, its size and construction gave it a dominant presence in the chamber. Jasmine had never seen a more imposing door before in her life. In some of the older parts of her university, Jasmine had seen huge wooden doors made from English Oak, but even they were small in comparison.

With slight nervousness, Jasmine pushed against the giant wooden structure. The little push was not enough to move it. Perhaps it was locked from the other side; although there was not a keyhole, handle, or anything on this side. 'Maybe I should knock first,' Jasmine thought to herself.

Jasmine pushed again; harder. This time, with a loud creak, the door reluctantly moved inwards. Jasmine's heart jumped at the sound and she stepped back, lost her balance on the uneven ground and fell. The door closed again with an almighty bang that seemed to shake the very foundations of the world. Dust fell from the roof and settled on Jasmine's hair and clothes.

Half stunned, Jasmine picked herself up and brushed off the grey/white dust. Her heart was now pounding hard in her chest, and beads of sweat appeared on her forehead. She plucked up courage, she was determined! For no apparent reason, Jasmine felt she must open the door. She lent her shoulder against the edge and used her whole weight to shove against the stubborn door. It creaked loudly and groaned again; but, at last, it moved.

It was actually beginning to open as Jasmine put all her strength into pushing the door. A faint light appeared through the gap as the immense piece of wood moved. The hinges screamed in pain, gone were the days of sitting dormant; now they had a life and a voice.

After a little more pushing, the gap was large enough to get through. In one quick movement, Jasmine jumped through, landing awkwardly on the other side and falling to the ground again. A mighty thud echoed through the world as the door closed.

Jasmine was through, but through to where?

In Hillcroft house, Benny and Mary had found the hole in which Jasmine had fallen. The incredibly loud noise of the floor collapsing had sounded throughout the house; alerting them as they hid.

Due to the cave-in, all they could see at the bottom was a basement floor littered with rubble and planks of wood. Unknown to the onlookers, the sidewall of the cellar had cracked and broken, allowing a stream of earth to flow inside. The earth had filled the sloping tunnel Jasmine had slid down. The extra planks on top that had fallen from the floor above during the cave-in acted to hide any trace to the chute.

'You don't think she fell down there, do you Benny?' Mary asked shining her torch around in the dark hole.

'Don't be daft; if she had fallen we would see her. It probably fell on its own, there's no sign of Jazz down there.'

At that moment, Toby showed up carrying a candle. 'I can't find her anywhere outside. Any luck in here?'

Benny shook his head. 'We haven't seen her at all. She

probably got scared when the floor collapsed and ran back to Durrey's. It was a really loud noise; it scared me for a while.'

'I don't want to stay any more, let's go home. Benny, I want to go back to Durrey's.' Mary pulled on her boyfriend's arm.

'Perhaps we should go. I'm sure we'll find her later on back in her room,' Toby added. 'Just think of the stories you could come up with about how Jasmine ran away scared.'

Benny was unsure what to do. He felt a little guilty as it had been his idea to come to Hillcroft house, his idea to play hide and seek and even his idea that Jasmine should seek first. Looking down the hole, he was convinced that Jasmine was not down there. 'Alright let's go home. If she isn't back at Durrey's we can come back here and look for her.'

The rest of the group nodded in agreement and they walked back to the main hall of the house. While they had been searching the house, some of the candles had burnt out leaving rings of white wax on the table. Toby picked up the remainder of the beer cans, and the group walked out of the door.

Outside, large clouds had hidden the moon and it was dark. Mary turned on her torch to help them see the narrow footpath. They had no idea that Jasmine had fallen into somewhere much darker without a torch or anything to light her way.

CHAPTER 2

The Great Corridor

Jasmine slowly lifted her head to look around the room she was now laying in. It was a perfect cube, no more than five metres across. All the walls and even the ceiling were covered in the same wooden carvings as the great door, although most had been decorated further with delicate gold leaf and small white beads.

The floor was hard; Jasmine had felt it when she had fallen. It was a strange brown/green colour, and perfectly smooth. It felt cold to the touch, like stone, but there was no sign of it being separate slabs, just one giant piece of polished rock. The light in the room was vivid yellow and the gold leaf of the walls and ceiling glinted brightly. However, there was no sign of where the light was coming from; no lamps or candles or anything to generate the yellow glow. There were three other doors in the room, one on every side and the great door behind making the fourth. The three other doors were much smaller and painted yellow and cream and did not have any carvings.

Jasmine gasped as she saw a man standing by one of the doors. She hadn't noticed him at first. That was very strange, how did she manage to miss seeing him standing there right in front of her? He was wearing a long red tunic and a strange red cap with gold lettering that Jasmine did not understand. In his left hand, he carried a small cloth bag in a similar material to his tunic but yellow in colour. He looked very old, grey hair appeared from under his hat and he had a long beard and moustache. His skin looked weathered and grey; his eyes were just small points peering outwards although he did not appear to be looking at anything in particular.

Standing up slowly and nervously Jasmine spoke to him.

'Excuse me, can you help me?'

'Move along!' The man said with a deep booming voice. 'I am waiting.'

'What is this place? Who are you? Where am I? Oh please help please…' Jasmine said sobbing. She was terrified and desperately wanted someone to help her.

'I am Rothgoe and I am waiting. You are here in this room,' the man boomed in reply.

'What are you waiting for? Oh I have so many questions.' Even when Jasmine stood right in front of the man, he appeared not to look at her.

The man did not move his eyes to look at Jasmine; he just stood perfectly still. 'I am waiting for my master; Balmore of Terrol. I am Rothgoe.'

'Please can you help me?' Jasmine said desperately.

'Move along. I am Rothgoe, I am waiting for my master; Balmore of Terrol.'

Jasmine did not know what to say. The man acted like a robot, saying only a few sentences over and over again in reply to any question.

'Argh!' Jasmine winced with pain. Her head began to throb with a pain like she had never felt before. A sharp pain seemed to ripple through every nerve in her body. It felt as if the room was squashing her, squeezing the life from her body. Jasmine's vision started to spin and she felt sick.

Without thinking, Jasmine opened the small door in the left-hand wall of the room. The room through the doorway seemed the same as the one she was in but every dimension was at least three times the size. She dashed through and the door swung closed behind her.

'What do you think you are doing going in there young lady? Did you not see the sign?' An old woman in a tatty dress came bustling over to her from a desk in a corner or the room. 'How long have you been in there? You people from the Catacombs don't have a single bit of sense in your heads. That's a Tamboli room; didn't you see the Tamboli symbol on the door?' The woman pointed to a blue symbol painted on the door Jasmine had just come through. Jasmine glanced briefly but did not look properly as she was frightened and her head was still throbbing with pain.

The woman knelt down and looked inquisitively into Jasmine's eyes. Her face seemed kind and she smiled gently. The pain in Jasmine's head seemed to be ebbing away after a minute or two, but she slumped down against the wall in floods of tears. 'I need some help!' She said between sobs.

'I am sorry that I shouted dear, but it was very silly of you to go in there. Not that you should be over here at all you understand.' The woman used the edge of her dress to wipe away Jasmine's tears. 'It's all alright. I imagine you're not feeling too good after being in there, and without your felostone as well. It is no wonder you're upset, I think you should go back to where you came from. I'm not sure if you are from the City or the Catacombs but you can't stay here. There is a door over there, go on now; off you go.'

'This is the way back?' Jasmine said pointing to the door. She did not know what to say or do anymore. She had met two strange people; one that only said a few sentences and the other that spoke more and quicker than Jasmine could keep up with. She wondered when she would wake up from this dream. Maybe she was on the ground after falling through the floor in Hillcroft House; her head spinning in a false reality after being knocked unconscious, but this all seemed so very real.

Jasmine wondered momentarily if she should stay and speak to the woman or just leave. If the door was a way back, she should probably take it.

The door the woman had gestured to; was opposite the door she had just come through and it was identical in every way except for a large gold leaf letter C embossed in its centre.

Jasmine thanked the woman and without saying another word she stood, opened the door and walked through; not quite sure what to expect on the other side.

It was a corridor about ten metres in length and decorated in the same carved wooden panelling as the square rooms. The light was a lot brighter in the corridor although, again, Jasmine could not see where it was coming from. The yellow/green light just seemed to appear out of the ceiling and flood the room. It was a strange light, not only in colour but in its brightness as well. It was very bright, as bright as a summer's day, but it didn't hurt her eyes. She did not have to scrunch her eyes up to protect them. It was strange to be in such a bright room that did not dazzle at all.

At the far end of the corridor was a door, again identical to the door the opposite end. If anybody stood in the middle and spun round a few times; they would never know which way they were facing.

The door opened into another identical room. In fact, this room looked more than just identical; it *was* the same room. The old woman she had just left was there; sitting at her desk.

'Oh my dear! What are you doing back here?' The woman stood again and came over to Jasmine. 'Don't you know how to use the conveyance corridors? If you people from the Catacombs are to keep coming into the City, then you should learn how things work up here.'

'What happened? How did I get back here? That doesn't make sense.' Jasmine was confused and a little worried; she had not turned around or turned a corner or anything. It was impossible to get back to this room by walking in a straight line. This had to be a bizarre dream.

'You just have to think about where you want to go and then you will get there.' The woman opened the door and stepped through. 'I can take you as far as the 'Great Corridor' but I can't go any further than that. You will have to find your own way from there.'

Jasmine followed the woman as she walked down the corridor and out the other end. Jasmine was surprised to find they did not end up in another room.

They were in a long corridor or gallery. The side Jasmine was facing was a series of wide columns; curved at the top to form wide arches. Each arch was decorated with a golden moon set in relief at its top. There were subtle carvings around each of the columns and a low brick wall at the bottom; turning each archway into a glassless window.

The door clicked behind her and Jasmine turned to see the old woman had gone. Looking left and right Jasmine saw that the corridor seemed never ending in both directions; it just went on and on into infinity. It was a complete contrast to the small rooms and corridors she had just come from. This place was huge; the ceiling was over the height of an entire house and you could easily drive a bus down its width.

There were people walking down the corridor in both directions. They were mostly men but there were a few women as well; all dressed in exactly the same long grey jackets and dark trousers. Their faces were expressionless as they walked.

One of the people bumped into Jasmine as she stood in awe at the strangeness of the people and the size of this impressive corridor. The man who had bumped into Jasmine did not seem to notice her and walked into the conveyance corridor that Jasmine had just come through. Jasmine had to step out of the way quickly to avoid being bumped into again, and she walked across to one of the arches on the opposite side of the walkway to avoid the people as they walked.

The corridor was divided in half by a gold line running down its centre. The floor of the side closest to the door was of smooth flat marble; white with pink and green flecks. The side running along by the arches where Jasmine now stood was made of rough-cut stone slabs of dark grey. None of the people in the grey jackets seemed to be walking anywhere except on the smooth marble.

As Jasmine turned around, she noticed there was more than one door. In fact, there was a whole line of them running as far as the eye could see in both directions down the corridor. Identical in construction but some had a gold letter C embossed on the centre and a few had a blue circle design painted on with blue paint. The paint looked as if it had been put on with a stick rather than a brush, as it was very rough and untidy. It spoilt the overall imposing effect of the corridor slightly but Jasmine was still impressed with its vastness. The old woman Jasmine had just met had said it was the symbol of Tamboli. Jasmine thought to herself that maybe they were rooms that were 'out of bounds' for some reason. The old woman did seem shocked that Jasmine had been in a room with the symbol of Tamboli painted on the front.

'Hello? Can you help me? Hello? Excuse me!' Jasmine tried to get the attention of one of the people walking up and down. They all looked at her blankly and walked on, saying nothing. One or two frowned heavily but most just looked blank and ignored her.

'How rude!' Jasmine thought to herself. 'Why won't they talk to me?' She had so many questions and she wanted answers.

Jasmine started to walk down the corridor looking for someone that was not wearing a grey jacket. She decided to keep to one side of the corridor away from the walkway where the people were. She did not want to get bumped into again.

Occasionally as she walked, Jasmine looked out through one of the stone arches, but there was nothing to be seen, just a bright light shining down from the top and darkness below. The light in this place seemed very different from what Jasmine was used to. The light from the arch windows was yellow/green in colour and seemed to get brighter every now and then would fade back to its normal intensity.

Jasmine must have walked for a good fifteen minutes without seeing any change in the corridor. At times there were more doors with the blue Tamboli symbol and at other times there were more blank doors, or more with the gold letter C. The number of men in grey jackets had also started to decrease, now there was only a few walking down the corridor. Jasmine had seen a lot of men go into different doors as she had been walking.

In the distance was something that caught Jasmine's eye, although she could not quite work out what it was. It was near one of the arches and it was big, far too big to be a person. As Jasmine walked towards it, she was aware of the sound of trickling water.

The object slowly came more into view and Jasmine saw it was round and made of stone and there was a figure sat on its edge. It was a fountain. The circular fountain was curved inwards at the top forming a little seat all the way round. In its centre was a large, dark brown rock from which water appeared at the top and tricked down. The water seemed crystal clear as it bubbled gently over the smooth dark rock.

Ignoring the figure that was sat looking out one of the stone arches, Jasmine splashed some water on her face to clean it. Then, cupping her hands together, Jasmine lifted some of the ice-cold water to her mouth and drank deeply. It was refreshing and tasted wonderful.

Jasmine drank a few more mouthfuls of the delicious water, and then her attention was drawn to the figure sat at the opposite end of the fountain. Although Jasmine could not see his face she could tell he was of similar age to her and had long blonde hair draping down over his shoulders. He was wearing a frayed brown jacket and three quarter length trousers held up with string. All of his clothes were full of holes and filthy dirty.

'Excuse me,' Jasmine said to the boy. There was no reply, or any sign that he had heard. Jasmine spoke again, adding a little tap on the shoulder to get his attention. 'Excuse me.'

The boy's head turned around instantly, his blonde hair flowing around his shoulders. He said nothing. His face seemed very cute to Jasmine, his skin pale and soft and he had bright, blue eyes.

'Sorry to bother you,' Jasmine continued. 'I was just...'

'Who are you? And why are you talking to me?' The boy asked inquisitively but not unkindly. His face had a rather puzzled look about it. Jasmine was confused to why the boy spoke so calmly but looked shocked.

'I'm Jasmine. I need some help. I just arrived here and...'

'Catacombs, right?' The boy questioned, interrupting her again.

'Well no, I...'

'Not surprised you need help, coming all the way up here.' The worried look about his face seemed to melt away and he started to beam with a cheeky smile. 'Lost are you?'

Jasmine sat on the fountain next to the boy. The stone was

cold and very smooth, and had almost a polished finish to it. 'Please let me explain.' Jasmine was getting tired of his interruptions; she was not going to get anywhere continuing on like that. 'For starters; I am not from the Catacombs, wherever they are. I was with my friends in this big old house near my university in…'

'Where?' The boy started to look puzzled again.

'Hillcroft house…England?' The boy shook his head as Jasmine spoke. 'You have no idea where I am talking about do you?'

'Sorry,' he said in reply with a slight smile.

Jasmine noticed that there were no longer any men with grey jackets walking down the corridor. They were alone in the great stone expanse.

'Maybe we should start again. My name is Jasmine, but most people just call me Jazz. What's your name?'

'Erm?' The boy seemed to have to think before answering. 'Malmayorkia. Why do you have two names?'

'Jazz is my nickname, like a short name. Do you have a nickname, Malmay…orpia? That's a very long name.' Jasmine was beginning to get a little bewildered.

'No I don't have a nickname. Everyone that speaks to me calls me Malmayorkia. What would my nickname be?'

'Well, Malmayorkia,' Jasmine said slowly; practising his name. She paused for a minute to think. 'How about Mal; it's just a short version of your name. What do you think?'

'I like it, but why do I need it?' Mal asked in reply to his new name.

Now it was Jasmine's turned to look confused. 'Have you never heard of nicknames before? They are names that your friends call you.'

'Oh I don't really have many proper friends. Only Kohrstan and his father, I used to live with them. I often see Kohrstan at the Givings but he calls me Malmayorkia.'

'The Givings? What is that? Is it somewhere near here?' Jasmine enquired looking down the deserted corridor.

Mal shook his head. 'No it's over the top of the City. Where did you say you were from again?'

'I'm originally from Bristol in England but I am away at university at the moment. I don't know how to explain to you where these places are. I'm from ...*outside!*'

Mal laughed loudly. 'Now I know you're from the Catacombs. There isn't anything outside the City, only Paluuka's Temple and you can't live there.'

As Mal finished speaking a distant bell chimed three times. He lifted his head instantly and started to look out of the arch windows. Jasmine still could not see anything except for light above and darkness below when she glanced in the direction Mal was looking.

Mal quickly jumped to his feet and grabbed Jasmine's hand. 'The stones are rising,' Mal said with urgency in his voice. 'We have to go now.'

Jasmine got to her feet to follow him without thinking. There was a loud rumbling as they started to run down the Great Corridor. Jasmine did not understand how Mal knew where he was headed; the entire corridor looked the same. To the right were the stone arches with their gold moons at the top, to the left was the line of identical doors.

Although they were running for a couple of minutes, the end of the corridor was still too distant to see. The corridor was still blurring into the distance with no sign of ending or altering in any way.

It took Jasmine a while to notice that the light from beyond the arch windows was slowly fading; becoming less intense, as if the sun was going down in this subterranean city.

A little more running and Mal slowed to a stop and opened a door. It was another corridor with the gold letter C on the front. The pair walked the length of the corridor and opened the door at the other end into a small room with a domed ceiling. The ceiling was made of a single piece of glass moulded into a perfect hemisphere and rested delicately on golden columns built into the circular wall. At the far end of the room; which was no more than a few metres away was another door, with two smaller doors to the left and right. The room was filled with the same yellow/green light that Jasmine had encountered in all the other rooms, but it was now slightly dimmer, like the light fading in the Great Corridor.

Mal opened the door to the right and ushered Jasmine in. The room inside was different to any other room Jasmine had seen so far. It was not as light as the others were. There was only a small amount of light emanating from the ceiling, but it was enough to see.

The room was square and similar in size to the first room Jasmine had been in, after getting through the big wooden door at the entrance to the City. The décor in this room was completely different though. There was none of the usual carvings or gold leaf patterning. The walls were bare, grey stone with scratches and chips on some blocks. The floor of rough-cut flagstones was uneven, but half-covered in dark brown blankets. There were more blankets made from the coarse, brown material stacked unevenly in the corner of the room next to a small battered wooden chest. Around the room were piles of dirt and rubbish that had been scraped up together as if swept with a broom, but there was not one in sight. A musty smell dominated the room, but it was not too unpleasant. Mal offered Jasmine a folded blanket to sit on.

It took Jasmine several minutes to get her breath back from all the running. Mal did not seem to be out of breath at all. Jasmine wondered if the air down here was thinner, and his lungs had adapted to this condition.

'Why did we have to leave there so suddenly?' Jasmine asked when she had enough breath to talk.

'I told you; the stones were rising.' Mal opened the small wooden chest and took out two small stone cups and a thin bottle; too dirty on the outside to see its contents. Mal had been between Jasmine and the chest so she could not see anything else that was in it.

Jasmine was very confused, a little scared and anxious, but most of all intrigued about the world she had quite literally *fallen* into. 'What are the stones? Remember I am not from around here I don't know anything about this place.'

Mal poured a pale blue liquid from the bottle into both of the cups. 'The stones rise at night and cover the lights in the roof. There aren't any other lights in the Great Corridor and you wouldn't want to get lost there in the dark.'

'Where am I Mal?' Jasmine asked after a short pause.

'In my room of course, I am not likely to take you anywhere else when the stones have risen, am I?'

'I meant this whole place, the big corridor we were just in, the conveyance corridors, the rooms, everything. What's it all part of?'

'It's the City of Martiblak. It's named after the man who dug out the main chamber that holds the lake.'

'Tell me more Mal, I am interested to know.' Jasmine tried a sip of her drink. It was very sweet and pleasant to drink although it did not taste like anything Jasmine had tried before.

'I'm afraid I don't know much. Just the name, and that people live here, and there's a lake in the main chamber surrounding the City. That's about all I know.'

'Ok well, tell me about the people. How many people live here and do any of them ever go to the surface?'

'The surface of what?' Mal asked in reply.

Jasmine's head was spinning with confusion again. Could it be possible that the people of this City had never been to the earth's surface? Just lived their entire lives underground in a strange city. 'The world above here, where you are outside, with no roof above you; just the sky.'

'You mean the Old World. Nobody would go there because it doesn't exist; it's only a myth.' Mal finished his drink and poured himself a second cupful.

'What if it's not a myth? I think I am from what you call the Old World Mal. This is the first time I have been here underground.'

Mal wiped a hand across his face and started to look nervous. 'You mean the Old World really *does* exist?'

'Yes I am from there. I fell down this big hole in this old house and found myself in a tunnel that led me here to the City.' Jazz spoke excitedly, thinking that Mal was beginning to understand where she came from.

It took many more hours of painstaking explanation for Mal to fully understand and believe where Jasmine had come from. She would describe every detail of the world outside; most of which Mal could not imagine, no matter how hard he tried. He had never heard of the sun or the sky. He had heard of the moon but did not know what it was; he thought it was just a symbol that people had carved on the walls in some parts of the City.

Mal listened intently to everything Jasmine had to say and asked many questions, and tried to answer all of her questions in return.

Jasmine learnt that the entire city was built upon a small island in the centre of an underground lake. Mal did not know how big the island was because no one had ever walked across it; they always used the conveyance corridors to get from one place to another. Mal explained there was a whole network of conveyance corridors around the City and you could travel to almost anywhere you wanted to go, just by thinking of the place you wanted to go to. As fictional as it sounded, Jasmine had already been through a corridor and ended up back in the same room she had just been through so she could quite believe it.

The City itself was one giant circular building that filled the entire island; there was not anywhere except the City that you could go to. The water from the lake lapped against the stonework of the City. Jasmine wondered if the City was on the island or if it, in fact, *was* the island.

'What about the Catacombs?' Jasmine asked at one point.

Mal explained that below the water level of the lake, the City's circumference was much bigger, although how big he did not know, and he did not know how many levels there were to that part of the City either. The area below the water line was not as developed as the upper parts of the City, just rough stone tunnels cut into the rock and no conveyance corridors. 'There are lots of corridors and tunnels leading in every direction and unless you live there and know your way around; you will get lost and never find your way out. You would be there forever.' Mal explained with a slight fear in his voice. 'The lesser people live there.'

After some explaining, Jasmine understood that the lesser people were a lower class of people and were supposed to live only in the Catacombs and never come into the City. The tops were the upper class and lived in the City. The two people rarely mixed and it was frowned upon for a lesser person to come into the City. It was completely unheard of for a top to go into the Catacombs so Mal did not know much about it.

Jasmine now understood why the men and women in the grey jackets had ignored her when she was in the Great Corridor; they thought she was a lesser person from the Catacombs. The old woman she had met also thought she was from the Catacombs.

The people in the grey jackets, Mal explained, were the 'tenders' of the 'Givings'; a massive expanse at the top of the City where trees grew and plants were grown for food. It was the job of the tenders to care for the plants and trees, pick the ripe fruits, and lay them out to be eaten. They would also collect seeds, and plant new trees and fruit bushes. They were a type of gardener/farmer all in one. Jasmine was interested to see trees growing underground but Mal told her they could not go out whilst the stones had risen so they would have to wait for them to fall.

The light around the City was generated by a chemical found in the rocks at the top of the cavern the City was built in. Long ago, when the City was being built; people climbed to the top of the cavern, collected some of the chemical, and covered the ceilings and some of the walls with it; so it was light inside. Apparently, the stones were giant covers that were lifted by a huge machine to cover the light source in the ceiling and make it darker. For some reason the lights painted on the ceilings and walls inside also dimmed when the stones had risen but Mal did not know why.

At a number of different times, Mal had spoken about the City being built or constructed but seemed confused when Jasmine asked him where the people had come from. Myth says they came from the Old World above the City but that, until he had met Jasmine, was only myth so had never really understood how the people started to live in the City. Mal still found it a little hard to accept that the Old World was anything more than Myth.

Jasmine was amazed when Mal spoke about the Great Corridor where she had met him. It was not a straight corridor that went on forever at all, but a circular one that ran all the way round the City. It was an optical illusion that makes it look like it goes straight on.

Mal became very quiet when Jazz asked him about his family, he said he had a younger sister, but would not give details about where she was now. He also explained that his parents had died when he was very young.

Jasmine was very confused, tired and hungry and slowly fell asleep on one of the blankets. It had been a very strange day and it had taken its toll on the young woman. She slept soundly all night. Oblivious to her as she slept, Mal covered her with the warmest blanket he had so she did not get cold, and out of decency slept in the domed room next door.

All of the corridors with all of their splendour were empty and quiet. The columns in the Great Corridor stood silent, watching in every direction for any souls that maybe about. There was nobody to be seen, and there was no creaking of doors or sounds of footsteps on the stone floor. The whole population were safe and sound in their home rooms, not wanting to wander around the communal areas of the City whilst it was dark.

When the stones had risen, Mal normally felt more alone than ever, but for once in his life, that he could remember, he had a friend sleeping in the adjacent room. Mal was very worried for her and understood little of whom she was or where she came from, but was pleased that he had met her and decided to help her as much as she needed. Mal thought that maybe one day she would take him to her world and see all the things she had spoken of; a sun sounded very interesting.

CHAPTER 3

A Strange World

Jasmine woke in the morning to a loud thud that rumbled through the walls and floors like an earthquake. The sound lasted only a brief second but in that time she was awake and terrified. She found out later that it was the stones lowering themselves back to their daytime resting-place.

It took Jasmine at least five minutes to remember where she was and how she had got there. Mal's face was the first thing she remembered and she wondered where he was; he was nowhere to be seen in the small stone room. The day before had probably been the strangest one in her life. Jasmine had seen many strange things and met some strange people, and she wondered what today would bring.

As Jasmine stood up and looked around the room further; her attention was drawn to the small wooden chest that Mal had gone into the night before, to get the cups and drink that they had drunk together. She was curious to know what other possessions Mal had in the chest, but felt it would be too rude to look. After all, Mal seemed very kind and Jasmine did not want to risk offending him in any way. She decided to go through the door and look for Mal, although she knew she would have to be careful or risk getting lost.

After her fears of getting lost, Jasmine found she did not have to go far to find Mal, he was in the next room yawning loudly. 'Good morning Mal.' Jasmine said cheerily, but froze suddenly as she saw another man in the room. He was taller than Mal and muscular although he looked similar age. His hair was short and dark, and his long green shirt was clean and well presented.

'Jazz, this is Kohrstan; the man I spoke of yesterday,' Mal

gestured towards the man who stepped forward smiling. 'Kohrstan; this is Jasmine, but we can call her Jazz. Jazz is a nickname.'

'Pleased to meet you,' Jasmine said to the man smiling nervously in return.

'So you are Jasmine, the woman from the old world. I was beginning to wonder if you really existed; Malmayorkia had told me about you and said you were asleep. I'm afraid I doubted what he said.' Kohrstan's voice was mellow and calm and did not seem as surprised as Mal had been when he had first met her. It appeared Mal had told Kohrstan about her and where she had come from.

'Do you live in the City too?' Jasmine realised the silliness of her question almost immediately, but she was trying to make conversation.

'Of course I do, do I look like I come from the Catacombs?' Kohrstan spoke, not with rudeness, but more with sarcasm or jest. Jasmine found that his way of speaking was confusing. It was difficult to know exactly what he was meaning.

'I'm sorry if I caused offence I didn't mean that, it was a silly question, I know that I am the only one here that doesn't come from the City or the Catacombs; but where I come from asking where someone lives is a normal every day question.'

'I understand. I live near the water.' Kohrstan noticed Jasmine's puzzled look as he finished speaking. 'That's down the bottom of the City at the level where the lake meets the walls of the City.'

Jasmine felt her stomach rumble slightly, she was hungry but did not really feel like eating. It was hard to know what to do or think in this strange underground world. Jasmine was deep in thought as she watched Mal putting ancient looking leather shoes onto his feet.

After Mal had finished buckling his shoes, he turned to Jasmine. 'What did you mean earlier when you said, Good Mourning? Mourning is what we do when someone dies. I guess you have a different meaning?'

'Oh yes, a very different meaning. To me morning is the

time of day just after we wake up and it has started being light.'

Kohrstan thought about what Jasmine had said for a moment. 'I suppose we would say 'Good Fall' then. This time is called Fall; when the stones have fallen and it is light. When the stones have risen and it is dark, it is called Rise.

'There are many differences here; I would like to learn them all. This place is so fascinating.'

Mal smiled. 'Good, because I have many things that I want to show you.' Mal took Jasmine's hand apprehensively in his own and started to walk to the door. Jasmine went with him without hesitation. She had begun to really like Mal; he had a deep kindness and caring personality that Jasmine admired. Kohrstan also seemed nice but Jasmine was unsure about him, maybe it would take a little while to get to know him.

Jasmine would not have the chance straight away to get to know Kohrstan. In less time than it took Jasmine and Mal to reach the conveyance corridor Kohrstan had said a quick goodbye and left through one of the other doors. As Jasmine followed Mal into the Conveyance Corridor she wondered where the door, Kohrstan had gone through, led to. It did not have the distinctive gold letter C on the front so it probably was not a conveyance corridor.

'They're very pretty Mal, but what are they for?' Jasmine asked as she looked at the purple stone. Mal had led Jasmine down to a room known as the room of stars. Jasmine felt the room had little to do with stars and perhaps the original meaning of the word had gotten lost somewhere. The room was an odd shape, almost round but certainly not a regular circle, the sides were uneven and one edge was almost flat rather than curved. The size of the room was amazing, at least as wide as two football pitches placed end to end. The ceiling was domed but it seemed as if the entire room had been carved out of solid rock. There were markings on the walls to suggest that they were made of individual blocks of stone but they had been carved into the surface.

It had taken Jasmine and Mal a long time to reach this

room. The conveyance corridor had taken them to a series of stairs and ladders leading down a dark shaft. This in turn led to a long winding corridor that wound this way and that in no particular direction, before ending up in the room of stars.

The floor was littered with dust and rocks, and small thumb sized gemstones; bright purple in colour and smooth all over as if it had been a pebble in a river.

Mal did his usual puzzled look as Jasmine asked her question. 'As I explained,' He said cheerily. 'The felostone is the only way of knowing if you're safe. If the vibrations stop on your wrist, you know you have to get into another room quickly.'

'I'm sorry Mal I still don't understand. Vibrations? Wrists?'

'Everyone in the City wears a felostone around their wrist.' Mal pulled up his sleeve revealing one of the purple stones carefully placed in a string wristband. 'Touch it.'

Jasmine ran her fingers across the purple stone on Mal's wrist, there were indeed slight vibrations coming from it. It was not vibrating hard enough to see the movement, but vibrating none the less. 'It doesn't feel like a normal stone. What did you mean by safe? How does this keep you safe?'

'Many times I have spoken about the Tamboli rooms, I am sorry but I haven't explained the full story to you.' Mal sat down on one of the larger rocks and invited Jasmine to do the same. 'Tamboli means lifeless or more precisely it means Life Stopped. A Tamboli room is a room where life cannot continue normally. The very essence of the room has been stolen and life stops.'

Jasmine signed, 'I really don't understand Mal, and it all sounds very complicated.'

'But it's important that you do understand, I know I am not a teacher but I will teach you about our ways.' Mal spoke with a confidence in his voice that Jasmine had not heard from him before. 'In a Tamboli room; time no longer exists. Nothing in a Tamboli room gets any older, or decays and most importantly; people forget everything except for the exact moment when time was stolen. Jasmine there are people trapped in Tamboli rooms they remember nothing about themselves or who they are, they only remember one tiny thought; what they were doing when time was stolen.'

Jasmine was a little distressed and again confused; everything she had ever been taught about science and technology seemed different here. Laws of physics that cannot be broken in the world above seem broken or simply not to exist. Jasmine's heart wanted to believe Mal but everything in her head was saying no. 'You keep saying stolen, is it a person stealing time? Moreover, how do you steal time? Perhaps we are misunderstanding each other.

Mal shook his head, 'There is no misunderstanding Jazz. Tamboli rooms are nothing like other rooms; time does not exist there because of an evil man named Paluuka who lives in a temple across the lake at the edge of the cavern. Until I met you, I thought he was the only person who didn't live in the City or Catacombs. It is not known if Paluuka is actually responsible or not, but there is no other explanation that we know of. Paluuka was a very bad man who once lived in the City but legend has it that he was cast out because of his dislike for order, and for working against the will of the people. Now he lives just to cause suffering in the City by making the Tamboli rooms'

Jasmine's head was starting to win the battle over whether to believe Mal's stories or not. It appeared to Jasmine that although Mal was not lying he was only speaking of legend and myth that had been passed down in stories over the ages and made into an abstract idea of what was happening. However, the idea of myth and legend appealed to Jasmine and she felt herself gripped to the story as Mal spoke.

'Mal, if there is no time in the Tamboli rooms, how do felostones work?' As Jasmine spoke, she picked up another of the bright purple stones and gently moved it through her fingers.

'I don't know exactly I'm afraid, but they do work. The felostones are tied to your wrist like mine is. All the time you can feel the vibrations on your wrist. If you ever go into a Tamboli room, then it will stop vibrating and instantly you know you must get out. If you go into a Tamboli room you have only a very short amount of time before you too, will forget everything and you will never leave the room.'

'It's like an alarm that tells you when you are no longer safe; I think I am beginning to understand.'

Mal took a thin piece of cord out of a pocket in his trousers. 'Jasmine I want to make you a felostone bracelet like mine so you will be safe.'

Still not totally convinced about Tamboli rooms Jasmine nodded and smiled at the thought of having one of the bracelets, they were indeed very pretty.

Jasmine watched as Mal carefully tied knots in the thin cord and made small loops to hold the purple stone in place. It took less than five minutes to finish the strap and Jasmine thought it looked very professional. Mal had obviously made straps like this before.

When it was finished; Jasmine held out her arm and Mal carefully tied it around her wrist, tightly enough so it would not fall off, but loose enough to feel comfortable. It felt strange to have the bright purple stone gently buzzing against her arm, but Mal put her mind at ease assuring her that before long she would not even know she was wearing it except in the peace of mind that it was there.

'I think I might have been in a Tamboli room before. The first room I was in; where there was the man that spoke like a robot and only said a few words to me. I had to leave that room because it gave me pains in my head.'

'It does sound like you were in a Tamboli room. Now remember if you ever feel like that again or the vibrations from your felostone stop; then you must get to another room as quickly as you can, I don't want you to get stuck like my...' He stopped speaking abruptly.

'Like your what?' Jasmine questioned a little puzzled.

Mal hesitated, 'Like the other people in the other rooms, never mind.'

Jasmine knew that Mal was about to say something else but she was not sure what it was, or why he changed his mind about saying it. Jasmine looked at Mal and smiled, he was looking a little sad for some reason although he was trying hard to hide it.

'What's the matter Mal? What were you going to say?'

Jasmine put her arm around his shoulders. 'Whatever it is, you can tell me.'

Mal stood up and walked away; Jasmine's hand fell back to her side. 'It really doesn't matter Jasmine. I wasn't going to say anything I...'

'Mal, look at me.' Jasmine said kindly. 'I know you haven't had many friends before but I am your friend now, and friends tell each other what is bothering them. I know you're upset about something and the Tamboli rooms remind you of that, but maybe I can help if you tell me.'

'You can't help, no one can!' Mal sounded angry as well as upset; Jasmine had never heard him speak like this before. After a few seconds he calmed himself; took a deep breath and said, 'I will tell you; or rather I will show you. Come with me and I will lead you to the Great Meeting Hall.'

Leading the way Mal took Jasmine back down the tunnel to the conveyance corridor, and through to a small dark room. The room was empty with blank grey walls and floor.

Jasmine kept twiddling with the felostone on her wrist; it was such a strange feeling to have a purple gemstone gently buzzing on your arm.

At the end of the room was an archway leading to a narrow balcony above a grand hall; filled with tables and cupboards. The room was immeasurably huge; the far side seemed a good five minutes walk away. The roof of the hall was arched and covered in white plaster, inset with wooden carvings; some too small to see any detail. Mal explained that this used to be the Great Meeting Hall, but it had not been used in many years. Jasmine thought this was strange, as the place seemed to be very clean and tidy; even the tables glinted as if they were highly polished.

The balcony had a spiral staircase leading down to the floor of the hall. As Jasmine followed Mal down the stone steps, she thought about the people of Martiblak and why they did not come here any more, this certainly was a 'great' hall.

The last step of the spiral staircase was badly broken and so Mal helped Jasmine down onto a red carpet that ran around the edge of the hall. Here, on the ground floor; Jasmine could see clearly that all the cupboards that lined the walls were empty, and the floor and tables were not as clean as she had first thought. There was a thin layer of dust on top of the tables and small pieces of rubbish littered the floor around the chairs and table legs.

'There used to be huge feasts here when I was young, with people eating, drinking and giving speeches,' Mal said as they made their way past countless tables. 'But then everyone stopped coming here.'

'Why did they stop coming here? This place is beautiful.' Jasmine ran her hand across one of the tables. It was incredibly smooth but her fingers made lines though the layer of dust.

'Because of this!' By this time, Mal and Jasmine had reached the far end of the hall, overshadowed by another balcony. In the centre of the end wall was a double door almost as grand as the door Jasmine had entered the City through. Mal opened one of the doors although it was marked by the Tamboli symbol. 'Look in here.'

Jasmine stood in the doorway and was horrified by what she saw. The doorway opened into the entranceway of the Great Hall. Gold shone brightly from the walls and a red carpet covered three huge steps that led up to the Great Hall. Light was shining brightly through a glass roof and lit up the faces of hundreds of people, all standing still or sitting on small chairs by large, round tables at the edge of the room. The people were silent, and still; except for a single figure rocking slowly backwards and forwards in a chair. Some people were holding cups of wine or carrying small children, but they were still and silent. None of the children were crying, no one took sips from their drinks, and no one was talking.

Jasmine felt a wrench in her stomach as if she was going to be sick. 'Oh Mal!' She cried. 'It's horrible, what happened here?'

'They are all stuck here, like everyone else in a Tamboli room.' Mal started to look pale. 'They all arrived for a feast and were waiting patiently in this entrance way for the doors to open so they could walk into the big hall, sit and start the feast. Sadly they never made it into the hall, the essence of this room, of their existence; was stolen. Since I was a boy, they have always been here. Sometimes you can see them blink or see them breathing in and out, but that is it, nothing more.'

'Mal close the door please, I don't like it. It looks like they are dead but still standing and looking.'

'No wait! There is more to see.' Mal pointed to a man and woman sat on one of the tables furthest away. 'Do you see the woman in the green dress and the man in a tall hat? They are sat down and the woman is cradling a baby.'

There were so many people it was, at first, hard to see whom Mal was pointing at, but Jasmine soon noticed the tall hat of the man and the green dress of the woman. 'I see them Mal. Do you…*did* you know them?'

Mal nodded slowly. 'The babies name is Reusomaesha; my little sister, the woman holding her is my mother, and the man is my father.'

'I'm sorry Mal, I didn't know. I am sorry I made you come here again. Close the door, please!'

Mal closed the door and a faint click echoed around the great hall. 'I can still remember running down the old arcade, and tripping over my shoes because I was running so fast. I was late and I was worried my father would be cross, but as I got to the entrance doors, a man grabbed my arm and held me back. He said I couldn't go any further. It was a long time before I truly understood what had happened, but now I know my family is gone forever.'

'But you don't truly understand Mal, you said so yourself; you only *think* that it is Paluuka stealing time from these places.'

Mal did not pay much attention to what Jasmine had said; he was still remembering everything that had happened after that terrible evening. 'After this had happened some men tried to go into the room and carry out some of the children. It took them many attempts as they felt pain in their heads and had to put down the child they were carrying and go outside to rest. It took a long time but at last, they got a child through the door, but he died within seconds of leaving the room. Its body could no longer live torn in two by the room. Nobody can ever leave here.'

Jasmine slowly and carefully sat down on a chair near one of the tables; stunned by the whole experience. 'I did not understand how terrible Tamboli rooms could be. I do not think I really understood what a Tamboli room meant exactly, until now. The Tamboli room I was in yesterday seems like nothing in comparison.'

Mal joined Jasmine around the table and they sat silently for many minutes. Jasmine was trying to understand the pain and suffering Mal must have felt when he was younger and he had found out what had happened to his family. Jasmine had lost her mother when she was very young and although she did not remember much about her, the memories were still painful.

Jasmine gingerly played with the felostone on her wrist, the gentle vibrations were still very noticeable, but not too bothersome. After a moment or two Jasmine felt a little more relaxed, perhaps the felostone can be relaxing. Moving her hands elsewhere, Jasmine brushed the dust off a small portion of the table. The dust fell to the floor slowly, leaving behind a bright polished surface. The polished wood reflected Mal's face and Jasmine wondered why this man had grown up so innocent, with a calm caring nature. He had grown up in a world without foster parents to care for him as she had had, and without many friends to rely on. Jasmine looked up to Mal and smiled, he looked proud and strong. Perhaps in the face of such sorrow, as he had seen, led him to a deeper understanding of compassion and emotion. Jasmine felt proud to call Mal her friend.

Jasmine spoke to Mal more about his past and his family, now he had shown Jasmine what had happened to his parents and sister; he seemed more open to discuss things.

Mal had lived on his own for a few years, before making friends with Kohrstan and living with him and his father. Mal had grown up under the strict control of Gryss, Kohrstan's father. Gryss is a kind and generous man but always expects the utmost politeness and hard work from his family. When Mal had 'turned to the older', which Jasmine guessed to be the Martiblak equivalent of becoming an adult, he moved away from Gryss and Kohrstan to find his own home. That is where Jasmine had stayed the night before. In the room, that Mal calls home.

Jasmine also spoke for a long time about her childhood and moving between foster parents. Mal was good at listening as well as telling stories about his childhood. He listened intently and politely asked questions whenever Jasmine stopped speaking.

Jasmine had no idea how long they were talking for, probably longer than they had last night. 'I am so glad I met you Mal, I was so afraid when I came to this City but now things don't seem so bad.'

'Perhaps I should show you some of the better things that are in the City,' Mal said after a short pause. 'I will take you to the Givings.'

'You have mentioned that before, isn't that where you get your food?' Jasmine asked following Mal back up the spiral staircase and along to the Conveyance corridor.

'Yes, the Givings is the place that we get our food, and it is the most amazing thing in the whole of the City of Martiblak. I promise you; you will be amazed!'

Mal was right; Jasmine was amazed, as soon as the door at the end of the conveyance corridor opened. A soft, warm light fell upon her hands and face; it was much more like sunlight than the lights inside the City. In front of the door and as far as the young woman could see was bright green grass broken only by the occasional gravel or stone path that wove gently around trees and bushes. Jasmine was truly in awe at the sight of the tall trees and leafy bushes growing underground, and looked up to see the light emanating from a patch of yellow in an otherwise black ceiling high above, too high in fact to properly see it.

The paths, trees and bushes were well kept and beautiful, but not laid out like an ornamental garden; more like an orchard or field. There was no order to the layout and even a few large boulders were dotted around; under trees or just sat by themselves surrounded by grass. Jasmine felt that this was a magical place, full of mystery and incredible beauty.

The conveyance corridor that Mal and Jasmine had just walked through was one of about fifteen that led to the Givings, and lines of people were walking in and out of them.

Mal took Jasmine's hand and led her away from the Conveyance corridor and along one of the little gravel footpaths.

Behind the first few trees was a small courtyard, made of stone slabs, with a stone column in each corner holding up a roof of pale tiles and blue glass. The floor of the courtyard was covered in rows of identical wicker baskets with curved handles. Each basket filled to almost overflowing, with fruits and vegetables. Some of the contents of the baskets Jasmine half recognised as being similar to something she would get at home, but most were new to her and she could not even guess if it was a fruit or vegetable.

Bustling about around the baskets were a few of the City people, picking up fruit, wrapping it in pink cloth, and carrying it away with them. A line of men in long gray jackets, whom Jasmine had seen in the Great Corridor, were walking towards the courtyard carrying more baskets, and another line carrying away the empties to be refilled.

'This is where everyone gets their food,' Mal said stopping just outside the courtyard. 'The Tenders pick the fruit and bring it here. Then you just pick up what you want to eat, but if you really want to; you can go and pick your own food from the trees.'

Mal led Jasmine further into the Givings, carefully keeping to the paths as much as possible. The further they got from the conveyance corridor the denser the vegetation seemed to be, more trees, bushes, and even some small shrubs.

'Have a look at these,' Mal said leaving the path and walking over to a bush with very long but thin leaves. The fruit growing on the bush looked similar in size to raspberries but were perfectly smooth and shiny on the outside.

'What are they called Mal?'

'They're called 'Bees', and they taste really sweet, but it's hard to pick them. If you don't pull them off the bush properly they will turn to liquid and drip through your fingers onto the floor. You have to grab the stem below the berry and squeeze it hard and pull, you will feel something stretch inside; then you let go and quickly pull the fruit off.' Mal demonstrated and deftly pulled the bright red fruit off its stem and handed it to Jasmine. 'Try it, it is really nice.'

Jasmine took the berry and popped it in her mouth. The outside was soft and the inside was softer still, like pure liquid. Mal was right; it was very sweet and delicious. Jasmine liked the flavour very much.

'Now you pick one. Remember when you feel something stretch in the stem; let go and pull the fruit really quickly.'

Jasmine tried to pick one of the small berries but as soon as she pulled it off it off the stem, it turned to a thick sticky liquid that dripped off her hand onto the grass below.

Mal laughed loudly, 'It does take some practice, and in fact some people can't pick them at all. You just have to keep trying.'

Jasmine tried a few more times but still could not master the art of picking the incredibly sweet but difficult to pick fruit. Mal was very good at it and gathered some more for Jasmine to eat.

After they had eaten quite a few Bees, Mal showed Jasmine around more of the fruit bushes. There were so many varieties of fruits and vegetables; each uniquely different to each other and most were completely different to anything Jasmine had eaten in the world outside.

The night stems, with long bitter/sweet leaves, were somewhat like lettuce but jasmine had never seen lettuce leaves growing from the top of two-metre high trees. Loujuij was a root vegetable similar to a potato. Jasmine could not pronounce the name properly even with Mal trying many times to teach her. Strangest of all the food at the Givings was the stone tree located in a small clearing inside a circle of Night Stem Trees. It was as tall as an oak tree and as wide as a road, with only one huge leaf hanging from the top of its trunk. There were no other branches except for the trunk; covered from top to bottom in fist-sized holes.

'It's called the stone tree because you can't cut it down, the bark is as hard as stone, the leaf is as strong as leather. There is only this one Stone Tree in the whole of the Givings,' Mal explained as he reached his hand into one of the holes. 'There is something special in here, it doesn't look particularly nice but it tastes good.'

Jasmine trusted Mal, but was not too sure if she wanted to try the mass of sticky fibres Mal brought out of the hole. He explained it was the soft wood from the inside of the tree. The tree was as soft inside as the outside was hard.

Mal pulled the clump of fibres into two parts and offered one part to Jasmine. 'Try it!'

Jasmine trusted Mal but was unsure about the white fibres he had just pulled out of a tree. 'Ok, I suppose it is worth a try,' she said after peering curiously at the insides of the Stone Tree. It was nothing like Jasmine expected it to be like, it tasted like chicken; part of a tree actually tasted like real chicken. Jasmine was unsure if it was part of a tree or part of an animal that lived in the tree. Mal put her mind at rest by assuring her that no one lives inside the tree. It was strange to Jasmine that Mal thought of a person when she mentioned an animal, and further discussion made Jasmine realise that there were not any animals in the City of Martiblak.

Sitting for a long time under the giant leaf of the Stone Tree, Mal and Jasmine chatted about life in the City. There was so much to see that Jasmine thought she would never get chance to see it all.

Whilst they were relaxing, Jasmine glanced down at her arm and saw the purple felostone. It had been there all day but she had forgotten about the strange buzzing sensation against her skin. Mal had been right, after a while, you do not even realize you are wearing it, Jasmine thought to herself.

After they had rested under the giant leaf, they continued their walk around the Givings before returning to the area where the Bees grew. Jasmine was eager to try to pick them again.

Jasmine felt so at ease with Mal, probably more at ease with him than anyone else she had ever known, and she had only known him for a day.

'What I don't understand Mal,' Jasmine said examining the stem of the Bees. 'Is that I got here when I fell though the floor of that house. If the roof of the cavern is way up there, where did I get in? I couldn't have fallen that far, without hurting myself.'

Jasmine pulled another berry off the bush and it squashed in her hand again.

'I don't know Jazz. I'm sorry. I don't even know about the rooms you spoke of with the carved ceilings, and the strange man and old woman.' Mal demonstrated again how to pull the Bees off the bush. 'I have been to a lot of places in this City and I don't remember seeing anywhere like that, especially with the door you spoke of.'

'Maybe the rooms were outside the City and the conveyance corridor the old woman took me through; brought me here.'

'I've never heard of that happening. As I said I have been to many places in the City but never out of it, and Paluuka's Temple is nothing like what you described, it is said to be cold, dark and damp. I'm sure I would know about those rooms if they existed.'

'They do exist, Mal, I was there. They must be outside the City, it's the only possibility,' Jasmine paused for a minute. 'If you never knew about the rooms; then you could never have travelled there in a conveyance corridor; you wouldn't be able to picture it in your mind.

Mal was busy eating a handful of Bees and puzzling over what Jasmine had said. 'It is possible, I suppose, that there are rooms that I couldn't get to, and it is possible that they are outside, but I'm not sure. Perhaps Grancathai would know; he knows more about the City than anyone.'

'Who?' Jasmine asked finally picking a berry that stayed intact.

'He's an old man I know, he looks after the Library of the City Books. He lives near the entrance to the Catacombs.'

'I didn't know that anyone read books, here.'

Mal shook his head. 'They don't, but Grancathai looks after them anyway. He is a very nice man I have spoken to many times, and Kohrstan's father makes ink and paper for him.'

'And we can go and see him, and ask him about the rooms I was in?' Jasmine started to get excited. Perhaps he would know about the Old World that Jasmine had come from.

'Of course we can go and see him, but it is probably better

to wait until later, just before the stones rise. He is easier to find then, most of the time he is in the library somewhere reading or writing, and he doesn't like to be disturbed. It is best to catch him after he has left the library and is in his home room. His home room is easy to find although it isn't near a conveyance corridor, we can take one most of the way but then we will have to walk. Don't worry it's not too far.'

'I wouldn't mind even if it was a long way, I like travelling around the City; there is so much to see. Everything is different to what my home is like.' Jasmine took Mal's hand. 'Thank you for showing me around and taking me places.'

Mal found himself a little shy whenever Jasmine thanked, or praised him, but he was happy to help and happy to have a friend.

Jasmine and Mal spent a little more time in the Givings before slowly walking back toward the Conveyance corridors. Jasmine was interested in speaking to Grancathai, whoever he was and hoped he would be more knowledgeable when it came to talking about the Old World.

'Mal?' Jasmine said as they approached one of the doors to the conveyance corridor. 'If I could practice using the conveyance corridors, could I get back to those rooms I was in? I can remember what they look like, so could go straight there.'

Mal smiled. 'Probably, but you will need to practice a lot; it's harder than it looks. We all learn when we are children but it is very difficult then, and I don't think anyone has ever tried to teach an adult before.'

'But it might be possible?' Jasmine suddenly remembered her first trip through a conveyance corridor where she had ended up back where she started. It was obvious to her now; she did not know about any other rooms so she could only return to where she had come from.

Learning to use the conveyance corridor would be more difficult than Jasmine could imagine.

CHAPTER 4

The Great Library

'Father, I have news.' Kohrstan called out as he exited the conveyance corridor into his father's workshop. Gryss, Kohrstan's father, was sitting at a large workbench carefully stitching a pocket onto a bright blue shirt.

Gryss' workshop, adjacent to his home rooms was a large rectangular room filled, almost, to bursting point with cupboards, shelves, boxes and crates. There was little order to the arrangement of things that were stored around the room. Racks of clothes were hung over pegs, glass jars and bottles were placed, either in crates on the floor or on shelves. Some of the cupboards were open and string, cloth, bowls, and odd bits of wood were poking out. The three main tables were littered with every type of tool any artisan would ever need. Saws, planes and chisels next to needles and thread, paint brushes next to files and metal snips. Gryss had made most of the tools himself. Metalwork was one of his best abilities.

'What have you heard? Tell me quickly Kohrstan; I am very busy.' Gryss did not even look up from his sewing as he spoke.

Kohrstan's father was middle aged but still in very good shape, strong and muscular. A green cloth cap poorly covered a mop of brown hair that was interspersed with the occasional grey. His hands, covered with calluses and scars, were old and beginning to wrinkle. However, they were amazingly skilled. Deftly and quickly, Gryss' fingers pushed and pulled the needle through the course blue shirt, pulling the thread behind it.

Kohrstan sat down opposite his father around the workbench. 'I met someone interesting today; she is a friend of Mal's...I mean Malmayorkia. She is from the Old World.'

Gryss put his needle and thread down carefully onto the

workbench. Most parents would have a hard time believing such a crazy story, but Kohrstan had been brought up by a man obsessed with honesty. Any tales or exaggerated story telling when Kohrstan was a boy meant being locked in his room until he admitted he had not told the whole truth. That had turned Kohrstan into someone who would only speak the honest truth to his father, but would still exaggerate and use plenty of sarcasm with him friends.

Gryss was, however, a little cautious to this news. 'Are you sure you mean the Old World Kohrstan? You are talking about a place that is said not to exist. Think clearly and tell me everything in detail and make sure you are accurate with your words.'

'Yes father, I am sure,' Kohrstan explained the whole story to his father in intricate detail, mentioning everything that Mal had told him. Gryss believed his son, even though the story sounded almost impossible.

'So where is this woman now?' Gryss said after Mal had finished talking. 'Is she still here?'

'Yes father she is still here,' Kohrstan replied. 'Mal is showing her the City.

'Who else knows about this woman?'

'No one, well I don't think any one else knows,' Kohrstan thought carefully.

Gryss stood and went to a small cupboard in the corner of the room and lifted out a small glass bottle. 'I would like you to take this bottle to Grancathai, and when you are there tell him what you have just told me and see what he has to say about this woman.

'Yes father I will.' Kohrstan grabbed the bottle and quickly went into the conveyance corridor.

'Now concentrate; see a picture of the room in your mind.' Mal held open one of the doors at the Givings for Jasmine to walk through. This was Jasmine fifth attempt to go to Mal's home room. 'Walk slowly and keep the picture in you mind, don't let it fade. Think of every little detail; some of the rooms here are quite similar, and remember if the corridor isn't sure where you are going it's just going to bring you back here again.'

'Oh Mal, I'm not sure I can do this; I keep thinking of other things. The more I think of your room, the more my mind tries to wander.' Jasmine turned to face her friend in the doorway. 'I'm scared I am going to do things wrong.'

'It's perfectly safe, I have told you so many times that the corridor always returns you to where you came from if it doesn't know exactly where you're going. If someone else tries to enter the corridor when you are in it, then that is fine too.'

'What do you mean fine? What happens exactly?' Jasmine asked.

'Nothing, you just won't see the other person. As long as the door is closed behind you, the next person to enter will just see an empty corridor; even if you are still walking along it.'

Jasmine turned to face the corridor again. 'I'm glad this all makes sense to you Mal. I don't understand at all how these corridors work. Where I come from we have cars and they are easy to understand.'

'Cars?' Mal asked.

'Never mind. Right, I am going to do it this time. I am going to get to your home room.'

Jasmine started to walk slowly down the corridor. She was concentrating hard to picture the small room with the domed ceiling that led to Mal's home room. She was picturing the curved glass in the ceiling, the columns and the doorways. In her mind, Jasmine could actually see the room. She looked around the room; seeing the stone floor and remembering meeting Kohrstan.

Jasmine was over half way through when suddenly she thought about the outside world, or the Old World as Mal would say. The image of the room, with the domed ceiling was lost. Quickly she tried to get it back, but it was too late, before long she was opening the door at the other end of the corridor and walking out onto the Givings Plateau.

'Don't be too disheartened Jazz, you'll get there in the end. Let's try again! If we keep practising you are bound to get the hang of it sooner or later.'

'Probably later,' Jasmine said grumpily sitting down on a

rock under one of the trees. 'We've been trying for ages and I can't do it, and I don't think I ever will.'

'Jazz, that was only your fifth attempt. It takes children days to get the hang of it.' Mal joined Jasmine on the rock. 'I might have an idea. It is something that parents do to help their children learn how to use the corridors. I will go through and wait for you on the other side. It might help you to get through if you can picture me on the other side.'

'But I tried that, I tried picturing meeting Kohrstan in the room.'

'Ah; but you don't know Kohrstan as well as you know me, and he isn't in the room, I will be. I will go through and wait on the other side for a while. If you don't come through I will just come back here to meet you.'

It took Mal a little while to persuade Jasmine that it was a good idea. She did not really want to be left alone for too long, especially in the Givings where many people were walking around. Jasmine did not like the way the people looked at her. Mal had been the only person she had spoken to or seen that seemed nice and friendly.

The feeling of being left alone gave Jasmine a new confidence in learning how to use the conveyance corridors and she sat down on a rock for minute after Mal had left to ensure he had reached the other side without any problems. Then confidently she stood up and marched over to the door, opened it and walked into the brightly lit corridor.

Jasmine walked down the length of the conveyance corridor, carefully picturing Mal's smiling face in the room at the other end, the light twinkling in his blue eyes as it shone through the glass dome. It took a lot of effort to think solely of one person in one room, nothing else could enter her mind or else it would not work. Jasmine did not understand how the conveyance corridors worked, but wanted desperately to be able to use them.

Jasmine felt tense as she twisted the door handle and pushed the door open. For a second Jasmine closed her eyes wanting desperately to see Mal when she opened them again.

Slowly Jasmine opened her eyes to see the bright light and

fresh green of the Givings. It had not worked; she still could not use the conveyance corridors. In frustration, Jasmine kicked a pebble across one the paths and slumped down next to the rock she had sat on earlier. Mal had said; it takes children a few days to learn how to use the conveyance corridors properly but Jasmine thought that maybe she could learn a little faster as she was an adult.

The Givings seemed a little less busy now; only a few people were walking in and out of the conveyance corridors. Jasmine held her face in the hands, and waited for Mal to return.

'Hello! Guess it didn't work.' It was Mal; he was standing in front of Jasmine with Kohrstan. 'Do you want to give it another try?'

Jasmine shook her head. 'No thanks Mal. Thanks for trying to teach me, but I think it is going to take me a while. I don't feel like practising any more today. It's nice to see you again Kohrstan.'

'Jasmine...I mean Jazz, what do you think of our City?' Kohrstan seemed to accept the fact that Jasmine was from somewhere other than the City, a lot quicker than Mal did. Mal had been convinced that Jasmine was from the Catacombs. Perhaps he believed what ever Mal told him. 'Malmayorkia tells me you are going to see Grancathai.'

'Yes that's right. We want to ask him about the old world and some rooms that I went into when I first arrived in the City.' Jasmine said standing up.

'You have chosen a good day; I am going to see him just before the stones rise. My father has made some ink for Grancathai and I am going to deliver it for him.'

'Your father makes ink?' Jasmine asked inquisitively. Mal seemed to be stifling a small giggle.

Kohrstan smiled flashing his bright white teeth. 'My father makes lots of things, and the things he can't make...he *acquires* to give to people. In return, they provide him with things that other people need. I guess you could say he's an exchanger.'

'That sounds interesting,' Jasmine replied, unsure about Kohrstan's father. Mal had said that he had grown up with

Kohrstan and his father, Gryss. Gryss sounded like he could be very strict, and *acquire* did not sound too good to Jasmine.

The three people slowly walked to the conveyance corridors and went through to the Great Corridor. The fountain, which Jasmine presumed to be the one she met Mal at, was still running with clear, cold water. Mal assured Jasmine that it was safe to drink and the three of them drank deeply. The food they had eaten at the Givings certainly had not quenched anyone's thirst. Possibly the air was much dryer underground than on the surface. There certainly was not any sign of rain or mist or sea breezes, or anything that could make the air feel clean and fresh.

'Is this the only place where you can drink?' Jasmine asked when she had finished drinking.'

Kohrstan wiped some drips of water from his chin. 'No, there are many other fountains and water courses throughout the City. Most of them are in the main dwellings. The old town where Mal lives does not contain very much any more. The people in the Catacombs live on drips of water that come through from the great lake.'

'And...' Mal added. 'It's from the chambers where the water drips through that they get all their food. A funny slimy plant grows on the walls and puddles on the floor.'

'Of course none of us have ever seen this so we don't know for sure,' Kohrstan finished, almost unhappy that Mal had joined in the conversation.

'At least we don't think anyone from the City has gone to the Catacombs, even Grancathai has lived his whole life in the City, although right at its edge.' Mal continued.

Jasmine thought that the relationship between Mal and Kohrstan must be a complicated one. They grew up together as brothers but did not always show many signs of brotherly love, and they certainly had completely opposite personalities. Perhaps when they were children they were more similar, but now Kohrstan was a proud, strong and intense person with a slight insensitive streak. Mal on the other hand was more sensitive and had a caring, polite and gentile manner.

'We should be leaving now,' Kohrstan said as Mal lifted

another handful of water to his lips. 'It won't be long before the stones rise.'

Kohrstan led the way through a conveyance corridor, which ended in another long tunnel. Jasmine had seen a lot of corridors and tunnels in the short time she had been in the City, but this one was very narrow and led gently down hill.

A gleaming silver door suddenly appeared as the tunnel ended. It was shiny, reflecting the yellow/green light in beautiful glints and shimmers. A square handle on the left was the only part of the door that was not silver; it was black and made from wood. It appeared to have been added later as an after thought and did not match at all.

Kohrstan turned the handle and the door swung outwards gracefully. 'This is the entrance to the Catacombs, Jazz.'

Entering the small square chamber Kohrstan pointed out a hole in the middle of the floor partially covered in wooden planks. A ladder made from bent iron rungs ran down one side of the hole that was deep enough that it could easily be called a well. 'I have been told there are three hundred steps to the bottom and it's at the bottom that the Catacombs begin.'

There was no visible light down inside the well, so it was impossible to see the bottom. Jasmine resisted the urge to drop a pebble down to see how deep it really was. There was a cold breeze wafting up from the well, bringing a chill to the air. Jasmine certainly had no wish to travel to the Catacombs; a shiver went through her body as she peered at the black hole. She had seen darkness like that before in the tunnel before she entered the City, and seeing it again made her feel uncomfortable.

Kohrstan opened another door at the opposite end of the chamber to which they had entered and ushered the others through.

'Kohrstan, I don't remember your father saying you were going to bring friends,' a loud voice echoed around the small stone chamber.

Sat on a low bench between piles of wooden chests and blankets was an old man. He was wearing a long robe and a cloth cap. Around his wrinkled brown eyes was a pair of half glasses, showing scratches and dirty marks.

'Grancathai, I have brought someone here to see you. This is Jasmine she is from the Old World.

Grancathai stood. 'First I hope you have brought ink, I can't be expected to write if there is no ink.'

'I have it Grancathai, here it is.' Kohrstan held out the small stone bottle. 'My father says it is even better than last time.'

'I should hope so boy.' Grancathai took the bottle and placed it inside one the chests, the only one that was open. It already contained a number of other bottles, in different shapes and sizes; some made of glass; but mostly stone. 'Now about your friend.'

'Her name is Jasmine. I met her in the Great Corridor,' Mal said carefully stepping forward.

Grancathai hummed quietly. 'Thank you Malmayorkia. So, your name is Jasmine? That certainly is not a name I recognise. You say you are from the Old World; from outside.'

'You know about the Old World? We thought maybe you may have known about other people coming here, or knew that it isn't just a myth; but real.'

'Yes Malmayorkia; I do know about the outside world, there are many pictures in the archives of things I could only assume came from the Old World, but until now I wasn't totally convinced that it really existed.' Grancathai spoke slowly with a low pitch and paused for a long time between sentences. As he spoke, he slowly moved back to his stool between the wooden chests. 'How did you arrive in the City Jasmine?'

'I fell through the floor of this house and landed in a tunnel. The tunnel led through to a big wooden door, much bigger than these doors.' Jasmine pointed to the three doors that were dotted around the room. 'It was hard to get through the door but I managed it and ended up in a small room with a man who didn't speak very much. Then there was an identical room next door with an old woman sat at a desk. The walls and ceilings were covered in wooden carvings and had a lot of gold decoration. I haven't seen any other rooms like that in the City.'

'Do you know of these rooms?' Mal asked when Jasmine took a break from speaking. 'I have been most places in the City but can't remember seeing anything like that.'

'Yes Malmayorkia I do know of those rooms, and it is not surprising that you haven't seen them. No one has been there in a long time. I saw them once when I was a young boy. A man named Balmore of Terrol was the Principal Guardian of the City and lived in the rooms there. Back then there were many more people in the City and a lot more things happening. The Principal Guardian of the City was an important person who oversaw everything and kept the peace. The rooms you spoke of are only part of an Outer City, with large galleries similar to the Great Corridor that looked out across the lake. It is a much smaller place than here and only a few people lived there all the time.'

'An Outer City, I didn't know there ever was anything outside the City except for Paluuka's Temple,' Mal said after a short pause.

'As I said, Malmayorkia, nobody has been there for a very long time.' Grancathai stood and moved towards one of the side doors. 'Come with me, I will show you some pictures from the archives.'

Jasmine was not prepared for what she was about to see. Through the door, Grancathai opened, was a short, arched corridor and beyond was an expanse; filled with light and colour. The circular room was three storeys high, with galleries running around the outside on each storey. The dry, dark colour of the wood that made the galleries was a striking contrast to a beautifully shining spiral staircase that ran up the middle of the room. It was made from an uncountable number of thin strips of metal; bolted together and painted green. Walkways, made from the same metal strips, ran off the sides of the stairs to the circular galleries. The floor of purple marble was shiny and glinted in the light that shone down from thousands of small crystals, suspended from the ceiling by gold chains.

The air was cool, but dry and had a slightly sweet smell to it. Jasmine took a few deep breaths of the cool air, as it felt fresher than the air elsewhere in the City.

'Welcome to the Great Library of Martiblak,' Grancathai said as he turned around to face Jasmine and the others as they walked from the arched corridor into the library.

It was indeed a library. Books of all different shapes and sizes were stacked tidily on shelves that filled all of the galleries. One or two bookcases were covered in large, white cloths; but most were visible. Jasmine glanced at some on the ground floor of the library where she stood. Some of the books were big and strong, bound in leather with gold and silver titles printed on the spine; others were no more than collections of papers tied to together with string.

'Its amazing Grancathai, there must be thousands of books here,' Jasmine said casting her gaze upwards towards the upper galleries. It was strange, there appeared to be nothing holding them up, except for the wall they ran around.

'45,812 to be exact and I have spent my whole life looking through them, and writing new ones on the things that happen in the City. Although recently I have not had that much to write about.'

Mal and Kohrstan had seen the library a few times before but were still impressed every time they came here and saw its inspiring beauty.

'Grancathai, are there books here with pictures of the rooms Jasmine saw?' Mal asked quietly, very aware of the loud echoes from the stone ceiling.

Grancathai had started to walk up the spiral staircase and did not look around to reply but firmly said. 'Yes!'

More crystals sunk into the wooden banisters lit the middle storey of the library. Grancathai led the group across the walkway and around the gallery. Jasmine thought about the library back at her university, and how happy the librarians would be to work in a place as spectacular as this.

'Here is a book that contains a few pictures of the Outer City. I wish I could remember its name,' Grancathai slid a thin brown book off a shelf and opened it. It was dusty and the pages were slightly crumpled. 'Here, is this one of the rooms you saw?'

Grancathai handed the book to Jasmine. Filling the right

hand page was a picture of an old man dressed in a blue tunic. He was standing in a square room, decorated with carvings and gold leaf decorations. It was indeed the room Jasmine had entered when she first arrived in the City.

'Oh yes, that is the one. I recognise the wooden panelling. Oh, and at the bottom it says it is the *home of the Principal Guardian*,' Jasmine read from the small hand written text at the bottom of the page.

Grancathai was startled and took the book from Jasmine's hands; closing it in a cloud of dust. 'What do you mean it is written at the bottom? These books are ancient, the text is from the old language; you can't possibly read it.'

'Of course I can read it,' Jasmine replied confused to why Grancathai thought she could not read it. 'The language isn't ancient it is what we are speaking now; English!'

'This language hasn't been spoken in over fifty generations. There is a new language now that I use to write in the books.' Grancathai looked a little angry and pulled some sheets of thick paper out of his pocket.

The writing on them was very different to English, or any other written language that Jasmine had ever seen. It was a series of short wavy lines with dots and the occasional circle.

'Grancathai, I am from the Old World as you call it. Your language might not have changed over all this time, but your writing certainly has.' Jasmine looked at Mal who smiled nervously back. 'I still don't understand how books were written in English such a long time ago, but I can read it. I can prove it too.'

Mal took Jasmine's hand. 'Perhaps we should go Jazz.'

'No! Wait.' Jasmine protested and began to look along the lines of books. 'Grancathai, this book here, the spine says *Anatomy* and so if the book has pictures it will be of the human body. This one, *Clock Makers and Time Keepers* will have pictures of circles with 12 numbers around them, and perhaps pictures of round wheels and cogs. This one will have pictures of trees and flowers because it is called *A Beginners Guide to Botany*.'

Silently Grancathai slid the Clockmakers book off the shelf

and opened it. It did indeed have pictures of clock faces and cogs of varying shapes and sizes, and although he did not know what a clock was he recognised it from Jasmine's description. Grancathai had looked at all the books that Jasmine had mentioned and could remember the pictures in them. He was amazed that Jasmine, this strange girl from a place thought to be a myth could read an ancient language.

'Jasmine how are you doing this? You couldn't possibly know what was going to be in these books, you have never seen them before. Malmayorkia and Kohrstan have looked at some books but I doubt they could teach you which books to point at. That truly is remarkable. You call this language English and you say it is spoken and written in the old world?'

'Yes, although we have other languages as well, but I don't know them.'

'Even I can't read these texts, Jasmine, and I have looked at thousands of books written in the old language. Many generations ago, the people here stopped writing books and this library became a mess; not seen by anyone. Slowly the people forgot how to read and write, until my Great Grandfather came here and started to look after the books. He developed a new way of writing to keep records of the happenings of the City.'

Kohrstan spoke for the first time since entering the Library and said exactly what Jasmine was thinking. 'So our spoken language has stayed the same but we have forgotten how to read these texts. Jasmine's people haven't forgotten how to read them and so knows what every word means.'

'Come with me Jasmine there are some special books for you to look at,' Grancathai said after Kohrstan had finished speaking.

The old man slowly climbed the steps to the top floor of the library. Here the light from the hanging crystals was more intense and the different colours in the books shone brightly. There was however, a lot more dust on the top of the books and on the floor.

'Perhaps you can tell me what is written in these books, Jasmine, they are very special.'

There were ten identical books neatly lined along the shelf.

They were faded yellow, turned almost brown by the years. On the spine of each was the word *Journal*.

'They are someone's diaries; a record of things they have done. This word says Journal.'

Grancathai seemed to turn pale, and covered his mouth with his hand in disbelief. 'These are the writings of Martiblak himself. I have never read them of course, but they are said to contain information about the carving out of the main cavern and the building of the City. Martiblak, the father of the City, these are his books, his writings.'

Grancathai took the left most book off the shelf and handed it to Jasmine. The cover was slightly torn and dirty, it must be extremely old.

The book seemed to creak as Jasmine carefully opened it. The pages inside were faded and felt loose. The first page contained only a couple of sentences.

I hope these journals will contain an accurate record of my life's work. They are the official records of the Dayvene Laboratory. Professor Martin Blake.

Jasmine read the words aloud to the three intrigued listeners. Grancathai had never heard of the Dayvene Laboratory but recognised the name Martin Blake.

'Martin Blake! That is why the City is called Martiblak. The name must have been changed over the generations,' the old man was very excited and his hands were shaking slightly. 'Jasmine, these are very special books and I will be very interested to hear more, but the stones will rise soon. It is with difficulty that I must ask you to leave the book and return to your home rooms.'

Jasmine quickly scanned a few more pages quickly before handing the journal back to Grancathai. It was all hand written with carefully drawn diagrams and even some mathematical equations. These journals were certainly records of a Laboratory, although Jasmine did not have chance to find out exactly what Professor Martin Blake was working on.

Grancathai replaced the yellow book back on its shelf. Its dust free top seemed out of place next to the other volumes. 'Jasmine, please return here when the stones have fallen again and you can read more of these books. Perhaps we can learn how the City was built, and if Martin Blake was originally from the old world. There is so much information here; it would be wonderful if you could read some of it to me.'

Jasmine smiled, 'I would be happy to do that Grancathai, I have many questions that maybe these books can answer too!'

The group descended the spiral stairs and moved through to Grancathai's home room. The aged librarian thanked Kohrstan for the ink and thanked Jasmine for her ability to read the ancient books in the Library.

Jasmine felt drained. She followed her friends out of the room, and walked with them back to the closest conveyance corridor. Kohrstan stepped in first to travel back to his father's home. Jasmine and Mal went in after a few seconds and went through to Mal's home rooms.

Their timing was incredible, the loud echoing rumble of stones rising thundered around the small domed ceiling room, as the two people exited the conveyance corridor and the door clicked closed behind them.

Across the City, Kohrstan sat down with his father around an old wooden table. Various pieces of metal were strewn across it from earlier when Gryss was making buckles for the trouser belts he was making.

Gryss looked at his son blankly unsure what information he was about to be told. 'Did you take the ink to Grancathai?'

Kohrstan nodded. 'Yes father I did, he was very thankful.'

'And did you speak to him about Malmayorkia's friend?'

Again, Kohrstan nodded but then stopped abruptly and frowned. 'Not exactly, Malmayorkia and Jasmine went with me, so Grancathai could meet her in person.'

Gryss thought for a moment. 'Did Grancathai believe she was from the Old World?'

Kohrstan scratched his head and paused for a moment

before answering. 'I think he was unsure at first, but when Jasmine started reading the ancient books in the library he...'

'She could read the ancient books in the library? I didn't think that was even possible. Are you sure you are getting the facts right Kohrstan?'

'Yes father I am sure! Although, I have to admit I don't fully understand everything she told us about how she could understand the writing; she says they use that language where she comes from. She also said some things about how the City was built.'

Gryss was shocked, a strange girl from a mythical place arrives, starts reading ancient books and speaking of the creation of the City.

Hours must have passed before Kohrstan and his father retired to their bedrooms to sleep. Hours of explanations from Kohrstan and hours of questioning from his father.

Gryss had always been curious about the goings on around the City. He did not leave his home rooms very often, but could rely on his son, and the people who stopped by to deliver materials or collect things he had made, to fill him in on the daily happenings.

Recently, however, there had been little going one and the City had seemed quiet and uneventful. More and more people seemed reluctant to participate in activities around the City. The number of people who worked apprenticeships to become tenders had dropped, and the small industries people had seemed to stop. Long past were the days when the City life was vibrant and productive. Every family had its own trade and would produce goods for others, or collect materials from the Givings and the quarries in which to exchange for things they needed. Nowadays people tended to keep to themselves, and live with the possessions they had rather than trying to create more.

The arrival of Jasmine could herald some much-needed interesting information to pass around the City.

CHAPTER 5

Books and Papers

Jasmine's second night in the City was more disturbed than her first. She had seen many things that were very different to her normal life back home. Her sleep was filled with strange dreams that woke her up often, and although she was exceptionally tired, she found it hard to get back to sleep.

Mal had slept in the room next door again, even though Jasmine had told him he could sleep in the same room as her. He slept soundly and did not wake until morning when Jasmine gently tapped his shoulder.

The stones had just fallen again with a loud thud, but that had not disturbed him. The people in the City were used to the loud sounds of the stones as they rose and fell to turn day into night, and back again.

Jasmine was still sleepy but excited about returning to the Library. The books would be fascinating to read. She hoped some would help to explain how the City had been built.

'Good Morning, did you sleep well Mal?' Jasmine asked when Mal had rubbed his eyes and sat up. 'I thought you were going to sleep all day…I mean *fall*.'

'Good morning Jasmine. I slept well thank you. Are you hungry, we can go to the Givings and get something to eat if you want?'

Jasmine's stomach had been rumbling for a while, she suddenly realised that she had only eaten one meal yesterday. 'Something to eat would be nice, and is there somewhere I can wash?'

'Yes of course, there is a pool of water where you can swim and wash; the water filters itself so it is always clean. I can ask Kohrstan if his father could give you some extra clothes, you can't live forever in those.'

Jasmine looked down at her shorts and t-shirt; she had been wearing them since she had gone to the party at the beach chalet. Since then, she had sat in the sea, fallen through a hole in the floor of Hillcroft house, walked down many dusty tunnels and slept in them for two nights. They were very dirty and ripped in a couple of places. Clean clothes sounded like a good idea.

Breakfast at the Givings was very busy, there were many people busily collecting foods from the baskets in the stone courtyard. Most of them were silent as they collected their daily food but some were talking quietly to each other. The tenders were efficiently bringing fresh baskets full of Bees, Night Stem leaves, Loujuij and many other foods, including the occasional basket of pulp from the stone tree.

A man, who was wearing a bright orange shirt, rather than the grey jacket of the tenders, was carefully arranging stone and glass bottles in a narrow basket. Mal told Jasmine that the glass bottles contained water, and the stone bottles contained the juice of the Light Fruit, a pale blue liquid squeezed from berries of the Light Tree. Jasmine had drunk the sweet juice the first evening she was with Mal at his home.

Mal and Jasmine picked up a handful of bees, some stone tree pulp and a bottle of water each, and went to sit on a rock in a circle of Night Stem trees to eat.

Jasmine's stomach was delighted to be full of delicious food again, and it was good not to have to try to pick every one of the Bees off the bush.

She had only been in the City for a couple of days and had a very disturbed nights sleep, but as she ate in the soft light of the Givings, Jasmine began to feel at ease in her new home. She would probably feel very different if she had not found Mal.

Mal and Jasmine sat contentedly, quietly chatting and eating their food. Although there were a large number of people walking back and forward to the baskets in the courtyard, it was surprisingly quiet at the Givings. Most of the tenders went about their work silently, only speaking to each other occasionally. It was amazing how they all co-ordinated themselves without speaking.

The warm air, cool water and delicious food were just what Jasmine needed to keep her insides going.

After they had eaten enough, Mal led the way through a conveyance corridor to the *Pale Water,* the pool that he had spoken about earlier, where people can wash. It was a large pool in a cavern, the same size and shape as the cavern with the felostone crystals. The floor however was completely smooth and gently sloped towards the pool of water. The floor of the pool was white, and the water, like its name was pale and almost looked opaque.

There were a couple of people already using the pool, a man and a woman, floating gently on the surface. The air was very hot in the cavern and Jasmine hoped the water would be warm too; it would not be pleasant to swim in cold water.

Mal took off his shirt and trousers and ran in wearing only his underwear. Jasmine was a little more cautious and kept her shorts and t-shirt on. The water was warm and smelt slightly of soap; perhaps there was a natural soap in the water.

As Jasmine walked about in the shallows of the pool she noticed that in a few places, the water seemed to be pushed out of the floor and in other places seemed to be sucked away. This was probably similar to a normal swimming pool where the water is pumped away to be cleaned, although Jasmine could not imagine how this pool worked.

The water was soothing. Jasmine had a few bruises and grazes from her fall that were slowly healing, but the water made them feel much better. It was probably very good for them in-fact as the water would help ensure they stayed clean and not get infected.

When Jasmine had finished swimming and thought her skin was sufficiently soaked; Mal showed her some large flat rocks on which they could dry themselves. The rocks were at the sides of the cavern, and very smooth; like glass. Mal stepped on first and sat down. Jasmine stepped on soon after and was instantly aware that the rock was warm on her feet. In fact, it was quite hot, although not too hot to be uncomfortable.

Jasmine laid down on the rock feeling the pleasant warmth

on her skin. Gentle wisps of steam slowly rose from their wet clothes and it did not take long for the warmness to dry them, and they left the pool feeling clean and refreshed.

Mal led Jasmine through the conveyance corridor and along the tunnel to Grancathai's home room. As they walked past the hole that led to the Catacombs, Jasmine thought she could hear a low buzzing sound but apart from that, it was dark and silent.

Jasmine did not like the hole. It seemed too dark and certainly unfriendly. She was happy when Mal knocked on the door, and after a few moments Grancathai opened it.

'Jasmine, Malmayorkia. I am pleased to see you both.' Grancathai held the door to allow his visitors to walk through, before closing it quietly. 'I hope you are well rested?'

'Yes thank you,' Mal said with a smile.

Grancathai ushered Jasmine and Mal towards the door to the Library. 'Jasmine, I have placed a small table and a stool on the top floor of the library so you can read the books in comfort.

'Please only take one book off the shelf at a time and replace it carefully before taking another. I think it is very important to keep the Library tidy and the books protected. Is there anything else that you will need?'

Jasmine paused for a moment. 'No I don't think so. Thank you.'

Grancathai led the way up to the top floor of the library and exactly as he had said earlier, there was a small square table and a round stool. They had been placed next to the shelf with the set of ten yellow journals. It appeared that Grancathai had dusted the top of the books, so they would not be too dirty when Jasmine took them off the shelf.

Jasmine sat down at her wooden table. The stool had been cushioned with layers of blankets cut into small squares and sown together.

'Malmayorkia and I will leave you in peace to read. It is important you concentrate; I find it very difficult to work if there is noise or distractions. When you have found something that is interesting call down to me. I shall be working on the ground floor doing some writing.' Grancathai smiled laying a hand on Jasmine's shoulder. 'Thank you Jasmine. You bring me hope of a new understanding of our City. If we can recover all this information that has been lost for a long time, perhaps we can better understand ourselves, and the way of life we have created here.'

Jasmine smiled back. 'I hope I can find what we are both looking for.'

Mal stepped forward, concerned about leaving his best friend alone. 'Jazz, I will visit you often to make sure you are alright and I will go to see Gryss, Kohrstan's father, to get you some more clothes to wear. Will you be alright here on your own?'

Jasmine was unsure what to say, she felt very nervous about being left alone again. She had found it quite uncomfortable when she was learning how to use the Conveyance Corridors and Mal left her at the Givings for a short while. However, Jasmine knew that Mal would never be far away and would be there to help whenever she needed it. 'I will be fine Mal, thank you. You are such a good friend.'

Mal and Grancathai began to descend the spiral staircase and Jasmine listened intently as the sound of footsteps on the metal steps grew quieter and finally stopped as the two men reached the bottom.

Jasmine looked at the series of journals on the shelf. They looked inviting, but at the same time; darkly mysterious and distant. 'I suppose there is no point in waiting,' Jasmine said to herself, carefully taking the left most book off the shelf and placing it on the table.

The books were very easy to read, although completely written by hand. The handwriting was tidy, the pencil drawings very clear and concise. The books were mostly records of experiments, or lists of ideas that Martin Blake had had. Occasionally there would be a few passages of a more personal nature. He would describe his feelings towards his work, or mention arguments with his assistant Dr. Paul Lewis. It appeared his working relationship with Dr Lewis was far from agreeable.

The Dayvene Laboratory was located underground and Dr. Lewis was not a fan of working without sunlight.

One particular passage was interesting:

Paul left today, taking all of his things. I know he will come back. As much as he hates working here, he understands the importance of these experiments.

Before Paul left we managed to get the second generator running, the magnetic field it generated was off the scale. If only we could keep the field stable, we could break through time and see.

That was the end of the book. Jasmine did not understand what the last sentence meant but guessed the Professor was working on a way to see the future, but it could mean many different things.

Jasmine carefully replaced the book and took another. There was more of the same scientific data and small scraps of personal information from the Professor. It was difficult to understand exactly what the professor was trying to say in his personal messages. He tended to write in long sentences that seemed to be missing some key words, replacing them with words like *it, the machine, the experiment,* or *the task.* What was it that Martin Blake was trying to build in his laboratory?

Pages of information, lists of data, sketches, drawings; it was all here. It certainly was the life's work of Professor Martin Blake, but very little of it made any sense to Jasmine who was reading the books meticulously. There must be some clues to suggest what he was doing in his underground laboratory.

Jasmine did begin to wonder if the professor really was the founder of the City, as the City was ancient, and the dates in the journals were from 1897. How could a man, who was in an underground laboratory little over a hundred years ago, build such an Old City? 'If he had been experimenting with time, perhaps he had built a machine that...' Jasmine suddenly realised she had been speaking out loud and stopped. It was a silly idea anyhow.

Jasmine had just finished looking through her fourth book when she heard the sound of footsteps on the spiral staircase. A few moments later, Grancathai's wrinkled face appeared.

'Jasmine, have you found any information about the creation of the City?' asked the old man excitedly.

Jasmine was a little worried because she did not have any information that he would find interesting. 'I am sorry; there is only information about experiments that Martin Blake was doing.'

Grancathai looked disheartened. 'There must be some information about the City's creation. When I was first learning about these books from my father, he always spoke of these books being about the builder of the City. You haven't looked through all the books yet, perhaps the others will contain more relevant information.'

'But I have looked through four books so far, and all there is, is information about scientific experiments with electricity and magnetism. If Martin Blake was the founder of the City, he certainly didn't write about it in these books. Anyway, these journals are only about a hundred years old. I don't know how much that is in generations. My mother's grandfather was born around then I think.'

'You must be mistaken about the age of the books, there are mentions of these books in my great-grandfathers archives, and he says they are much older than anyone can remember. Grancathai sighed. 'Is it possible the information is in one of the other books?'

Jasmine sat down on her stool again. She decided not to pursue the argument about the age of the books. 'Yes, I suppose there might be information in one of the other books, but it is going to take time to look through them. There are six more books to look through.'

'Very well Jasmine, I will leave you to your reading.' Grancathai said, walking towards the spiral stairs. 'And I will instruct Malmayorkia to go to the Givings and fetch you something to eat if you want?'

Jasmine nodded. 'Yes please that would be nice. Thank you.'

Grancathai descended the stairs and Jasmine was on her own once more. She picked another book off the shelf and started to flick carefully through the pages again. There were only more pictures of experiments and the same complicated equations.

The next book was the same, and the next, and all the other books; there was no mention of the City of anything to do with it. Only one paragraph in the second to last book had anything to do with being underground.

I feel my work is beginning to become my life and my life is becoming my work. Hillcroft is growing more deserted each day as the servants leave. I do not have time to employ more, I must continue with my work.

This underground laboratory is more like a prison rather than somewhere to work. The walls seem to stare at me and my experiments give less than positive results.

Talking to Paul is the only way I have to stop going mad, but everyday he seems less interested in my work.

This paragraph seemed to suggest that the laboratory certainly was near here, as it mentioned Hillcroft. That was the house Jasmine and her friends had been in before she fell into the City.

Jasmine closed the book. She suddenly remembered her friends and was worried about them, and the world outside. She hoped they were safe, and wondered if they were looking for her. It would have been a shock to find that their friend had disappeared.

Benny and Mary had returned to Hillcroft house the following day to try to find Jasmine, as they had not seen her back at the university.

Benny had climbed down into the hole where Jasmine had fallen and found himself in a dark basement. By the light of Mary's torch, he found a mound of wooden planks from the broken floor, but found no evidence of Jasmine or the slope she had slid down.

After their search, they were convinced she had not fallen down the hole and had just simply; run away.

Mal was having a lonely day. After leaving Jasmine at the library; he had gone back to his home room and tried to make it a little tidier. If Jasmine was going to stay with him for a while, he thought it important she had somewhere nice to live.

Painstakingly, he scraped up all of the dirt on the floor and carefully took it to the rubbish chutes. The rubbish chutes were three large holes, believed to be bottomless that led steeply down into darkness. It was here that the City people had thrown their rubbish for generations; there had never been a sign that it was getting full.

Although Mal was pleased with the state of the room after he had finished cleaning, he desperately wanted to be with Jasmine again for company.

After a quick snack, he remembered that he had told Jasmine he would ask Gryss for some new clothes for her. Perhaps he should take something to give to Gryss in exchange for the clothes.

Gryss often used the thin fibres from the Dauger plant leaves to make thread for his work.

Dauger plants were one of the few plants in the Givings that could not be eaten, but were very useful for making cloth and thread. Its large flat leaves could be soaked and scrapped until only the tough inner tissues remained or the fibres at the ends of the leaves could be pulled out and woven into thread. Both were very time consuming but had good results in the end.

Mal spent, what seemed like, a long time collecting the Dauger leaves. They were strong and needed cutting with a knife to get them off the trunk of the plant. There were tiny barbs at the edge of the leaves that were too small to cut through skin but they made Mal's hands feel very sore.

When Mal had collected a large bundle, he carried them in a cloth sack to the conveyance corridor and travelled to Gryss' workshop.

Mal went through the door to Gryss' workshop as quietly as he could, as he did not want to disturb the artisan if he was busy working.

'What can I do for you Malmayorkia?' Gryss said before Mal was fully through the door. Mal jumped slightly, as he was not expecting Gryss to speak so soon.

Mal closed the door quietly. Gryss was red faced and looked busy trying to hang a shelf that had obviously fallen off carrying its contents with it. The collections of small metal tools were now strewn about the floor.

Mal felt uneasy, it appeared as if Gryss was having a bad day. 'I am sorry to bother you; if you are busy I can come back later.'

Gryss dropped the shelf on the floor and sat down. 'I only put a small knife down on the shelf and it fell. I have been trying to re-hang it for ages. Maybe I should have a break. What can I do for you?'

Mal held out the cloth bag for Gryss to look at. The bright green leaves protruded from the top of the bag and Gryss instantly knew what they were. 'I thought you could do with some Dauger leaves.'

'Thank you Malmayorkia, they will be useful.' Gryss took the bag and placed it on a small table at the edge of the room. 'Now, I guess there is something you want in return?'

Mal went red. 'Only if it's not too much trouble. It's just I needed some things and I knew you might have some and...'

'What is it that you want Malmayorkia? Speak clearly, don't mumble.' Gryss' voice was direct but not unfriendly.

'My friend, Jasmine, needs some new clothes; she only has the clothes she is wearing and nothing else. Her clothes are very nice but they are getting dirty and need fixing.' Mal felt himself mumbling again and stopped speaking.

Gryss smiled. 'I have some nice clothes in the store room, quite a lot in fact. If you want you can come and choose what you think she will like.'

'Thank you very much. It will make my friend very happy.'

'Grancathai, I have something. Grancathai!' Jasmine was standing at the top of the spiral staircase calling down to the old man at the bottom. The young woman was excited and waved frantically as the aged librarian walked slowly up the steps.

'Have you found something?' Grancathai asked when he reached the top.

Jasmine nodded. 'Yes I have, but not in the journals. I got a little bored looking at them as Martin Blake only talked about his experiments and about his friend, Paul Lewis. I started to look at the other books along the shelves and found these papers tucked in at the end.'

'I have been meaning to find a better place for those papers, they seemed so untidy there, and they are very fragile,' Grancathai mentioned, glancing at the papers on the small table. 'I hope you have been careful with them.'

'Very careful,' Jasmine replied. 'And I have kept them all in order.'

Grancathai seemed a little unhappy about her looking through the papers but was excited to hear about what she had found. 'What is written on the papers? Is it the information we have been looking for?'

Jasmine grinned. 'Yes I think so. I will read you a passage. The handwriting is difficult to read and some parts of the pages I can't read at all but I will do the best I can.'

I do not know why I continue to write these notes; I now believe it is impossible to break through the barrier my experiment created. I have tried everything I know to return time to normal but we still seem too fast. It is hard to explain and I am not sure I understand it myself, but believe me when I say that we are no longer experiencing time like the outside world. Through the eastern exit, I can see the oil lamps alight with flames after 14 days. No one has been there to refill them and yet they still burn. Flakes of dirt from the tunnel ceilings seem to hover rather than fall to the ground.

What have I created? Since my experiment went wrong, I have felt a deep grief in my heart. There are 67 of us down here, including all of my staff, and the excavators working in the tunnels nearby. They are trapped as well; the barrier my experiment created has trapped us here forever. We have water and food for about two months and then I do not know what we will do.

Paul has not spoken to me in days; he just spends all of his time in the back office consoling his wife. Margaret is not taking things well. Some of the excavators are trying to dig their way out and have broken through into an underground lake.

I have moved the tower of light to the lowest chamber to try and reduce the strength of the barrier but that doesn't seem to help. There are many natural tunnels in that area, perhaps I will find a deeper one.

I hope one day someone will find these diaries and will know how we were all trapped here. Throughout the ...

'I can't read the rest of the page; I think it must have got wet.'

Grancathai looked pale he had never before heard words about the creation of the City and he had always longed to. 'So the City people *were* from the old world, this proves it. Jasmine what is the Tower of Light that he speaks of?'

'I don't know, perhaps it was the name of his experiment, or the equipment he used.' Jasmine stopped and thought for a second. 'I think there might have been a picture of something in one of the journals I thought it was a statue or something. I suppose it could be a tower.'

Jasmine picked one of the yellow journals off the shelf and flicked through it carefully. Although a lot of the information was very similar, Jasmine was good at remembering things and got the correct book first time. Flicking through the pages, she came across a double page that contained only a single drawing. The picture seemed to be of a cylindrical tower, although the size of the tower was impossible to guess. Around the base of the tower, were numerous lines joining small circles on the outer edge of the page. The top of the tower and around the side of the tower were thin arrows in groups, as if depicting lines of magnetism. There were other features to the tower but it was hard to make out what they were. To Jasmine, they were just squiggles or small shapes that decorated the tower.

At that moment, the now familiar rattle of someone's feet on the metal staircase could be heard around the library. They started faintly and grew louder as the person climbed towards the top. It was not long before the cheery face of Mal appeared at the top of the spiral steps.

Jasmine was delighted to see her friend's face. Although he had spent less than three hours away, it seemed like much longer. Grancathai was friendly but it was Mal who was her first friend in the City and she trusted him almost completely.

'Mal, I am so glad you're back. I have just found something really exciting and I must tell you.' Jasmine was beaming with a smile that nearly matched Mal's always-cheery face. 'These papers explain how people from my world were trapped here.'

Jasmine carefully explained everything she had found out about the beginning of the City, which in total was not very much, but it took some careful explaining. Mal did not really understand at first. There seemed to be a lot of terminology that did not mean anything to the people living in the City.

Their written language had changed beyond recognition over the centuries as people had forgotten how to write and had to relearn. However, their spoken language had changed little in the way of grammar, general vocabulary and even accent, but some words; common place in the world above were meaningless here. Words such as day, night, autumn, winter and sunlight were all words that Jasmine had found that Mal did not understand. Now there were more words and some were very complex to understand.

The idea of a scientist was particularly difficult to explain. Everything in the City seemed to work. The stones rose and fell, water flowed from the fountains and the felostones gently buzzed continuously without fail. The City had survived this way for centuries; there was nothing new that the people of the City wanted.

Why should they learn and practice science to invent

something, when you are happy with everything that you have, and why try to understand the truth about how something works if it has never broken and works exactly how you want it to? To these people science would be to seek the truth about something, but they feel the myths and legends they have created have much greater meaning and interest than the truth ever could have. The people of the City, Mal included, were content with their stories of how things work and did not care to analyse any further.

This was Jasmine's interpretation of the City People's thoughts and attitudes. Although she was perfectly correct in nearly every way, there was one detail she had not thought of. In one very important way, she was wrong in her assessment. There *was* one truth the people longed to know, but probably would not admit it, the truth about the creation of the City and their way of life.

Legend tells of a wise man who led his people into caves after a great apocalypse that threatened the extinction of the human population. Here the people lived for a long time happy with their way of life, not wanted to return to their original homes, even after the apocalypse had past.

It did not take long before they out grew the caves, and so the Wise Man; Martiblak spent the rest of his life digging out the great cavern and building the foundations of the City.

The people who now live in the City both believe and disbelieve this story at the same time. They know it could not be true as it would take a thousand men their whole lives and more to dig out the cavern, but most importantly they believed that the Old World did not really exist.

On the other hand, all the people of the City had grown up being told that story, and there was no other explanation to the creation of the City, so everyone just seemed to unquestioningly accept it.

These contradictions; present within the minds of all the people here, was the reason that they would seek the truth, or more accurately, wait until the truth came and displayed itself.

When Jasmine had finished speaking and Mal and

Grancathai understood everything she had said, they stood silent in disbelief.

'Jasmine, I never thought I would see the day that someone would read these books in the library. I have devoted my whole life to their up keep, and now you are able to read about the creation on the City.' Grancathai was truly stunned as he tried to come to terms with what Jasmine had read.

If everything in the papers and books were true, Martin Blake and his staff that worked in the Dayvene Laboratory had in fact built the City.

It had been little more than one hundred years ago that it had happened. August 19th 1894, Martin Blake and his Principal Associate Paul Lewis were working on a machine to look into the past. It never worked, but the tower of light; the machine filled with over a thousand lenses, mirrors and diamond refractors did do something. The electromagnets that controlled a flow of super charged light particles around the device were so powerful that instead of looking into the past, it actually damaged time.

The machine created a boundary in time. On the outside everything continued as normal, whilst on the inside, time was too damaged to pass properly. Over one thousand five hundred years had passed for the underground city and the descendants of the people originally trapped underground had never been taught about what had happened. Therefore, over the generations, thousands of people had lived and died in the City, oblivious to the fact they were stuck in a bubble of time.

CHAPTER 6

<u>Essence of Tamboli</u>

It was Jasmine that slept-in late the following morning, and Mal had quietly come into his home room to wake her. He was unsure about waking her, she seemed very peaceful as she slept; face calm and her hair lying smoothly over her shoulders.

Jasmine had had a long day the day before; reading books in the library had turned out to be quite tiring. After the revelation about the creation of the City, she had gone on to read more notes written by Martin Blake after the accident. It went into more details and described the tower of light. Of course, everything had to be explained to Grancathai and Mal who were intrigued by every little detail.

As the day had gone on, Kohrstan had come to the library to bring food. Grancathai welcomed the food but insisted that nobody ate or drank anything in the library.

Everyone had sat down on stools in Grancathai's home room to enjoy the delicious meal. There were the foods that Jasmine had already tried; Bees, Loujuij, and Stone Tree pulp but there was also a couple of new ones that she had never seen before. Jasmine had eaten especially heartily as her brain had been working hard looking at the books and papers. She was again a little wary at first of trying some of the new foods as they looked very different to food she would have back home but after a little persuasion from Mal she tucked in and enjoyed every mouthful.

Everyone seemed to speak little about anything else apart from what Jasmine had found in the books. Grancathai and Mal had been particularly interested. Kohrstan, although less confused about the whole matter than Mal, seemed it hard to believe. In his mind, he still believed that the Old World did not exist, even with Jasmine as living proof sat right in front of him.

The Tower of Light slowly started to feature more in their conversations. Jasmine had had an idea about it and tried for a long time to explain. She believed that the Tower of light could be responsible for the Tamboli Rooms, either on its own or with Paluuka.

The Tower of Light was a mysterious idea, the small group of people had very little information about it, but slowly Jasmine's suggestion that it was the source of Tamboli began to sink in. Even more disturbing, however, was where the Tower of Light was located. Martin Blake had mentioned that he had moved it to the lowest chamber to reduce its effects, there was one plausible place it could be and that was in the Catacombs.

As the day drew to an end and the bell sounded the imminent rising of the stones the small group departed each other's company to return to their home rooms.

'Jasmine?' Mal whispered quietly. 'Jazz, it is time to wake up.'

Slowly Jasmine began to stir, her mind gaining control after its long sleep. 'Mal? Have I been asleep for a long time?'

Mal smiled and offered some water in a cup. 'The stones fell quite a while ago, but you haven't been asleep for too long. I have something to show you.'

Jasmine sat up right on her blankets, and felt the calming vibrations of the felostone on her wrist.

Mal had opened his wooden chest and was taking out a small cloth bag, no larger than an average woman's handbag. It had been repaired many times with various colours of thread, but it did not look too peculiar against the mottled brown and yellow fabric. The top was drawn to a close by thin laces that were tied together in a bow. A long strap for wearing over the shoulder was firmly tied to the corners.

'I would like you to have this.' Mal said holding the bag out to Jasmine. 'My mother made it for me when I was very young, but I don't seem to use it now.'

Jasmine smiled a thankful smile. 'Mal, are you sure you want me to have it? It's very beautiful, and must mean a lot to you.'

Mal's face lit up with a smile. 'It does mean a lot to me, it reminds me of my mother; not the way she is now but how she used to be when I was young. Nevertheless, it would mean more to me for you to have it and see it used everyday. I have put a bottle of water in it, but you could put anything you like in it.'

Jasmine was very pleased with her new bag and carefully hung it on her shoulder after she had dressed and was ready to go back to the library. She did not have anything to put in the bag just yet, but decided to carry it anyway, as it obviously meant a lot to Mal that she should have it.

Jasmine had only been to the library a couple of times but she was beginning to remember how to get there, and although she still could not use the conveyance corridors on her own, she would carefully think of where they were going. She thought that if she practised whenever she could, then picturing the rooms in her mind would be easier next time she tried to use the Conveyance corridor on her own.

Grancathai was busily tiding his home room when Mal and Jasmine arrived. Clouds of dust were floating in the air and there was a slight stale smell. One of the racks on the end wall had had all of its contents taken out and carefully laid out on the floor. Obviously, they had been moved to allow the rack to be dusted.

'Fall to you Jasmine,' Grancathai said with a dusty smile. Jasmine quickly remembered that Fall was the City's name for morning. Mal had adopted the word morning from Jasmine but no one else in the City really knew the term, except perhaps Kohrstan.

'Good Fall to you too Grancathai. I would like to read some more books if that is alright?'

Grancathai shook off some of the dust that had clung to his clothes. 'Yes Jasmine, it is alright. In fact, I am happy you have come; I have found another book that maybe of some interest. It is an old book, bound only by string and it is very delicate. It has pictures in it that look similar to the drawing of the Tower of Light that you saw in Martin Blake's Journal.'

Mal glanced across the biggest table in the room expecting to see the book. It was not anywhere to be seen, or at least what Mal expected the book to look like was not anywhere to be seen. The table had only a few sheets of loose paper on it, and three heavy looking volumes bound in red leather.

Grancathai smiled. 'It is in the Library Malmayorkia. I seldom take the older books out of the library as there is too much moisture in the air out here.'

As the small group had done many times before, Grancathai led the way through the door and short corridor into the Library.

Jasmine always enjoyed walking into the library, the bright lights hanging above and the glint of the metal stairs seemed magical. In all her life, she had never seen anything like the wonders that were contained within the City.

Occasionally Jasmine would find herself thinking of the world outside and what she would have been doing if she had not found her way into the City; this was one of those moments. The books that Grancathai had laid out on the little table reminded her of the time she had spent studying at her university. There had been numerous textbooks that she would refer to before an exam. She would lay them out on one of the tables in the university library or in her room in the same way.

'I have prepared a few more books for you Jasmine as I guessed you would come here again.' Grancathai was slowly walking up the spiral stairs as he spoke, his boots gently clanging against the metal. Grancathai was obviously very happy that Jasmine could read the books; otherwise, he would not have prepared so many books for her. She thought back to a couple of days before, when she had first started to read the journals of Martin Blake. Grancathai had insisted that only one book be removed from the shelves at a time, now he would take four or five off at a time.

Walking to sit down on her stool, Jasmine suddenly jumped as the door to the library flew open with a bang. Rushing through the door was Kohrstan, gasping for breath as if he had just run a marathon. He was sweating profusely and shaking from head to toe. Something bad had happened. An unimaginable shock had sent him running across the City to find Mal.

Crippled by exhaustion he collapsed on the floor by the foot of the spiral stairs, his lungs struggling to supply oxygen to his body. Mal turned pale and dropped the book he was holding to run down the stairs, quickly followed by Jasmine, both fearful for their friend. What had happened to put him in such a panic?

Kohrstan's face was flushed red, his eyes wide and alert. He tried to speak but the extreme speed at which he was gasping for breath held the words back and only groans came out.

Mal took his friends hand and gently squeezed it to let him know he was there and would help him. 'Kohrstan? What has happened? Are you hurt?' Mal's questions went unanswered for a long period of time.

'I will fetch some water to calm him,' Grancathai said, walking towards the library door. The suffering of the young man was too much for him to bear.

Tears began to roll down Kohrstan's face, and he took a couple of slower, deeper breaths. Jasmine used the edge of her shirt to dab the tears, and the sweat from his forehead.

The first word Kohrstan managed to say was simply, 'Tamboli.'

Mal went white. 'Where? You must tell me what room has suffered Tamboli. Did you get caught in a Tamboli room?'

Kohrstan frantically shook his head and struggled with more words. 'Not me, my father, our home room. Tamboli!'

Mal slumped on the floor next to Kohrstan and began crying in sympathy for his friend and in incredible sadness for his childhood carer. Gryss had taken Mal in when his own parents had been struck by the evil effects of Tamboli. Mal knew what Kohrstan was feeling, he had felt it before. Memories of his own tragic loss started flooding back and fixed with his new sadness.

Slumped on the floor, the two friends put their arms around each other and hugged. Jasmine sat still next to them, unsure what to do or even say. She too was saddened by the thought of Gryss being stuck in a Tamboli room, but she knew her grief was mild in comparison.

Grancathai had returned with the water and was standing motionless in the doorway. Jasmine stood and made her way over to him. 'Grancathai what should we do?'

Grancathai laid a hand on Jasmine's shoulder. 'I fear that there is nothing that we can do, we must let them be for a time. They have always been friends and are practically brothers. I know they don't show it much but they are close. Their grief will be terrible, but they will help each other in the end. Perhaps we should leave them in peace for the moment.'

Jasmine could see the pain in Mal's eyes, the same pain as the time he had shown her the entrance hall where his family was detained by the effects of Tamboli. Quietly, she took the cup of water from Grancathai and placed in carefully down next to her friends on the floor. Mal and Kohrstan did not see her, or even hear the click of the door as she and Grancathai left the library.

Mal and Kohrstan held their embrace for a long time, taking comfort from the closeness, but slowly they released and lay down on the floor staring at the lights hanging from the ceiling at the top of the library.

Kohrstan was the first to speak after a long period of silence. 'It's all my fault.'

Mal sat up and looked into his friend's eyes. 'No, it can't be your fault, you did not create Tamboli. You shouldn't blame yourself.'

'You don't understand,' Kohrstan continued. 'It really is my fault. I should have gone back for him, I should have warned him earlier. I should have spoken to him more often about taking his felostone off. If only I had...'

Mal interrupted. 'Tamboli happens too fast, there was nothing you could have done.'

'But I have to think about it, you weren't there, you didn't see what I did.' Kohrstan stood and walked away from his friend. 'I could have saved him.'

'Kohrstan, what happened?'

Kohrstan turned and faced his friend. 'I ran away.'

Mal listened intently as Kohrstan explained what had happened.

'I returned home after going to the Pale Water. My father was in his workshop repairing one of his shelves. He was stood holding the shelf and adjusting a bracket or something, I didn't really pay much attention.

'I sat for a while tidying some of my fathers tools on the work bench, when I was struck by a strange sensation, my felostone felt still and cold. It had stopped vibrating.

'I don't remember exactly what I did. I panicked, and shouted something at my father about Tamboli. I was making for the door as my father let go of the shelf. It fell and knocked him to the ground. I was about to go back, but I had pains in my mind and I just ran out of the door. I didn't look back I just kept running. I could hear my father's screams from down the corridor, and then it just seemed to go silent. It was then that I stopped and realised what I had done. I should have helped him to the door, but I was afraid, and when it went silent, I knew Tamboli had taken him and there was nothing I could do.

'I didn't return to our home room, I couldn't face standing in the door way, and seeing my father stuck in Tamboli. I simply ran here. You must think badly of me; I have done a terrible thing.' Kohrstan closed his eyes and hung his head in shame.

Mal stood and went to his friend but Kohrstan tried to turn away. Mal grabbed his arm to hold him. 'If you had returned you would have been stuck there with him. Tamboli takes hold too quickly for anyone to do anything. There was nothing you could have done for your father.'

Kohrstan put his arms around Mal and again they hugged each other. 'I am so sorry Mal; I don't know what to do. I wish there was a way to help my father.'

'There isn't...' Mal stopped mid word. If Jasmine was right and the tower of light was responsible for creating Tamboli Rooms, then maybe they would stop if they could switch off the machine, but that would mean going into the Catacombs. It had been Jasmine who first thought of the idea of travelling to the Catacombs and finding Martin Blake's creation, but he had told her it was not possible to go into the Catacombs. That had been a lie of sorts, it was not impossible to go into the Catacombs, just dangerous. He was afraid to go into the Catacombs, no one knew exactly what was down there, but if they could help Gryss and possibly his own parents, they should try.

'Jasmine said something to me earlier about finding one of Martin Blake's inventions; the Tower of Light. If we find it, Jasmine thinks, we could switch it off and stop Tamboli rooms.'

Kohrstan was struck by a glimmer of hope. 'Is it possible? Can we find the tower of light?'

'I really wish we could Kohrstan, I really do, but the Tower of Light is probably in the Catacombs.'

Kohrstan's glimmer of hope faded at the mere mention of the Catacombs. 'Can you tell me more about what Jasmine has found out?'

Kohrstan listened attentively as Mal explained more about the tower of light, its power, and its probable location in the Catacombs. It seemed more like a fantasy story than real life but they both hoped everything was true.

Jasmine had gone with Grancathai back to his home room. They sat and spoke about Gryss and the Tamboli room he was now in. Grancathai could understand Jasmine's desire to find the tower of light and told her about books that had been written by his grandfather about the Catacombs. 'There isn't much information but he describes small pockets of people that live among the maze of tunnels and chambers of the Catacombs.'

Jasmine was interested to know more about the Catacombs, but Mal had seemed nervous when talking about going there. 'What are the people like who live there?'

Grancathai opened a small draw under the edge of the desk and took out a bundle of papers, joined together in the top corner by a small metal stud. 'These are accounts that my grandfather wrote about the Catacombs. It doesn't say much about how he found out this information, but I imagine he must have gone there and met the people.'

Grancathai handed the papers to Jasmine who looked through them. The paper was thick and creased but seemed more fragile than paper she was used to. The pages were written in the modern City text that Jasmine could not understand but she flicked through the dozen or so pages, stopping to look at the occasional colour drawing.

Most of the drawings were depictions of rooms, or stone carvings within the rooms, although very few of the rooms had any carvings at all. The style of the carvings differed from that of the City, they were poorly made without the symmetry and grace of the carvings Jasmine had seen. It was possible the drawings had not accurately copied the carvings, but they seemed intricate and detailed.

The picture on the last page was of a small boy, perhaps about 10 years old, dressed in a white tunic and carrying a bucket. He seemed sad or at least a little apprehensive about something. Grancathai's grandfather had drawn the picture, and probably got the boy to stand there while he worked.

There was a small paragraph written under the picture, which again was written in the modern City text, which Jasmine could not even begin to understand. After she had carefully studied the picture, Jasmine handed the papers back to Grancathai asking him to read the paragraph.

Grancathai nodded and began to read. *'Armiche is the closest approximation of his name that I can write. I met him in the third tunnel past the stream. He was carrying water. I spoke to him but his replies were difficult to understand, some words were not what I expected.'*

Jasmine listened carefully, numerous questions brewing in her mind. When Grancathai had finished he placed the bundle of papers back down on the table, so Jasmine could again see the picture.

'Grancathai, do the people of the Catacombs speak a different language to us?' Jasmine asked studying the picture again.

Grancathai rubbed his chin. 'I do not know. This is the only place in the account that mentions someone speaking. My grandfather could obviously communicate with the boy enough to ask him his name.'

'Maybe there are just some words that are different. Some of the words that I say seem to have different meanings here. Is there any mention of a tower of light? Or are there any descriptions of the layout of the Catacombs?'

Grancathai shook his head. 'There is no mention of the tower of light, but that isn't a surprise, he says it wasn't possible to travel too far within the Catacombs as all rooms look alike, and nothing leads to where is should.'

Jasmine was puzzled. 'What does that mean, nothing leads to where it should?'

Grancathai turned over a couple of pages and began reading the text again.

'The tunnels beyond the green room are long and have many turns, some lead nowhere, while others lead back the way they came. The more I try and progress the further I seem to go back.'

'My initial thoughts were perhaps there are Conveyance Corridors in the Catacombs but less organised and move you randomly without knowing other places you are going to. You could not progress further because you would not know what the rooms further on looked like, and therefore not be able to picture them in your mind.'

Jasmine's heart sank; she desperately wanted to do something to help the people stuck in Tamboli rooms. 'It seems like the Catacombs are well named. Do you think we would be able to find the tower of light?'

'Going to the Catacombs will mean going to a place without maps, where every corridor and tunnel may return you to where you started. You would meet people who may never have seen someone from the City, and there is no telling how friendly they will be. You may have to walk huge distances and there may not be a supply of water or food down there, you would have to carry everything with you.

'It sounds difficult and dangerous, but I do not think it would be impossible. I can help you prepare, I can find as much information as there is written in the library, you can take plenty of food with you. Nevertheless, Jasmine, no one here will think less of you if you decide not to go. It will be very difficult regardless of the amount of preparation you do. Are you sure you want to go?'

Jasmine took a deep breath. 'This is something I must do, you have all shown me such kindness, and asked for nothing in return.'

The library door clicked as the ornate handle was turned, and the door opened. Mal and Kohrstan walked through silently. Jasmine desperately wanted to throw her arms around Mal and let him know that she was there for him and would be his friend, but she decided it was best to stay sat at the table.

'I am going to go with Kohrstan up to the Givings, for a walk. Will you be alright Jasmine, staying here for a while?' Mal asked quietly as he went towards the door.

Jasmine nodded, 'Of course Mal take whatever time you need. And Kohrstan I am really sorry about what happened.'

Kohrstan smiled slightly but said nothing in reply as he left with Mal.

The exit door closed and Jasmine was again left with Grancathai. 'Jasmine, I think you are doing the right thing by waiting to tell Mal of our plans. Now certainly wouldn't be a good time; he needs time to himself, and time with Kohrstan.'

Jasmine nodded in agreement and sighed. It was difficult knowing your friend was hurting and having to wait before you could do anything.

Grancathai had decided it best if Jasmine did not continue reading that day, although she was quite insistent that she should start planning their journey to the Catacombs. 'There will be time tomorrow, Jasmine,' he said as he carefully rolled the piles of papers on the table.

Jasmine felt a little lost without Mal. Grancathai was friendly and polite, but Jasmine missed the warmth and fun of her best friend in the City.

As the day went by, Jasmine frequently thought about Mal and Kohrstan and what they were doing, as she helped

Grancathai finish the cleaning in his home room. It was a long task as a thick layer of dust covered everything in the room.

When they had finished, Grancathai took Jasmine to the Drop Tunnel where they could throw away all of the dirty rags and pieces of rubbish. Little more than a two metre wide hole in the ground Jasmine was unsure why they would throw rubbish down there, but was amazed as the rubbish disappeared into the darkness of the deep hole. Listening for a long time Jasmine tried to hear it hit the bottom; but there was no sound. Either the landing was soft enough not to make any noise, or the bottom was far too deep to be able to hear the rubbish hitting it. It was yet another element in the City of Martiblak that Jasmine found a mystery.

On returning to Grancathai's home room, Jasmine again started to think about Mal. She kept expecting him to walk through the door, but he did not come; he was still with Kohrstan. They had walked for a long time at the Givings and later went to sit on a fountain in the Great Corridor.

They talked for long periods and then sat silently for similarly long times. They reminisced about their childhood together and spoke at length about Gryss; not only a father to Kohrstan but also a father figure to Mal.

Kohrstan's mother never wanted children and left as soon as he had been born. His father had never spoken of her, and in all possibility, Kohrstan had probably seen her around the City, but they never would have recognised each other and neither really had any interest in meeting.

At the end of the day, Mal still had not returned when the bell sounded to signal the rising on the stones.

'Grancathai, I should go back to Mal's home room, but I don't know how to use the Conveyance corridors. Would you be able to take me there?' Jasmine asked as she heard the bell chiming.

Grancathai smiled. 'Of course Jasmine, but one day you will need to learn how to use the conveyance corridors on your own.'

Jasmine frowned slightly. 'I have tried many times before, and Mal has been teaching me different techniques but I just can't do it.'

'With practice you will learn in time.'

'I hope so; it would be nice to travel on my own if I need to.'

Grancathai nodded. 'Thank you for your help today Jasmine. When you see Malmayorkia, will you tell him your plan to go to the Catacombs, and ask him to go with you?'

'Yes, I am sure he would come with me, we have briefly spoken about it.'

'I think it would be best if you didn't ask Kohrstan to go, his grief is still too fresh.'

Jasmine had not thought about asking Kohrstan to come, in her mind it had just been Mal and herself going to the Catacombs. 'Perhaps it would be best; he will find things difficult for a while.'

Grancathai escorted Jasmine back to Mal's home room. When they arrived, he quickly made his way back to the library as the loud rumble of the rising stones echoed around the City.

Jasmine waited in the room with the glass dome and watched Grancathai leave; before she opened the small door into Mal's home room and was greeted by the sight of Kohrstan and Mal asleep on blankets on either side of the room. They had become tired after their long walk across the Givings and had returned come home to rest. Kohrstan had fallen asleep first and Mal had covered him with a blanket to stop him getting cold. Mal had fallen asleep a few moments later.

Jasmine closed the door quietly and lay down next to Mal. She had tried very hard not to wake him but his eyes flickered open as she lay down.

'Jasmine, I am sorry. I didn't mean to fall asleep, I was going to come back and get you.'

'It's alright Mal; Grancathai brought me back. We have been talking a lot.'

Mal rubbed his eyes. 'About the history of Martiblak?'

Jasmine nodded and continued; they were both talking as quietly as they could to avoid disturbing Kohrstan. 'Partly, but mostly about the Catacombs, and we have decided something.'

'Decided something?'

'Yes, but I need you to agree as well, I think we should go to the Catacombs and find the tower of light. I have spoken to Grancathai a lot about this. He agrees it may be possible.' Jasmine sat up on her blanket.

Mal again looked horrified as he did every time Jasmine mentioned the Catacombs. 'We're not supposed to go down there. We have always been taught that the Catacombs were a bad place and dangerous to go there. Even if we could find the tower of light, how do you know stopping it will stop the Tamboli rooms? We shouldn't go to the Catacombs.'

Jasmine looked cross. 'But none of that makes sense Mal. Who says you can't go to the Catacombs? There isn't anyone in-charge here, no one to get you into trouble if you did go down there.

'Don't you see Mal? Nothing about the Catacombs makes any sense. You all think you know what people from the Catacombs look like, I know because everyone thought I was from the Catacombs. However, who do you know that has ever seen someone from the Catacombs? Everything seems to be rumours; someone thinks they saw a Lesser from the Catacombs but no one really has. If they had kept coming up here surely you would know how they spoke.' Jasmine paused momentarily, expecting Mal to speak but he stayed silent. 'And Mal, if the Lessers are so dangerous why did people just ignore me and look away when they thought I was from the Catacombs? Why weren't they scared of me? You see Mal; none of this makes sense, and while I do believe the Catacombs to be a dangerous place, I don't think it is as bad as everyone here makes out. It appears that encounters with the Lessers are just stories.'

Mal was reluctant to agree to go to the Catacombs but trusted Jasmine. 'When I think about going to the Catacombs it makes me feel sick, and very scared, but I feel worse when I think about Gryss. If we can find Martin Blake's invention, it would be worth going to the Catacombs. I will go with you Jasmine.'

Jasmine smiled. 'We will face the Catacombs together, we can do this.'

Mal did not share Jasmine's enthusiasm and dedication to finding the Tower of Light but understood the importance of trying.

'We should get some sleep, we will have a busy day tomorrow planning everything, and getting what we will need.' Jasmine lay backed down and pulled the blanket over her. Mal did the same on the other side of the room. Both of them found it very difficult to sleep that night, as they were thinking about the Catacombs and trying to imagine what might be down there.

Mal Shivered as he carefully wrapped strips of cloth around his hand. He had always been taught that the Catacombs were not somewhere to go to, ever! It was a place that children would talk about going to, and tell scary stories about what might be down there, but in reality, they would not dare venture into that dark pit.

As Mal stood at the top of the vertical tunnel looking into the darkness below, he felt a strange coldness come over him.

It had taken them the whole of the previous day to prepare for their trip. Jasmine wanted to reread the small amount of information there was in the library. Grancathai assisted her and read the papers written in the new text.

Mal and Kohrstan had gone to the Givings to collect some fresh food. They wanted to get the freshest there was as they might be carrying the food for a long time. They also filled some bottles with water.

News had spread around the City that Jasmine and Malmayorkia were planning to go down into the Catacombs. Kohrstan had told only one person, but it did not take long before many more people had found out and passed on the information. The people had mixed feelings about their trip, they knew nothing of the reasons, but most felt it was not a good idea. Mal and Jasmine found they got strange looks from people when they went to the Givings to have lunch.

They tried to ignore the looks they got and concentrated on their preparations; returning quickly to the library to pack Jasmine's small bag with equipment that they needed.

Jasmine was very pleased to have, at last, things to put in the bag that Mal had given her.

They decided Jasmine would carry her bag and Mal would carry an oil lamp that Kohrstan had found.

It had taken him a very long time to find the lamp; he knew he had seen one somewhere but could not remember exactly where. After much searching, he found it tucked into a large coil of rope in a small room his father once used to store things.

The lamp was old and rusty, and only half filled with precious oil. There was a special lighting rod on the side of the glass lamp. Once turned the lighting rod sent a small shower of sparks onto the wick in the centre.

Kohrstan tried the lamp briefly. He had to make sure that the lamp worked, but did not want to use up too much oil. There was no telling how long his friends would be in the Catacombs and it was impossible to know how light it was going to be.

All the equipment they collected was brought to the library and carefully packed into their bags. Amongst the food, water, and the oil lamp was a length of rope and some blank paper and pencils in case they needed to make any notes. The food had been carefully wrapped in small squares of cloth or carefully placed in metal tins to keep it fresh, and the water had to be put into bottles with lids that fitted lightly to stop them from leaking.

Jasmine was surprised when Grancathai handed her something to put in her bag. It was a small folded piece of paper, torn out from one of Martin Blake's journals. On the paper was the picture of the Tower of Light. Grancathai was normally very protective of his books and never let them leave the library, but he felt it was important that Jasmine and Mal had a picture of what it was they were looking for.

'You must look after this piece of paper Jasmine,' he said as he watched Jasmine put the folded page into her bag. 'The air outside the library is not good for the ink; it will fade quickly. You should keep it folded in your bag and only get it out when necessary. Be extra careful when you unfold it, while the folds help to keep the ink away from the air, they will damage the paper and make it tear.'

Jasmine and Mal slept well that night, which surprised them both. They were expecting to be too nervous to fall asleep but after a few last minute discussions, they slowly drifted off and slept late in the morning.

It did not matter that they got up late, they had little to do except eat well and dress in warm clothes. They had agreed to leave half way through the day and so sat chatting for a while in the Givings until it was time to leave.

The time for preparation and planning had now passed and after long goodbyes with Grancathai and Kohrstan; Mal climbed down onto the first metal rung; testing it carefully to ensure that it would support him before allowing his full weight on it. A moment later, he lowered himself down onto the next rung, again testing its strength. After he had descended a few more rungs, Jasmine began her descent, carefully watching the distance between herself and Mal, as she did not want to step and his fingers.

The metal rungs were bent at odd angles and were covered in rust. The rags around their hands helped protect their skin a bit, but occasionally a sharp edge would prick their fingertips or scratch through the rag.

As they descended into the darkness, the air seemed to get colder and chills ran through their bodies. At least they thought the chills were from the cold, but they could easily have come from fear.

Jasmine had experienced this fear before, when she had first arrived in the City, and gone into the unknown. Mal, on the other hand, had always lived in the City and had little experience of going anywhere particularly new. There was the added fear from being told on numerous occasions, that you should never go into the Catacombs. Jasmine had helped Mal considerably when she had mentioned the Catacombs being made of stories and legend; it gave him the chance to be open minded about the Catacombs and not to expect the worst.

The rungs continued to descend into the darkness.

At the bottom was a small stone chamber; the light was dim, and the air was cold and stale. The chamber, in which Jasmine and Mal now stood, stretched for about twenty metres towards a dark tunnel.

The walls were grey, but the remains of brightly coloured plaster could be seen in some places. This tunnel was once beautifully decorated with painted walls and illuminated by oil lamps hung from metal brackets along the walls. None of that was now visible except for the plaster remains, and small twisted strips of rusted metal hanging off the wall or fallen to the ground.

The floor was littered with uneven stones and fallen plaster from the walls. Walking in the half-light would be difficult, but thankfully not too treacherous.

Mal turned the lighting rod on the lamp; it clicked but failed to light. Again, he turned it, a little quicker this time but still the flint failed to ignite the oil on the wick. A shiver went down Mal's back, either from the cold of the Catacombs or from anxiety from the lamp refusing to light.

Taking a deep breath Mal turned the lighting rod a third time. It fizzed momentarily and burst into light. The glass ball diffused the light beautifully. Suddenly the room seemed friendlier in the graceful glow from the lamp.

Mal adjusted the wick, turning down the light slightly to prolong its burning time. There was no telling how long it would take to find the Tower of Light.

Nervously they began their journey into the mysterious Catacombs.

CHAPTER 7

The Catacombs

There was not a choice in the route they took from the chamber at the bottom of the metal rungs. A single tunnel led straight for about twenty metres, then turned sharply to the left and exited into another stone room.

This room, although much larger than the first one, appeared very similar, even down to the crumbling plaster and rusted lamp brackets. Here there was more choice, as there were three tunnels leading in different directions. They all looked the same; dark and featureless.

Mal and Jasmine looked at each other and without saying a single word; walked towards the centre tunnel.

The light from Mal's lamp, although turned down low, produced enough light to see that the tunnel ended abruptly in a stone wall. There was no point in exploring a tunnel with a dead end and so they made their way towards the left tunnel.

This tunnel was very different, but equally impassable. It sloped downwards for about ten metres and widened dramatically into a chamber with a high ceiling.

The tunnel narrowed again at the far side of the chamber and continued downwards but the space in-between was not a floor. It was a large well with steep rocky sides. There was barely a hand's width between the edge of the well and the sidewalls. Jasmine looked carefully around the inside edge of the well, hoping to find metal rungs similar to the ones they had just climbed down, but there were none.

Jasmine and Mal were already starting to feel their expedition was not going to plan.

The third tunnel was even worse. It ran up hill slightly, curving around to the left. At first, it seemed promising as Mal and Jasmine walked along it for about five minutes, but they were disheartened to find it slowly grew narrower. After a little while, it was so narrow that even Jasmine could not squeeze herself between the walls. They had to go back.

Mal was already thinking about returning to the City, but Jasmine was much more determined. She returned to the chamber with the well, down the left-hand tunnel. On closer inspection, she was convinced it might be possible to walk around the tiny edge next to the wall. It would be extremely difficult; relying on holding on to small rocks that protruded from the wall and narrow cracks that fingers could just be squeezed into.

'I'm not sure we can get round there Jazz, the ledge is too small and there isn't even anything to tie the rope onto for safety.'

Jasmine was busy at the edge of the well cautiously looking at the narrow ledge and evaluating the possibility of being able to walk round it. 'We can do it Mal, we *have* to do it. If we can't get round here we have no chance of finding the Tower of Light.'

'I believe you Jasmine, if you say we can do it then I believe that we can.' Mal had a strong admiration for Jasmine's determination and personal strength. Instead of just seeing defeat, Jasmine found a way around any problem.

Looking around the edge Jasmine could see some well-defined footholds and some good cracks. 'I think we will be alright as long as we take it slow and make sure our feet and hands are in good positions before we make our next move. I think climbers only move either one hand or one foot at a time; keeping the other three firmly attached to the wall.'

'What should I do with the oil lamp? Mal asked. 'It will be very dark in here without it.'

Jasmine thought for a moment, the glass would break if they tried to throw it to the other side and it would be too hot to be strung over their backs. 'I think we should be ok if we pass it between the larger areas on the ledge. If I go round to that large area there; you can pass me the lamp then when I am further round and you have got the lamp, again you can pass it forward.'

Mal nodded in agreement.

Taking a few calming breaths; Jasmine stepped across the first part of the ledge. Some small stones were dislodged, as she placed her foot on the uneven surface, and they went bouncing down the edge of the well. It was not possible to hear them hitting the bottom; it must be very deep.

The first larger section of the ledge was only one more step away. Jasmine held out her hand and fitted her fingers into a small crack. Holding on tightly, she swung her leg across. Her foot landed exactly on target and she was able to shift her body weight to help move her over onto the tiny platform.

Mal had moved his first foot onto the ledge and held out the lamp. They both had to stretch their arms out fully, but they just managed to pass the lamp across.

Shuffling her feet slightly, Jasmine managed to create enough space for the lamp to sit securely against the wall, its soft light flickering gently against the rough stone.

Jasmine took another step and it was the biggest step she had taken so far and her foot was a little out of place; it did not hold in position when she tried to put her weight on it. Luckily, Jasmine had a tight grip with her hands and her left foot was still firmly in place. Climbers were certainly right when they came up with the idea of keeping three points of contact.

The air was dry down in the Catacombs and it was hard work climbing along the narrow ledge. Jasmine wished she could have a break and drink from the water bottle in her bag.

Another step was taken, and again the lamp was passed a little further round the outside of the well.

Mal was a lot stronger than Jasmine but he did not have her dexterity or balance; he found it difficult to position his hands and feet. Fortunately, Jasmine was able to help by looking round and pointing out good places that his fingers could go, or checking that his feet were in the correct position.

It was slow painstaking work, and extremely tiring. Each step or movement of a hand had to be carefully thought about. Professional climbers would probably have got round in less than half the time, especially if they did not have an oil lamp to pass along every other step. However, Jasmine and Mal were not professional climbers and the lamp was proving very tricky.

They had passed the half way mark; each step got them closer to the other side and the floor where they could stand normally.

Their hands were already sore from climbing down the rusty metal rungs, now they were being forced into narrow gaps and gripping rough outcrops. Their knees were suffering too; they were frequently being knocked against protruding pieces of rock or being scraped across the wall if they stumbled or lost balance for a moment.

'Mal, you can pass me the lamp again,' Jasmine said as she reached another stable position with enough space to put down the lamp.

The part of the ledge Mal was standing on was not particularly big and the surface was rough and covered in dust and stone fragments. Jasmine had slipped a little when she had been there, but Mal almost lost his balance completely.

He picked up the lamp from where it had been left against the wall and reached out to pass it onto Jasmine. She was a long way off and Mal had to shift his body to lean as far as he could. Jasmine did the same, stretching out her arm to grab the lamp handle with her fingers.

The lamp was almost in reach; Jasmine's fingers could just touch the edge of the metal handle. Mal leaned over a little further and at that instant, his right foot slipped on the loose surface.

In the blink of an eye, he reached up with his right hand to grab a small outcrop of rock. By some miracle, he managed to grasp the rock tightly in his fingers, stop his body from sliding further, and allow him to quickly reposition his foot. If he had not reacted so quickly he would have tumbled off the ledge and fallen down the deep hole, but his reaction came at a high price.

Jasmine's fingers had almost grasped the metal handle of the lamp as Mal had slipped but Mal could not have kept hold of it and saved himself from a deadly fall. The lamp had slid from his fingers and gone clattering down the side of the wall to the dark depths below.

The light had ceased almost immediately as the glass ball at the top of the lamp hit the ledge and smashed into a thousand pieces. The force had flattened the wick against the metal surround, at the top of the oil reserve, and had been extinguished.

The rattle of the broken lamp echoed into the abyss below and disappeared into the sound of Jasmine and Mal's heavy breathing as they realised what had happened.

Mal's face had turned white with the sudden shock of his narrow escape, but the faint light that was left emanating from the bioluminescent chemical in the ceiling, showed him as a deathly grey.

'Mal? Are you alright?' Jasmine cried as she watched her friend clinging for dear life on the ledge.

Breathing heavily, Mal looked towards his friend. 'I'm sorry, I dropped the lamp. I'm sorry.'

Mal was still too shocked to say much more than I'm sorry. Jasmine knew there had been nothing he could have done to save the lamp. If he had kept hold of it, he would be tumbling down the well with it.

'We must keep moving; we can't stay on this ledge. Don't worry about the lamp; there is still some light in here.' Jasmine was a little distressed at losing the lamp; there may be light here, but further into the Catacombs it could get much darker. Mal was not to blame though and she wanted to comfort him, as she knew he would feel guilty about dropping the lamp, even though it had just been an unfortunate accident.

'Yes, we must get to the other side.' There was an understandable shakiness in Mal's voice. He was trembling from head to toe, but he was strong and held on tightly to the rock face.

Step by step the two people traversed the remainder of the ledge. Although it was darker without the lamp and the hand holds were harder to see, they no longer had to concern themselves with passing the lamp between them and they made good time across the last few steps.

Jasmine stepped onto the ground at the far end of the ledge and held out her hand to help Mal across. He took it and pulled his shaking body off the ledge to stand in the exit tunnel.

The climb around the edge of the well had been very tiring and so Jasmine suggested the have a rest and eat some of the food they had packed into their bags.

In the half-light, they sat on the dusty ground and ate heartily, and drank the cool clear water they had collected from the fountain in the Great Corridor.

The food and drink had calmed them both down and they started to feel rejuvenated and relaxed. Far above them in the City, the stones were beginning to rise and both Mal and Jasmine knew it was beginning to get late but they wanted to press on further.

They began to walk along the exit tunnel, which led slightly uphill for a while and then more steeply down hill. The walls were bare and rough, as if they had been crudely carved out of the rock. There were no carvings or decorative arches that were everywhere in the City.

As they walked along the length of the tunnel, they stopped occasionally to look at small openings on either side. They were little more than small holes that ran at random directions for a few metres and then stopped abruptly. They were probably natural rock formation that the miners had come across when they were excavating the tunnel.

The tunnel was very long and showed no sign of ending. Mal and Jasmine had been walking for a long time and were beginning to feel tired. They needed to stop and have some sleep or their bodies would become too exhausted. They were both worried about how far they would have to walk. The Catacombs could be much bigger than they could have imagined and to find the tower of light could take days or even weeks.

They stopped at an area of the tunnel that seemed a little lighter than in most places, and a bit wider, making it easier to lie down next to each other. They agreed that they could both rest, but only one person should sleep at a time; the other should keep watch in case anyone or anything came along the tunnel and found them.

Mal volunteered to stay awake first. He sat up and leant against the wall. Jasmine was exceptionally tired and laid her head in Mal's lap. She was asleep almost instantaneously.

After sleeping for a while, Jasmine woke and swapped places with Mal. He found it a little more difficult to fall asleep and lay with his eyes closed for a long time with thoughts of what they would find in the Catacombs, buzzing through his mind.

There was no morning in the Catacombs. The dim light that shone from the ceiling was constant, too far away from the stones in the roof of the City cavern for them to have any effect. In total, they had each slept about two hours, but they had no way of knowing this.

Continuing their journey, they walked single file down the tunnel. It had become narrower and Jasmine was concerned that it might become too narrow; like one of the tunnels they had gone down previously. If it did, there really would not be any other way for them to progress further into the Catacombs.

Jasmine's concerns were alleviated when the tunnel grew wider and expanded to form a chamber.

It was similar in size to the chamber with the well, but luckily the floor was complete; no hole to fall down and no ledges to climb across.

The room was much lighter than the tunnel and glowed brightly green. The walls and floor appeared to have been painted green and were smooth to the touch. This was probably the room that Grancathai's Grandfather had called the Green Room.

At the far end was a carved archway leading to another tunnel. There was no choice except to walk down it. It led for about twelve metres and turned sharply to the right and led for another twelve metres and turned to the left.

The tunnel continued zigzagging backwards and forwards for many hundreds of metres, each turn at right angles alternating left and right. There were no openings or doorways, no carvings or decorations on the walls and no sign of people, the tunnel was plain and empty.

Jasmine began to remember the time when she had first fallen through the floor in Hillcroft house and had walked through an endless tunnel; scared and afraid of what she may find. This tunnel was similar in many ways; dark and eerie, cold and lifeless, but Jasmine took comfort in knowing Mal was walking beside her. They had become close friends, although they had known each other little more than a week; they already felt a strong connection between them. They trusted each other; one of the most important aspects of a close friendship had blossomed quickly and grew to create an unbreakable bond of trust and deep understanding between them. Jasmine knew she would not have been able to cope in the City had she not found Mal sat on the edge of one of the fountains in the Great Corridor.

Rounding another right hand turn in the long tunnel Mal suddenly stopped, Jasmine had lagged slightly behind and had not seen around the corner when her friend had stopped. Peering around edge of the stone wall; Jasmine could see why Mal had stopped. Expecting to see the tunnel to continue for another ten metres and then turn to the left, Jasmine was surprised to see an opening up ahead, less than five metres away. Beyond the opening was a room filled with green light, although not as bright as the green room they had previously left. A gentle breeze seemed to be wafting its way down the tunnel, the air smelled sweet and was refreshing after the dry, stale air of the last few hours in the zigzag tunnel.

Quietly, Mal and Jasmine approached the opening. The walls had been carved into an ornate arch with carvings depicting vines climbing to the ceiling and finishing in beautiful flowers interlocking at the top of the arch. The roots of the vines had also been carved into the floor and stretched out across the smooth flat marble of the room ahead.

'Long has passed since any Top has walked along the paths in our realm,' a voice echoed around the vaulted ceiling of the room. Mal and Jasmine froze in the doorway; the room ahead appeared empty. The smooth green walls ended at a flight of steps into a bright tunnel beyond.

'You need not fear us. We do not fear you,' the voice was clear, although it had a strange accent. It gently echoed around the room and faded into silence.

Mal looked around the room checking every corner and each section of the ceiling. At the far end was a small window high above the tunnel entrance with the steps. The window was dark but the outline of a person could just be made out. Mal nudged Jasmine and pointed.

The long silence, since the voice had last spoken, was ended by the faint sounds of bare feet upon stone steps. The figure in the window had gone, presumably now descending the steps into the room.

'You need not fear us,' the voice repeated, as a figure now appeared in the tunnel entrance to give a body to the voice. He was older than Mal and Jasmine, possibly around mid thirties, and not very tall. His hair was fair and his skin pale. A long, white robe flowed from his strong shoulders and gathered in layers around his waist before continuing to his knees. It appeared that he was wearing a loose shirt under his robe that had short sleeves ending at the elbow and open at the front revealing his pale chest. Around his wrists and ankles were thin cords threaded with glass beads and coloured stones.

The figure continued down the steps onto the floor of the room, his bare feet slapping gently against the smooth stone.

When he reached the bottom, he held out both of his arms towards Mal and Jasmine who still stood motionless in the archway.

'I am the Hallier. I am of the name; Tantan. By what name are you known?'

Mal was fearful of the man, his mouth not attempting to speak an answer, Jasmine was also afraid but plucked up courage and stepped forward and spoke, her voice shaky. 'I am Jasmine, and this is Mal.'

The figure smiled. 'I am happy to meet you. It has been many years since any Top has come here.'

Jasmine was surprised that Tantan had used the word; years. Mal and everyone else she had spoken to in the City had no words for the passage of time except for the word; day. 'You count time in years here?'

Tantan nodded. 'The moon crests here glow brightly for one day at the start of each year, but I don't think it is a term used by the Tops in the City. How have you heard of this word?'

Jasmine knew it would be difficult to explain that she was from the old world and decided to keep things simple, at least for the moment. This was the first time they had met someone from the Catacombs and she did not know if they had ever heard of the old world. 'Where I am from we use the word, but we don't have moon crests.'

Tantan accepted her answer and did not feel the need for further detail. 'I am the Hallier; I am a caretaker of the Catacombs. I must ask you why you are here.'

Jasmine thought for a moment, unsure if she should tell this man that they had only just met about the Tower of Light and their mission to destroy it. 'We are looking for a machine called the Tower of Light.'

Tantan looked startled, his usual beaming smile relaxed to an apprehensive frown. 'It was foretold that this day would come, the day that the Tops would come to the Catacombs and ask for the Tower of Light. Hundreds of years ago a Truth Slayer taught the Lesser people about the history of our world, the building of the City and the machines that ran everything. He even taught our ancestors about the Tower of Light, but years later, he forbade anyone from passing on the knowledge to their children. The knowledge was lost. We cannot help you.'

Mal's heart sank; their only hope was to find the Tower of Light and destroy it, but if it has been hidden and even the local people cannot find it, then their mission was at an end. Jasmine, as always, was less deterred. 'So the Tower of Light does exist down here?'

Tantan paced across the room, deep in thought. 'There are many machines here, and we know the names of all of them, but none of them are named the Tower of Light. I am not sure if I can be of any help to you. Nevertheless, there is one man who knows the machines better than I; it is possible he could help.'

'Is it possible to see this man?' Jasmine asked politely.

Tantan nodded. 'Yes, I can take you to see him. His name is Zieen and he is very wise, but please understand, although this day was foretold you are still strangers here. I must ask you not to disturb the people; they may not accept you as easily as I.'

Mal spoke for the first time since meeting Tantan. 'We would appreciate any help you could give to us, and we won't do anything to disturb anyone. May I ask a question?'

Tantan smiled again, flashing his white teeth. 'Yes, I am happy to answer any questions.'

'What are the Truth Slayers?'

'The Truth Slayers are the ancient words to describe the people who were once the rulers of the Catacombs. They had been expelled from the City and had come to live here. They ruled for many years but slowly they died and none were left from their line to continue ruling. There is more I can tell you, but not here. If you will follow me, I will take you to Zieen.'

Mal and Jasmine knew they were risking a lot by agreeing to go with Tantan, they knew precious little about him. The Catacombs had already proved a strange place, even stranger to Jasmine than the City had been when she had first arrived. Tantan seemed to be kind and helpful but, for all they knew, this could be a ruse. It would have to come down to trust. They had to trust Tantan, and trust the man he was taking them to see.

Mal was already confused about what Tantan had said. He didn't understand what the Truth Slayers were or how the people of the Catacombs had evolved from the time the Truth Slayers had been around.

Tantan led them up the steps into the entrance at the far end of the room. The steps wound in a spiral to the small window where they had first heard Tantan speaking from. From there the steps led to a narrow corridor and into a huge cavern. Jasmine and Mal were speechless as they stood in awe at what they saw.

They were high up on a ledge looking down on a cavern the size of a football stadium. The floor, far below, was littered with small stone houses, with streets in-between. It looked like a small town. Along the walls of the cavern were more houses and walkways, either built into the rock face or constructed on angular pillars rising up from the floor. Tunnels and bridges ran around the outside like a giant spiral connecting different levels of the town.

The stone houses had sloping roofs and chimneys, and were decorated with white pebbles. The streets were cobbled and littered with boxes and odd shaped wheelbarrows. If there had not been a stone roof above them, Jasmine could have imagined it to be a town like any other in the outside world.

In the centre of the town was a round courtyard of small, smooth paving slabs of brilliant white.

'This is the Old City of Martiblak. It was here that the first people built their homes. Only after the population grew too big did they build the City where you live.'

'It's incredible!' Jasmine exclaimed in wonder at the sight.

Tantan shook his head. 'A gold mirror may look bright on the surface but you cannot always see the cracks behind it. That is an expression we have here; it means that this may look like a nice place, but unfortunately, no one lives here.

'There is a Truth Slayer who comes here. He takes people with him to his temple and they are never seen again. He always comes to this City, so the people decided to leave and live in the lower tunnels. This town is deserted; no one lives here. I only use it as a path from the lower tunnels to the Observation Room, where I met you, and the higher tunnels.'

'I thought there were no longer any Truth Slayers around?' Jasmine asked cautiously.

Tantan sighed. 'I don't think I have explained things very well, there are no true Truth Slayers left in the Catacombs, but there is one other who lives a long way away. I will not speak of him here.'

'How long has it been since the people moved away from here?' Mal asked Tantan as he moved to go along a short bridge across one side of the cavern. Mal was eager to change the conversation, as Tantan seemed uncomfortable talking about this *other* Truth Slayer.

'No one has lived here since my grandfather was a child.' Tantan stopped shortly at the edge of the wooden bridge. 'We must go quickly; we cannot stay here for long.'

The bridge was constructed along the edge of the cavern, its wooden supports jutting out from the rock. The wood creaked and groaned with every step.

As they traversed the bridge, Jasmine took the chance to get a better look at the houses below. Some of them had begun to crumble slightly; their stone blocks scattered in piles around their foundations. Many of the roof tiles had slipped and shattered onto the ground, and the streets were dusty and covered with rubbish.

The bridge ended at the mouth of a short tunnel that led steeply downwards towards the bottom of the cavern. Glass-less windows on the right looked out across the roofs of the houses.

Tantan marched out in front, walking briskly. His feet were used to the uneven surface of the tunnels in the Catacombs. Mal and Jasmine were less agile and took time to avoid the holes and protuberances in the floor.

The Catacombs were proving very different to what they were expecting. Grancathai had spoken about mazes of interconnecting tunnels and endless corridors. They had not been expecting caverns with houses and streets. Perhaps the mazes were yet to come, in the lower tunnels.

On the floor of the cavern, the tunnel briefly exited into the wide expanse of the City. From this level, Mal and Jasmine could see other tunnel entrances in a line around its edge leading in a variety of directions. In the dust, that covered the floor, was a well-defined path where Tantan had obviously walked many times. It led to the fourth tunnel in the line. It was the only tunnel not in complete darkness.

Again, they found themselves descending, only this time it was steps. Mal could not imagine how far below the level of the City they must be now; they had gone down the iron rungs from the room near the Martiblak Library, and then down the long winding tunnel into the green room and now even further down; below the Old City. They had been travelling nearly all day and except for briefly heading upwards from the observation room to the top of the Old City cavern they had descended the whole time.

As they descended further into the earth, they began to hear strange noises. They were heading towards the origin of the sounds, far below them, presumably in the lower tunnels. There was a faint clanging, like a hammer hitting something metal in a forge and fainter still; the sound of running water.

The sounds grew louder as the tunnel levelled off and turned sharply to the left. On either side were small dark passages leading steeply downhill, but it was not possible to see more than a couple of metres along them.

The tunnel opened into a large chamber. It was here that the sound of water originated. Along the whole length of the chamber was a stream, bubbling steeply downhill over rocks and pebbles. It flowed from a small waterfall that fell from an opening in the rocky ceiling.

The water was clear and fresh, but growing along the side of the stream was masses of bright green moss. It grew in thick layers, clinging to the rocks that lined the water's edge.

Mal wanted to stop for a short while and enjoy a refreshing drink, but Tantan was already on his way out of the room through an archway on the left.

The corridor beyond the arch led both left and right and was easily as wide as the Great Corridor. Along its length were people sat on stools at high tables. Scattered around the tables were metal tools, carved stones and strips of cloth. There were at least twenty people in total. They were all busy using hammers and chisels to shape the rough stones into smooth blocks.

At the side of each table were wicker baskets, where the workers occasionally threw small pieces of stone they had chipped off their block. They appeared not to notice the new visitors to the Catacombs and continued busily with their work.

At the far end of one side of the corridor was a furnace, its thick black smoke rising through a grate in the ceiling. Workers were zealously stoking the coal as others poured fragments of metal into a scorching cauldron.

'These are the workshops, we are expert builders; we cut stones to line new tunnels and cast metal to make new tools,' Tantan informed them as they walked left down the corridor towards the furnace. The heat was intense as they passed a line of blacksmiths hammering red-hot pieces of metal.

There were more tunnels up ahead leading off to the right. The Catacombs were beginning to be true to their name as Tantan led them down a tunnel to a room with five further tunnels.

Finally, Tantan led them down a short tunnel to a small wooden door. He knocked loudly before pushing the door open.

A man was sat on a stool in the middle of the room; the rest of the room was empty.

'Zieen? I have visitors from the City, they are here to find the Tower of Light,' Tantan said bowing in front of the man. Mal and Jasmine copied in respect to the aged man. He was sat with his hands on his knees; he wore a similar robe to Tantan and wore a cloth hat upon his head.

The man stood from his stool and bowed to Tantan glancing briefly at Mal and Jasmine. 'As Hallier you have done the right thing by bringing them to me.'

'They believe the Tower of Light is here in the Catacombs,' Tantan said in reply. 'But I have told them we do not know where it is.'

The man turned his attention to Mal. 'I am the See-Smith and I am of the name Zieen. Why do you seek the Tower of Light?'

Mal swallowed and spoke nervously. 'The Tower of Light is trapping people in the City, we want to destroy it.'

Jasmine sighed, she thought it better if they did not mention their intent to destroy the Tower of Light but luckily, Zieen did not seem shocked by this information.

'That is an interesting idea. Perhaps you would walk with me and tell me more about what you have said. I am interested to know more about how the Tower of Light is trapping people in your City.

'Hallier? Would you please find something for these people to eat, they look half-starved. We will meet you at the Ring.'

Tantan bowed again and left the room briskly.

'What are your names?' Zieen asked as he motioned towards a small door at the side of the room.

'My name is Malmayorkia and this Jasmine,' Mal replied politely.

'Well Malmayorkia and Jasmine I am happy to meet you both, walk with me along the stream and tell me your story.'

Through the door was a long tunnel, with a stream running through a stone aqueduct about the level of Mal's waist. A narrow path of cobbled stones ran along next to it. The tunnel was straight and very long, disappearing into the distance.

Jasmine and Mal accompanied Zieen along the path and explained as much as they could about the Tamboli rooms, the books in the library and their mission to destroy the Tower of Light. Zieen listened intently to everything they had to say and spoke only occasionally to ask questions.

As Mal and Jasmine explained the story, it became apparent that Zieen had a good understanding of the history of the City. He knew about Martin Blake and the building of the Catacombs and the City, although he did not know that Martin Blake was originally from the old world. It turned out that the old world was also a myth to the people of the Catacombs.

The concept of Tamboli rooms was difficult to explain; it had taken Jasmine along time to fully understand them, and she had been in one and seen Mal's family and many other people trapped in them.

Zieen was amazed when Jasmine and Mal showed him their felostones gently vibrating on their wrists, there was not anything like them in the Catacombs.

The tunnel ended in a small round room, where the water flowed from a gap next to a wooden door. Jasmine wondered if this stream was the same stream, they had seen with the green moss before entering the workshops.

In the centre of the room was a group of small chairs carved out of large blocks of stone. Zieen sat down and gestured for Mal and Jasmine to join him.

'I wish I could help you, the Truth Slayer forbade anyone from passing on the knowledge of the Tower of Light, and its whereabouts was lost many years ago. There are many machines here; perhaps if you could describe the Tower of Light to me I could help you further.'

'We can do better than that,' Jasmine said reaching into her bag. 'We have a page from Martin Blake's Diary and it has a picture of the Tower of Light on it. It's a bit faded but you can still see it.'

Jasmine carefully unfolded the piece of paper and handed it to Zieen. Grancathai was right in saying that the paper would not last long outside the library. The ink had already begun to fade and the paper felt like it could crumble at any second.

Zieen took the paper and looked at it inquisitively. At that moment there was a click behind them, and Tantan came walking in through the small door. He was carrying a basket in which was placed a variety of metal pots, each containing leaves. They were all different shades of green, some large and some small.

Tantan placed the basket in front of Jasmine. 'You may eat; these are some of the best foods in the Catacombs. I did not think you would enjoy eating boiled algae; these are the foods most similar to what you are used to. Although it has been hundreds of years since the last time anyone here has seen the Givings.'

Mal and Jasmine were indeed very hungry; they still had some food in their bags but had not eaten since entering the zigzag tunnel. They ate heartily. The leaves tasted sweet and were soft like lettuce.

'Hallier?' Zieen said after examining the piece of paper Jasmine had handed to him. 'Do you recognise this?'

Tantan looked at the See-Smith and then looked at the picture of the Tower of Light. 'No I'm afraid it doesn't look like anything I have seen before. Is this a picture of the Tower of Light?'

Zieen nodded. 'Yes, but look more closely, do you see these lines here?'

'I'm sorry, I do not recognise it, but I am only a Hallier, I do not have the eyes of a See-Smith.' The lines, Zieen was pointing at, were at the base of the machine and appeared to depict pipes or wires running into the Tower of Light.

'Imagine two stone pedestals in front of here, and a bright light here.' Zieen used his fingers to point out where he was meaning in the picture.

'The room of shadows! Could it be that simple?'

Mal and Jasmine were still busy eating but listening intently as the two men spoke.

'Do you recognise this machine?' Mal asked picking up some more of the large dark green leaves.

The See-Smith looked up at Tantan who answered. 'The picture is difficult to make out but there is a room we know of called the Room of Shadows, there is a small machine there but it is called the Renara; The Shadow Maker.'

'Continue Tantan,' Zieen instructed. 'I think they should know more about Renara.'

Tantan sighed but continued speaking. 'Renara was the daughter of one of the Truth Slayers. When she was born, the Truth Slayer built her the Shadow Maker and named it after her. He said the Shadow Maker would be for her to look at when she was older and so could always see light in her life.

'Renara died before she was old enough to even stand up and never really saw the machine. Her father was so saddened by her death that he made the room a dead room and stopped anyone from ever going in there. We can go to the doorway but not inside.'

Zieen took over from Tantan. 'We have both seen this room many times, although never entered it, the machine on your drawing does look similar. However the machine cannot be both the Tower of Light and The Shadow Maker.'

Jasmine pondered for a while. 'Is Renara's Father the same Truth Slayer that forbade your ancestors from speaking about the Tower of Light?'

Both Tantan and Zieen gasped and looked at each other. 'Yes,' they said in unison.

'Is it possible he made up the story of his daughter in order to help keep the secret of the Tower of Light?'

Tantan frowned. 'While the stories of the Tower of Light and the Renara both descend from Paluuka the Truth Slayer; it would be impossible to know if either is true. These stories are more than a thousand years old, maybe even two thousand.'

'But,' Mal interjected. 'If this Truth Slayer wanted to keep the Tower of Light a secret, what better way than to create a completely different story about it. If the new story was passed down from generation to generation, it wouldn't take long for the old story to be forgotten.'

As Mal spoke, Jasmine remembered something that Tantan had said previously. He had talked about a Truth Slayer named *Paluuka*. 'You know about Paluuka? Before we learnt about the Tower of Light we thought Paluuka was creating the Tamboli rooms, although again he was little more than myth and stories.'

'This is a puzzle; an ancient puzzle. We are trying to decide what stories are real and which ones are fake. Which stories actually happened and which ones have been exaggerated over the years or had their meanings lost in time. If Paluuka built the machine for his daughter and that meaning was passed on to your City folk through a story, and then that story was changed over time to miss out the part with the machine; then in your minds Paluuka created the Tamboli rooms.' Zieen had an air of wisdom when he spoke. He had described himself as a See-Smith, and Tantan had spoken about himself not having the eyes of a See-Smith. It was likely that this was a term to describe someone who had knowledge and wisdom, and the scholastic ability to use that knowledge.

Tantan was first to speak after everyone had taken a moment to think over what Zieen had said. 'But you didn't know about the machine until you read about it. Does it say in the book if Paluuka made the machine?'

'No,' Jasmine replied. 'It says Martin Blake Built the machine, with the help of Paul Lewis, but it was Martin Blake's invention.'

'If we trust your books then it seems unlikely that Paluuka made the machine for his daughter, and the machine we have seen in the Room of Shadows is the Tower of light. But if we trust our stories then the Renara machine is nothing more than something pretty to look at; a light giver and shadow maker.'

'Did Paluuka want to stop people going to the machine because he was devastated at his daughter's death or because he was using the machine to make the Tamboli rooms?'

Jasmine had something pressing on her mind, ever since they had first starting talking to Tantan in the Observation room there was one thought that continuously popped into her head. If the Truth Slayer had forbidden anyone from talking about the Tower of Light, why would Tantan and Zieen help them? After a few seconds carefully pondering, she decided she should ask them. 'I don't mean any disrespect, but I need to know why you wish to help us if you have been forbidden to talk about the location of the Tower of Light?'

'You are wise Jasmine; we can see you have a strong heart,' Zieen said in reply. 'We are helping you because we no longer respect Paluuka or want to follow in his ways. There are some rules we will not break but some we will bend a little. Anyway, we are simply going to take you to the Renara; The Shadow Maker, not the Tower of Light. We no longer regard Paluuka as a true Truth Slayer.'

'Then you will take us to the Machine?' Mal asked.

Tantan looked at Zieen and they seemed to share a moment of questioning. It appeared they were unsure what they should do.

Finally Zieen spoke. 'Tantan will take you to the Renara machine, or the Tower of Light; whichever it may be. I will return to my room as I have many other matters to attend to.'

'Thank you,' Jasmine and Mal said in unison.

Zieen smiled and turned his attention back to Tantan. 'You know what needs to be done, I cannot decide further than I have. You understand?'

Tantan nodded. Jasmine and Mal had no idea what they were talking about, but hoped it would not cause them any problems.

The route to the Room of Shadows was complicated. Tantan led them through a series of small rooms and tunnels to a large room with a low ceiling and at least thirty tunnels leading away from it. As they walked towards the tunnel at the far end of the room, Tantan explained that they were entering the oldest part of the Catacombs and it was from this area that the Catacombs got their name.

'The tunnels lead in every direction and around in circles. You could be lost here forever,' he explained. 'You must know where you are going if you want to get there. If your mind wanders from its goal; then you will never find your way.'

This all sounded very complicated but Grancathai had read a section of his Grandfathers notes that mentioned tunnels that acted like Conveyance corridors and took you to random places.

The Catacombs was a justified name for this area. Tunnels led in every direction, some to dead ends, and some back to the start. Every tunnel looked identical, and with the exception of junctions and occasional 90-degree turns; were straight and flat. The walls were smooth, but the floor was covered in brightly coloured pebbles. They were every colour you could imagine and shone brightly in the light from small lamps that lined the walls.

The chamber Tantan had led them to was narrow and very tall. It had a smooth floor but rough walls and an arched ceiling. At the end of the room was a stone archway.

Tantan pointed towards the archway. 'Here lies the Room of Shadows. You can only see into the room, you cannot go in there.'

'Why can't we go in there? Is there a door or something?' Mal asked looking towards the doorway at the end of the room.

Tantan shook his head. 'No, there isn't a door, but you cannot go in there. It is a dead room.'

A shiver went down Jasmine's back as she listened to Tantan speak. His unusual accent made everything he said seem more dramatic. 'Many years ago,' he continued. 'When Paluuka, the Truth Slayer, was last here he made the room so no one could go into it. It is a dead room, perhaps it is the same as the Tamboli rooms you mentioned to me earlier.'

'It sounds similar; do people forget everything when they enter the room?'

Tantan shook his head and frowned. 'No one has ever entered that room so we don't know what would happen, we only go by what the Truth-Slayer said to us.'

'Can you tell me more about the Truth Slayers?' Jasmine asked after a short pause.

'The Truth-Slayers are the first ones. They were the ones who had the knowledge to build the Cities here.

'In the beginning there were many of them. Martiblak was their leader, and it was from him that the City above got its name, but there were so many more. Paluuka and Martiblak spent a long time designing things for the City, building big machines that made water fall from the Fountains and the Walkways to move from one place to another.

'But slowly the Truth-Slayers grew old and died. The people in the City were sad, but were also afraid of what would happen if there were no longer any Truth Slayers to run the machines. So Paluuka made himself part of the machines so he wouldn't die, and he would make the machines work forever.'

Jasmine and Mal both listened intently, but Jasmine understood more of what Tantan was saying. Truth Slayer was the name the Lessers gave to the original people from Martin Blake's Laboratory and it was quite probable that they *had* built the machines to run the City. The only part that Jasmine did not understand was the part about Paluuka made himself part of the machines.

Jasmine was still thinking things over in her mind as Mal started to ask questions. 'How do you know about all this? We have a library full of books and none of this is mentioned. Do you have books as well?'

Tantan looked puzzled. 'I do not know about a Library or Books, the information we have is passed down from father to son. And Paluuka has walked here in the Catacombs many times, even after he was told to leave the City. He is no longer our true Truth Slayer but he still tries to control how we live, and what we are allowed to think. Now, come with me and I will show you the Room of Shadows and Renara; The Shadow maker.'

CHAPTER 8

Room of Shadows

The Room of Shadows was an appropriate name for the room Jasmine and Mal now found themselves looking at. It was a huge expanse like a cathedral nave with a vaulted ceiling and massive pillars in rows down the sides, although the pillars seemed to be more ornamental than actually holding the ceiling up.

In the centre of the chamber were two short, stone columns less than a metre tall, with the shape and appearance of beer barrels or water butts.

At the end of the chamber was a bright light, shining from a large, complicated machine. It resembled nothing that Mal or Jasmine had ever seen. Countless mirrors and lenses suspended by gold rods were arranged around a large spinning disc. The disc was at least half a metre is diameter, and spinning horizontally below a mass of wires and metal filaments. A dark green surround enclosed the mechanical working at the top and bottom and so they could not be seen.

The light appeared to be generated somewhere behind the machine and struck mirrors as they span round on the disc. The light was scattered around the machine and was finally focused onto polished metal plates set in a rack on either side of the machine.

Steam was rising from small copper pipes that rose from the ground in front of the machine and curved around either side and met again at the top to be fed into the inner workings behind the upper surround.

The machine was built into an alcove in the rock. Attached to metal brackets set into the rock were large coils of wire and high current electrical cable. These were the electromagnets that had become so highly charged they prevented the machine from being shut off, but over the years this effect has lessened considerably; leaving the machine vulnerable.

Although most of the light from the machine was focused on the metal plates, there was one bright ray that looked outwards into the chamber. It hit the small barrel columns and cast long shadows, almost to the end wall where Jasmine and Mal were now standing.

Tantan stood next to them in the doorway. 'Paluuka came here many times. The light used to be much brighter, but then the white air came from the pipes and the light faded. When the light was at its brightest you could not look at it, it was too bright for your eyes.'

Jasmine turned her attention away from the machine towards Tantan. 'White air? You mean the steam?'

Tantan frowned. 'I do not know about steam, you can see the white air coming from the pipes.'

'We call that steam. If the machine needs steam to work and some of it is escaping from the pipes it makes sense that it doesn't work so well.'

Deep below the room of shadows was a generator that used heat from inside the earth to turn water into steam. The steam fed along pipes to the top of the machine, and in turn fed into a turbine that turned the disc and generated electricity for the laser lamp behind the machine.

Martin Blake and Paul Lewis had built the machine when they worked in the Dayvene Laboratory. Although little over one hundred years had passed in the outside world, one and a half thousand years had passed here and the machine was now ancient. The copper pipes had corroded inside, and finally worn through allowing the steam to escape. The metal mirrors inside the machine had tarnished and the lenses had become coated in a thin layer of dirt and dust. The light was no longer being reflected properly around the machine and coupled with the disc spinning slower caused the focused light beams to become dimmer and less intense.

The machine had lasted hundreds of years longer than Martin Blake would ever have expected, the unique conditions in the Catacombs had preserved the moving components more than they would have been in the outside world. If the machine had been built outside, the bearings on the spinning disc would have worn out by now and would have forced the disc to break off its spindle and crash onto the floor of the machine, shattering the mirrors.

Jasmine was hoping that the damage done to the machine over time would have reduced the magnetic field and would allow people close enough to stop the machine.

Jasmine and Mal had travelled a long way to reach this room, and the machine was only a stones throw away. The machine, although at the end of the chamber seemed to be amazingly close, close enough to reach out and touch it with your hand. If only they could find a way to reach it.

Tantan turned towards the machine momentarily and then back towards Jasmine. 'This is as far as you can go, the room is dead; none may enter!'

Jasmine reached out her hand, as she had a thought of what Tantan meant by a 'dead room'. Her hand passed the edge of the doorway and as she extended her arm fully, her sleeve pulled back slightly from her wrist exposing the bright purple felostone.

'Jazz!' You must not enter the room,' Tantan shouted, but it was already too late. Jasmine's arm was in the room, the bright light glinting off the felostone.

Jasmine shuddered. 'I can't feel it, I can't feel the felostone. This room is Tamboli. Don't worry it doesn't hurt, it just feels strange; slightly cold.'

Jasmine dropped her hand back to her side, and Mal breathed out. He had been holding his breath the whole time, concerned for his friend. 'Does your hand feel alright now?' Mal asked gently touching the back of her hand.

'Yes, it feels fine.' Jasmine held her hand up for Mal to see. 'There is something I don't understand though, when I was first in a Tamboli room; it took a little while before I felt its effects but here I felt them instantly.'

'Perhaps it is because this room is so close to the machine that makes Tamboli,' Mal suggested. 'Or maybe Paluuka made this one particularly bad to stop people even being able to get close to the Tower of light.'

Tantan moved back from the doorway taking Mal and Jasmine's gaze away from the Room of Shadows. 'As you can see, it is a dead room; you cannot enter.'

Jasmine was saddened by this news; they had worked so hard to find the Tower of Light and now there seemed nothing could be done, or was there? Jasmine looked at Mal and took a deep breath, then without any warnings she ran into the Room of Shadows.

'JAZZ!' Mal screamed in horror and turned to run after her, but Tantan grabbed his arm to hold him back.

'No Malmayorkia, you be trapped as well.'

Jasmine felt a sudden shock run through her body, followed by a strange coldness. Everything went deafeningly quiet and she found herself running very slowly, her legs failing to move at normal speed.

As she moved through the room, breathing became more difficult and her heart pumped loudly, filling her ears with a slow regular beat. The felostone on her wrist had stopped vibrating the moment she had passed the doorway and Jasmine missed the comforting buzz against her skin.

More time passed and she was still only halfway across the room and nearing the barrel shaped rocks. She did not look back; she did not know if Mal had followed her but hoped that he had not. This was their only chance to destroy the machine and there was no use both of them becoming trapped in the Room of Shadows under the evil grip of Tamboli.

In reality, it should take less than a couple of seconds for her to reach the machine as she passed the barrel rocks. Time to put her plan into action, she reached down and picked up a small rock by her feet, barely slowing down as she leant over and grabbed the rock with her right hand.

The light from the Tower of Light was more intense here, but Jasmine's eyes became less aware of the brightness. Her whole body began to feel numb except for a sharp pain in her head. Random thoughts flashed before her as her mind tried to overcome the powerful effects of Tamboli. A second later, it was over.

In the grey light of Paluuka's Temple, an aged man sat on a stone chair. In his hands, he held a small bag of black stones. A frown came across his withered face; he felt something. It was like nothing he had felt before; it was a strange feeling and it made his feel very uncomfortable.

The man stood, dropping the bag of stones as he suddenly realised what the feeling could be. The stones scattered across the floor like marbles. He reached behind the chair and pulled on a metal chain that was hanging on the wall. A loud thud echoed around the chamber followed by a shrill whistle.

Leaning heavily on his staff, the man walked towards a doorway and left the room, moving as quickly as his worn out muscles would allow.

Beyond the door, he manoeuvred around some large wooden boxes that were strewn across the floor and made for a flight of stairs.

The shrill whistle stopped as he pushed open a door at the bottom of the long steps and walked into a narrow tunnel. The door closed behind him with a thud.

The felostone buzzed gently on Jasmine's skin and it felt good. It had seemed like an eternity ago that the vibrations had stopped but now they had returned. Jasmine was laid on the ground in front of the barrel rocks. Fragments of glass were scattered around her from the mirrors and lenses of the Tower of Light. The small rock had hit its target; the centre of the machine and sent the glass flying in all directions. The disc had begun to spin irregularly; its weight no longer distributed evenly. It had not taken long for the disc to break its bearings and smash onto the base of the machine. A cloud of steam had exploded into the air and dissipated on the ceiling.

The machine now stood motionless, the bright light had disappeared the moment the disc had fallen and the steam escaping from the copper pipes was little more than a faint wisp.

Jasmine opened her eyes to see Mal's face and he looked terrified. 'Jazz, are you alright? How did you know you would be able to do that?'

'I didn't know for sure,' Jasmine said standing up and dusting herself down. 'I just figured I would have enough time. People in Tamboli rooms only remember what they were doing at that exact moment they succumb to the Tamboli effects. I thought if I could time it right, I could throw the rock even if I forgot everything else.'

Mal sighed thankfully. 'As long as you are not hurt?'

'I'm fine, I guess I wasn't here long enough to do any damage to myself. I'm sorry if I scared you, but I Tantan would have stopped me if I had planned it.'

Tantan walked over to the machine looking at its broken inner workings. 'Jasmine, may I see that drawing again that you had. There is something wrong here.'

Jasmine took the folded piece of paper out of her bag and handed it to Tantan. It was now very faded; the ink lines barely visible on the delicate paper.

'I now know why I didn't recognise this machine when I first saw this picture.' Tantan held the picture up in front of the machine. 'The top part is missing along with some of the inner workings.'

Jasmine and Mal looked intently as Tantan pointed out a section on the picture that was missing from the top of the machine; there were holes and clamps where it originally fitted above the spinning disc. It was difficult, with the machine in its broken state, to see that the top section would have protruded down towards the centre of the spinning disc, but it was clear something was missing.

Jasmine thought back to Martin Blake's diaries and the other papers she had read about what had happened after the people had become trapped underground. 'I don't understand something; Martin Blake said he had moved the Tower of Light to the lowest chamber he could find. This machine looks like it was built here, you couldn't move this, and even if you could why would he reattach all of these copper pipes if he didn't want the machine to work?'

Tantan refolded the paper and handed it back to Jasmine, who put it carefully back in her bag. 'I fear that this is not the Tower of Light, at least, not the important part.'

'If that's true, why did this stop being a Tamboli room?' Mal asked utterly confused with the situation.

Tantan walked away slightly and turned to face Mal and Jasmine, he looked troubled. 'There is more I haven't told you. It is difficult to explain, but I couldn't tell you everything; not all at once.'

Jasmine looked puzzled, 'What do you mean?'

'When you threw the rock at the machine, it wasn't its destruction that stopped this being a dead room, I mean a Tamboli room. It was me; I moved a handle above the door.'

'What?' Jasmine and Mal said in unison.

Tantan rubbed his hand across his face. 'I'm sorry I didn't tell you everything.

'Many years ago when Paluuka stopped us from talking about this machine, the people were fearful that he would be angry if anyone approached and so they asked him to make this a Dead Room. Only the Halliers and the See-Smiths know about the handle to switch off the machine. It was there in case Paluuka returned to the machine.'

'But why didn't you tell us about it before?' Jasmine asked.

'I'm sorry, I couldn't. To tell anyone about it is punishable by death. It is one of our rules. I really wanted to help you, but I was afraid of what Paluuka would do.'

'But you pulled the handle, and you are telling us about it now?' Jasmine said glancing at the door where they had entered.

Tantan paused momentarily. 'When I saw you run in here, I didn't want you to get trapped. I had to do something to save you. I also remembered something else but I please don't ask me to explain, I can't tell you more.'

'Tantan I don't understand,' Jasmine was confused.

'Much more was foretold than simply someone would come looking for the Tower of Light. Paluuka calculated many things; this is just the start of something much bigger. There are going to be many changes here and there is something important you should do.'

Jasmine looked at the broken machine. 'We want to stop the Tamboli rooms; we thought destroying this machine would do that. Are you saying that it hasn't?'

'I honestly don't know Jasmine. I hope so, I really do. Now you must go quickly, there is more for you to do,' Tantan walked towards the entrance to the room. 'Come with me, I will explain on the way.'

Jasmine and Mal were baffled, suddenly their mission had come crashing down around them and they did not know in what direction they should go now. They had little choice but to go with Tantan and hope he would be able to help them further. It was obvious to Jasmine that although he had lied to them, he had a genuine desire to help them.

Tantan led the way back through the maze towards the stream, the faint light again dancing across the coloured pebbles on the floor as they walked. As he walked, he spoke about a woman called Anarlia who lived in the Outer City. Grancathai had already told them about the Outer City, and it was probably there that Jasmine had first entered the underground realm of Martiblak. She wondered if the woman that Tantan was describing was the same woman that she had first met after leaving the Tamboli room with Rothgoe, servant of Balmore of Terrol.

Tantan spoke quickly as he walked, looking back only occasionally to check that Mal and Jasmine were following close behind. 'Anarlia is the link. She is the only one who has lived in both the City and the Catacombs. She must be told what has happened, and she will be able to tell you what to do next.

'I will take you to the Arch of Guilt, an entranceway to a flight of steps which leads to the lookout, a giant window high above the City. From there you can get into the Outer City. I wish I could tell you more, but there isn't time and there are many things I cannot tell you. I know it doesn't make sense, but the less I tell you the better it will be.'

Jasmine and Mal followed in silence; listening carefully to what Tantan had to say. They were confused to why he was being so elusive about some things; he had already broken his rules by telling them about the handle to make the Room of Shadows safe, why was he not telling them more?

They continued past numerous rooms and tunnels, heading back towards the workshops and on to the Old City.

'I cannot go further than here,' Tantan said as they arrived at the bottom level of the Old City. 'This entrance here will take you along a short passageway to the Arch of Guilt. Go quickly and do not stop. I know you don't understand, but I hope, soon, you will.'

'Will we see you again?' Mal asked as he walked towards the entrance Tantan had pointed to.

'I don't know, there will be many changes and I don't know exactly what they will be.' Tantan raised his hand to wave. 'Goodbye people of the City, I hope we will meet again.'

'Goodbye Tantan. Thank you.' Mal took Jasmine's hand in his own and walked into the tunnel.

Tantan watched from the entrance until they disappeared into the distance. He knew they had a difficult path ahead of them. The steps to the lookout were long and treacherous. The dust on the floor clearly showed only two sets of foot prints walking into the tunnel; no one had entered this tunnel for many years.

Tantan returned to the Room of Shadows and waited for Zieen.

The steps started exactly as Tantan had described under a low archway of green marble. Jasmine could just walk underneath without ducking, but Mal had to bow his head.

Jasmine now understood why it was called the arch of guilt. It made most people bow their heads as if in shame to walk under it.

The stone steps beyond the arch led steeply upwards, but not in a straight line. They curved to the right, as if in a gigantic spiral. Most of the steps were worn and some were cracked and chipped.

The light seemed dimmer here and intermittent in some places, causing strange shadows to be cast across the uneven steps. A slight nervousness came over the two friends as they began to climb the steps.

The tunnel that the steps had been cut into was wider at the top than at the bottom, and had been hacked out of the rock without much consideration for aesthetics. The sides and roof were rough and uneven, with holes and protuberances. These could be dangerous, and both Mal and Jasmine hit their shoulders, elbows, ankles and even their heads on these sharp pieces of rock.

The air in the steps' tunnel seemed hotter and dryer than anywhere else in the City. It appeared that whoever had made this tunnel had done everything they could to make climbing the stairs a very uncomfortable and unpleasant experience.

Hundreds of steps, followed by hundreds of steps, onwards and upwards, towards the lookout the steps continued to climb. Like the emergency stairs in a tall skyscraper the steps went forever upwards. It must have taken an age to dig out a tunnel like this and even longer to carve all of the steps, although they were obviously not done with great patience or care. Some parts of the City had also been cut from solid rock, however, talented artisans had painstakingly shaped them into perfectly smooth surfaces of intricate patterns and shapes, and made to look even more impressive by gold leaf decorations or additional carvings and plaster work set into the walls or ceilings. Here there was nothing but rock, chipped and broken but nothing more.

Jasmine and Mal climbed the stairs almost silently; they had not spoken since passing the Arch of Guilt and proceeded on their long upward journey. Their minds were too busy concentrating on the steps in front and the walls around, to think about talking. Only the sounds of their shoes upon the cold stone, and their breathing broke the absolute silence.

The steps although equally treacherous further up, seemed to be getting more difficult to climb, each step became more tiring. Jasmine started to notice it first, but believed it to be her legs becoming more tired and therefore each step more difficult. However, it was not long before Mal started to feel it too, and notice that the steps were actually getting larger. The change had been so gradual that it had taken a long time to notice. Each step, only a fraction larger than its predecessor, but after hundreds of steps, meant a much more tiring and challenging ascent.

'This is taking forever,' Jasmine said breaking the silence and stopping momentarily to catch her breath. 'I wish we could tell how much further we have to go.'

Mal stopped just in front of his friend and turned to face her. 'Tantan did say it would take a long time to reach the lookout from the Catacombs, but the Outer City door would only be a short climb from there.'

Jasmine breathed out heavily in a long sigh. 'What if he is wrong and it takes days to reach the lookout and days to reach the Outer City door? We only have enough food and water to last us for today and it is really hot in here and we won't be able to continue if we run out of water.'

Mal stepped down to the step just above Jasmine. He placed his hand on her shoulder and for a brief second she felt comforted. Mal's presence always made Jasmine feel better. It was as if he could draw ill feelings out of her body just by smiling or by the gentle touch of his hand in hers or on her shoulder.

'Jazz, if people used to come up here all the time, then it must be possible to walk it. Why build a huge staircase if people collapse from exhaustion before they reach the top?'

Feeling slightly happier, the couple continued their climb up the treacherous stairs. They must have climbed very high by this time, as many hours had passed and except for a few short breaks they had carefully and painstakingly continued forever upwards.

The ever-spiralling steps with their ever-increasing height did not show any indications of ending. There were no windows in this tunnel, and it was far from an open plan stairwell that could give any impression of how far up you were. It only continued.

Jasmine's legs began to ache more, and her feet had become sore and blistered, making every step difficult, tiring and uncomfortable. She tried to imagine what it must have been like for the stonemasons who had the hard task of actually cutting this tunnel. In the world Jasmine had come from, people had the luxury of powerful machines to build tunnels but this would, most likely, have all been chipped away by hand. The waste rock would also have had to be carried by hand all the way down, or perhaps up, the stairs to be disposed of. It must have been back breaking work.

Jasmine stopped, her hope had diminished, and her feet were sore and her legs tired. Mal was much further ahead and Jasmine could only just see him around the curve of the stairs, but suddenly he turned around and came bounding back down the steps. 'Jasmine! I can see a light up ahead,' Mal said as he descended. 'It can't be too far.'

Jasmine felt a moment of excitement at this news, but the excitement soon turned to horror, as Mal's legs, too tired to work properly refused to move as fast as he had wanted them too. He began to tumble forward in slow motion, as if time had stopped. All Jasmine could do was watch as the body of her dear friend fell forwards and hit the stone steps with a hard thud, unable to stop himself with his arms.

'Mal!' Jasmine screamed as she raced upward towards the motionless figure, laying awkwardly downhill, with trickles of blood on the stone beneath his head.

The tunnel felt even more silent and strangely cold as Jasmine approached her friend. Chills ran endlessly up her spine and tears began rolling down her face. She knelt beside him, the pains in her legs gone for the moment in a rush of adrenaline.

Mal's face was lifeless and pale. His normally bright eyes were closed and his normally smiling mouth lay open dripping blood. The blood was pouring from two large gashes on his chin and jaw; it ran like water over his face and dripped onto the floor in dark red puddles. Jasmine felt helpless and alone.

Hundreds of steps below in the Room of Shadows, Tantan was sitting on a rock at the base of the tower of light. The mirrors and lenses were scattered in shards across the sand by his feet and long wire strands lay twisted and mangled in a heap.

'Now is the right time,' Tantan said to himself, tossing a small pebble onto one of the larger pieces of broken mirror, it broke further into numerous pieces with a high-pitched clink.

'There will never be another time for us here Tantan,' a deep voice said from the back of the room. 'We know Paluuka will come here now.'

Tantan stood, being careful to avoid touching the shattered glass with his shoeless feet. 'I did not tell them everything Zieen, they have a hard journey ahead of them, and there was no point in troubling them further. I told them only what they needed to hear.'

Zieen was tall and strong and seemed huge in comparison to Tantan as they stood facing each other.

'Then we have set in motion the events that will ultimately end our life here. As you said, now is the right time. We must get ready.'

'Mal? Can you hear me?' Jasmine cried as she tried desperately to wake her friend. The cuts on his face seemed deep and his body seemed twisted at an awkward angle. Jasmine hoped there were not any broken bones. Thoughts seemed to run through her mind like water. Mal was still breathing, which hopefully meant his neck, was alright; a broken neck normally killed instantly. Even so, a broken leg or broken back could cause huge problems in getting back to the City. Jasmine tried to remember what she had learnt about First Aid, which was not much. Carefully she felt along his body, feeling for anything that could indicate an injury. Her hands were shaking as she carefully moved them over his body. Starting from his head she worked her way down to his feet, there was nothing that felt broken or injured, but then she was not a doctor.

Jasmine moved back to his head to check his breathing. She pushed back a lock of Mal's hair from around his face and to her astonishment Mal's eyes flickered open for a second and then closed again. 'Mal…Mal? Can you hear me?' Jasmine sobbed. 'Can you open your eyes again?'

Slowly Mal's eyes began to reopen. His vision was blurred at first but started to clear after a few seconds. Mal felt a sharp pain down the side of his face and strange sensations in his head. 'Jasmine?' he said after a moment to recover his senses.

'Oh Mal I am so glad you are alright, I feared the worst.' Tears were again rolling down Jasmine's cheek. 'Where do you hurt?'

Mal lifted his head slightly. 'My head, just my head, it hurts all over.'

Jasmine tore the end of the sleeve off her shirt and dabbed Mal's face. 'You have to take things easy, you blacked out for a moment. We should rest here for a while.'

Jasmine helped Mal into a more comfortable position on the uneven stairs and talked to him about her world and what she did there. She knew it was important for him to stay awake Mal always listened intently whenever the Old World was spoken about. He loved hearing about all things that were different from what he was used to; even if he did not fully understand a lot of them.

Jasmine thought of nothing else except her friend as she spoke non-stop about her home; she did not even realise that she no longer missed the outside world.

CHAPTER 9

The Outer City

An hour had passed since Mal had fallen and he had begun to feel a little better; his face was still very sore but the rest of his head ached a little less. Jasmine had torn off more of her sleeve and mopped up most of the blood from his face, although a little still dripped from time to time.

After a drink from their water bottle, Mal felt strong enough to move. Jasmine helped him up and put his arm over her shoulder.

It was very awkward trying to walk up the steps side by side. Luckily, for them, the steps were getting slightly wider and the walls were sloping backwards more.

They made their way slowly up the last few steps and found themselves in a small chamber with an archway leading to more steps on the left and a hole near the ceiling on the right.

'I think the lookout must be up there.' Mal pointed to a hole in the tunnel opposite the doorway. It was high up near the edge of the ceiling and all Mal and Jasmine could see was darkness beyond the boundary of the hole. Carved below the hole were four small foot and handholds, allowing a person to climb up the wall easily and crawl into the small space.

Jasmine helped Mal to sit down and made him as comfortable as possible on the hard uneven ground.

'I will have a quick look and then come back to you.' Jasmine felt a little guilty about leaving her friend in his injured state, just to look at the City, but she really wanted to see what was there. They still had more steps to climb to get to the Outer City and Mal did not look very good.

'Take as long as you want Jazz. I will wait for you here. I am just sorry I don't have the strength to see for myself.' Mal held Jasmine's hand for a long time, looking deeply into her eyes. 'You will have to describe it to me.'

Jasmine nodded and went over to the wall under the hole. She had to climb only about two metres and there were handholds to help her up, but Jasmine did not like the idea of crawling into the small hole at the top.

It was not as hard as Jasmine had predicted to get into the tight space. It was large enough for her to crawl inside on all fours. The hole was more of a tunnel, led horizontally for a few metres, and ended in a carved wall.

Cautiously Jasmine crawled forward. The floor of the tunnel was rough and hurt her knees slightly. The muscles in her legs were complaining, as they had to work hard again. The rest they had received after Mal had fallen was not enough for them to recover fully.

Jasmine approached the end wall; it had subtle carvings of people on each block. Above the wall was nothing, just darkness. Almost as dark as the dark tunnel she had walked through when she first arrived underground.

This was the lookout. Hundreds of metres below Jasmine's feet was the City. This lookout had been used for only a short period, until the Outer City had been built. It was small and cramped, and could only fit one person. The ledge used to have a soft cloth top fitted to it, to allow the watchmen to lay there comfortably for hours, peering over the ledge just behind the wall.

No one had been here for years but now Jasmine was here and brought herself upright to look over the wall.

Peering over the ledge, Jasmine looked down on the City. It was nothing like she had imagined. Even after the long and gruelling climb up the lookout stairs, she was unprepared for the immense, black distance below. A void, of nothing as far as the eye could see. The dark rock around the lookout disappeared into nothing along the edge of the cavern roof. The sparkling jewels of light from the City and the emerald plateau of the Givings were the only breaks in the otherwise boundless void.

At this height, the City seemed small. The people walking

about at the Givings were nothing more than ants on a patch of grass.

Jasmine leaned over further and could just make out the edge of two of the huge stones that rose and fell to cover the phosphorescent light. However, to Jasmine's disappointment, it was impossible at this angle to see the light itself, just a gentle, yellow glow against the brown and black rocks behind.

After a few more minutes staring at the impressive emptiness of the cavern, Jasmine crawled backward off the ledge and returned to Mal who was still sitting on the steps. His chin was still bleeding a little and slowly dripping fresh blood onto his shirt. His face looked pale and in pain.

'I don't know how much further I can go Jasmine,' Mal's voice was slow and uneasy. He so wanted to walk with Jasmine to the top of the steps and see the Outer City, but was unsure if his body would make it.

Jasmine took the strip of cloth out of Mal's hand and gently dabbed the dark red drops from his chin and neck.

'But you must Mal; it is too far to walk back. I know you are hurt and tired, but we must keep moving. Why don't we rest for a short while, maybe you will feel better.'

Mal nodded in agreement but Jasmine could tell he was not convinced he could make it. There was not another choice though; Jasmine knew she must help Mal to get to the Outer City. Once there they could use the conveyance corridor to get home.

That was a strange thought. Jasmine was thinking to herself as she sat down next to Mal. She had thought about getting home to the City. Not too long ago her home had been Durraton Hawthorne Hall, now she was beginning to think of the City as her home.

The two people leaned against each other. Mal closed his eyes and fell into an uncomfortable sleep. Jasmine found that whatever she did, she could not fall sleep; her mind was fixed on speaking to Anarlia and getting Mal home.

Only a few minutes had passed when Mal awoke and glanced over towards Jasmine; blinking to clear the sleep from his eyes. 'You looked sad Jazz,' he said quietly.

'I don't feel particularly sad, just confused and thinking too much, I just hope our plan works Mal. I hope we can speak to Anarlia in the Outer City.' Jasmine sat down next to Mal. 'I wonder if she will remember me?'

'I imagine so, if she has lived there as long as Tantan has said, and not returned to the City she would remember every person she saw, and that could be you alone.

'I am sure everything will be fine, I feel a bit better now and we will speak with Anarlia and she will be able to tell us all about Paluuka.'

Jasmine had started to hate that name, ever since Tantan had spoken about the type of man, if he could be described as that, Paluuka was and what he had done.

A few more minutes passed and Jasmine knew they must keep moving. 'Mal we should go, it can't be much further to the Outer City.'

Mal nodded slowly, just managing to smile. 'If you are determined for me to go with you, then I will.'

Jasmine helped her friend to his feet and held his arm as they left the lookout and proceeded up the stairs towards the Outer City.

Luckily, the final flight of steps was very short, little more than thirty steps that sloped gently upwards with only a single turn halfway. Mal felt tired and cold, his head ached and his face felt sore, but the final leg of the journey was not too taxing.

At the top of the stairs was a small door; cream and white in colour with gold leaf decoration in the centre. The gold leaf was depicting two people walking up steps, a pictogram of what you had done to reach this door. The artist who created the gold leaf picture obviously had little in the way of a sense of humour.

Cautiously, Jasmine turned the handle and pushed the door open. A light, much brighter than in the tunnels, met their eyes and at first they could not see what was in the room. As their eyes adjusted, they could make out a shape in front of them. Nervously Mal and Jasmine walked towards the shape, its figure clearing as their eyes fully adjusted to the light level. Behind them, the door shut with a click.

It had been two whole days since Mal and Jasmine had descended the iron rungs into the Catacombs, and ever since then Kohrstan had waited at the entrance. Except for the occasional break once or twice a day, and a few hours at night when he had slept, he had looked down the hole constantly. His friends were down there, and nothing meant more to him now than his friends who were desperately trying to find a way to free his father and all the other people from the vicious grip of the Tamboli rooms.

Kohrstan felt guilty that he had not volunteered to go into the Catacombs, but he had been too afraid to ask to go with Mal and Jasmine. The Catacombs were a place that no one normally went to, and Kohrstan feared for his friends. He knew he could have tried to persuade them not to go, but they probably would not have listened. Mal and Jasmine were determined to find the tower of light and to stop it from making the evil Tamboli Rooms.

Grancathai had spoken to him soon after Mal and Jasmine had descended into the darkness of the Catacombs. The old librarian was wise and made good use of comforting words. 'Your pain is still too fresh Kohrstan.' Grancathai had said. 'It would only bring you more suffering, and Malmayorkia and Jasmine will feel no bad feelings towards you for staying here. You must take time to mourn your father, you are a strong man and time will help you. Be patient and wait for their return.'

At first Kohrstan found Grancathai's speech a little over powering but as the words organised themselves in his mind he found that it made sense. He was not mentally strong enough to face the Catacombs at this time; if he had tried, it would have made things more difficult for Mal and Jasmine.

Therefore, Kohrstan had decided to wait at the Catacombs entrance for as long as was necessary. It gave him the time to himself that he needed to fully accept what had happened to his father. Grancathai was right, he was a strong man, and it would just take a little time for his strength to return.

Wherever his friends were in the darkness below he wished they would find a safe path and easily return after completing their task.

Kohrstan had no idea that Jasmine and Mal were, in fact, somewhere far above him, standing in a small room. The room had wooden panelling and was similar in size and construction to the room where Jasmine had met Rothgoe many days before.

The bright light in the room showed up a figure in front of them. It was an old woman wearing a tattered dress. Jasmine instantly recognised her as the woman who had taken her to the Great Corridor when she had first arrived in the City.

'Are you Anarlia the Hallier?' Mal asked after a long pause.

The woman had been looking puzzled at the new arrivals in the Outer City but smiled slightly as Mal spoke. 'I have not heard that name for a long time. Yes, I am the Hallier of the Outer City, but I have not been called by my real name in a long time. I didn't think I would ever hear it again.'

'My name is Jasmine and this is Malmayorkia. Tantan sent us here to speak to you. I don't know if you remember me; but I was here once before.'

'I rarely see anyone these days; I remember when you arrived and however unlikely it seemed at the time I thought you were from the Catacombs. Now I know that you are from the City. If only I had known when you first came bursting into my study it could have saved so much time.'

The woman spoke quickly, barely pausing for breath. Jasmine recalled their first meeting and how much she had spoken when she was scared and confused about being in the City.

'You know why we have come here?' Jasmine asked. 'Were you expecting us?'

'I don't think expected is the right word. There is a See-Smith in the Catacombs called Zieen and he told me that one day he would send some one to me through the lookout stairs. I didn't know when that day would come; I had begun to think it may never happen, but then, while I was gazing out of the glass windows; I saw you at the lookout and came here to meet you. What is it that I can help you with?'

Jasmine signed, she did not really know why they had come to the Outer City. Tantan had just ushered them in the right direction and told them that the woman living in the Outer City would be able to give them more information.

Mal looked at Jasmine and saw her puzzled expression. She had always been his source of strength and now she seemed not to know what to do.

Mal's head felt sore and he wanted, more than anything, to have a good meal and to sleep in his home room. Their expedition was starting to become too much for him, but he managed to say something that made Anarlia seem worried. 'We are here because of the Tower of Light.'

Anarlia thought for a moment, remembering back to when she was young and the meeting she had had with Zieen. That meeting had been a long time ago but Anarlia knew it had been important, and although she had not understood it at the time she knew her role in future events, would be vitally important.

'You should follow me. There is much we have to discuss.'

Anarlia led them through a door into another room that was similar in design. Jasmine recognised the desk in the corner of the room stacked with pieces of paper and small stone tablets.

There were four doors in the room, one had the distinctive blue Tamboli symbol; beyond that door was Rothgoe. Jasmine wondered if it was still a Tamboli room or if the destruction of the Tower of Light had ended that hideous creation.

She did not have time to check. Anarlia took them into a Conveyance corridor that opened into a circular room. There were numerous tables and chairs scattered around the room and shelving units on each side holding various carved statues; made from wood and stone. They depicted people standing in formal poses. Some had been decorated further with small glass beads and thin strips of silver wire.

The floor of the room was carpeted, a rarity in the City, which was deep red in colour with a deep pile.

'Please have a seat at the centre table and I will fetch something for your injury Malmayorkia.'

Jasmine and Mal sat down on the cushioned seats and cast their eyes around the beautiful room. The domed ceiling was covered in white plaster imbedded with light crystals similar to those suspended from chains in the library.

Anarlia went to a small wooden cupboard and took out a thin glass bottle, a small drinking glass and a grey cloth bag.

'You should drink this, Malmayorkia,' the old woman said as she poured the thick clear liquid into the glass. 'It will give you your strength back, and this will help to clean your face.'

Mal took the small white towel that Anarlia offered him from the cloth bag. It smelt sweet and was cool to the touch.

'It is made from the pulp of the Stone Tree, pressed into a special fabric. Hold it against your face for a moment and drink your soup.'

The liquid was not anything like the soup where Jasmine was from, it looked little more than thick water, completely transparent.

Mal sipped some of the clear soup from the cup. It tasted bitter and almost made him gag. Anarlia saw his expression as he drank and laughed loudly.

'It will give you your strength back, but you will have to endure the taste, it is better to drink it as quickly as you can; then its all gone in one go.'

Mal did so, and coughed loudly as the bitter drink stung the back of his throat. The ill effects passed quickly and Mal sat back in his chair. The drink felt warm in his stomach and he did begin to feel a little better.

Anarlia sat down at the opposite end of the table. 'This will be a difficult discussion. I know some things about the Tower of Light, perhaps slightly more than Zieen but my knowledge is still limited. Perhaps it would be better if you begin by telling me your story. Why are you interested in the Tower of Light?'

Jasmine explained the story, as she had done before to Zieen in the Catacombs. However, the story was longer now as they had found what they believed was the Tower of Light and had irreversibly damaged it.

Anarlia understood most of what Jasmine was saying. In the past, she had lived in the City and in the Catacombs and had experience of Tamboli rooms and she herself wore a felostone, although it was hanging in a pendant around her neck.

Jasmine was now experienced in telling the story of the library and the books written by Martin Blake, and like Tantan and Zieen; Anarlia knew more about the City's creation than the people who actually lived there. Jasmine did not feel it would be important to mention that she was from the Old World at this stage, although Anarlia must know about the huge wooden door that she had used to get into the City.

It was a tale that could have been from a film back in Jasmine's home in the Old World, but this was real and Jasmine was now a major part of the story.

As Jasmine neared the end of the story and spoke about meeting with Zieen and Tantan, Anarlia nodded as if she already knew what the Hallier and See-Smith had told them.

The story ended with their arrival in the Outer City. Throughout the story, Mal had rested in his chair. The drink had given him a strange feeling throughout his body and he wanted to sleep, for a moment he had closed his eyes but sleep did not come. The soft towel on his face was soothing and helped to take away the pain. Jasmine looked at him after she had finished speaking and he smiled back at her as if to say he was feeling better.

'Jasmine, that certainly is a complicated story and I now understand why Tantan sent you here, rather than Zieen. Zieen may not have wanted you to come. I will now tell you my story, at least the parts that are relevant to yours.

'When I was very young; the Outer City that we are now in was home to the Principal Guardian; a descendant of Balmore of Terrol. The Principal Guardian was the head of the Council of Guardians that used to run the City. Paluuka had been thrown out of the City hundreds of years before and life was good except for one small problem, the first Tamboli Room.

'It had been created a long time ago to stop anything from entering the City; unfortunately two people were trapped in that room. Jasmine, you have seen that room, it is from there that you came into my study when we first met.'

'But there was only one person in that room,' Jasmine interjected.

'There were two originally, Balmore of Terrol was also in there and he and his servant, Rothgoe, were about to embark on a journey out of the City through the large wooden door. You probably saw it when you were in the room.'

Jasmine, of course, had seen the door and had gone through it, but again she decided not to speak about her original home.

'No one knew what a Tamboli Room was back then and they tried to get Balmore out; he was after all, the Head of the City. But as you probably know, no one can be taken from a Tamboli room and survive.'

'Didn't this all happen hundreds of years ago?' Jasmine asked.

'Yes it did, but it was an important event. It made the people realise how vulnerable they were, and when new Tamboli Rooms started appearing when I was a little girl the people started to panic, they feared what would happen to their way of life.

'It didn't take long before the Council of Guardians could no longer keep order around the City; people stopped working and simply kept to themselves.

'After a little while the Council of Guardians was abolished all together, and the Principal Guardian stayed here in the Outer City and didn't allow anyone to enter; he was a very wise man and re-opened the lookout stairs and met the people of the Catacombs.'

Mal sat up in his chair; he was beginning to feel much better and was taking a greater interest in what Anarlia and Jasmine were talking about. 'If you don't mind me asking, how did you come to live here in the Outer City if the Principal Guardian didn't let people come here?'

'You don't need to look so worried Malmayorkia; you can ask any questions you like.' Anarlia had a very kind nature and spoke with grace and wisdom. 'The man was called Chan-chey;

he was my father. I lived here with him and my mother and befriended a young man from the Catacombs named Zieen; the same Zieen that you met.

'Zieen was training to become a Hallier at that time so I joined him in his training and also became a Hallier.

'We spent many happy years together. After my parents had grown old and died I lived with Zieen in the Catacombs, but one day our lives were changed forever and this is where my story meets yours.

'Zieen was a strong and intelligent man and had become a great Hallier; but the people knew his skills would be better used as a See-Smith.

'The See-Smith he replaced was very old, but before he died he told Zieen all the knowledge and wisdom he had learned in his life. One piece of information was a dark tale about Paluuka. Jasmine, you already know most of this story; as it is about Paluuka forbidding anyone from speaking about the location of the Tower of Light.' Anarlia paused for a minute and went back to the small wooden cupboard to fetch some water for them all to drink.

Jasmine was particularly thirsty and Mal was glad to have some water to remove the last remnants of the bitter soup taste from his mouth. When they had finished drinking, Anarlia continued her story.

'The See-Smiths normally kept their secrets to themselves, but we were in love and we shared everything, and he knew so much more than any of the See-Smiths that had come before him; he had met Paluuka.

'It was a dark day that he has had nightmares about every day since. Paluuka was walking through the maze below the stream carrying part of a large machine. This was before Zieen had become a See-Smith and was only a Hallier and therefore; responsible for the tunnels and took it upon himself to confront Paluuka. To his surprise, Paluuka agreed to speak with him.

'They sat and spoke for hours; possibly even days, Paluuka spoke at length about being thrown out of the City and tried to convince Zieen that he had done nothing wrong. Zieen was a good match for Paluuka's intelligence and knew he was lying but went along with it to gain his trust.

'By some miracle it appeared to work and Paluuka began to speak more freely. This was a deception, their whole conversation was based on deception; both of them trying to out deceive each other. Paluuka reinforced the fact that no one should ever talk about the Tower of Light or discuss where it was. He also said that one day someone would come looking for it and if they found it, it would be the end of the people in the Catacombs.'

'I'm sorry Anarlia, I don't understand,' Mal said apprehensively. 'If Zieen and Tantan knew all that information; why risk helping us?'

Anarlia smiled. 'Zieen never trusted anything Paluuka said, he always believed he wasn't telling the truth. If Paluuka kept telling them not to help anyone who was looking for the machine, then maybe something good would happen if they did.'

'That's a big risk to take,' Jasmine added. 'If Paluuka found out that Tantan and Zieen helped us, then it could cause problems for everyone in the Catacombs.'

Anarlia lost her smile. 'My dear, he already knows. There are stones that can sense the goings on in other places. The instant you broke the machine; he knew. And it won't just be the people of the Catacombs that will suffer, but the people of the City too.'

Jasmine was stunned, had destroying the Tower of Light really caused so many problems?

'You look unwell dear, are you feeling alright?' Anarlia asked with a caring motherly tone.

Jasmine shook her head. 'This is all our fault, we destroyed the Tower of Light and now we are to bring suffering to the Catacombs and the City.

Anarlia smiled. 'Do not worry yourselves; you have done the right thing.'

'How have we done the right thing?' Jasmine asked looking more and more sorry for herself.

Anarlia leant over and pushed a lock of Jasmine's hair back away from her face. 'You have started in motion a series of events that will change our way of life forever. There is one task that needs to be done, and soon. If it can be done well; then the City will be made new again. If it cannot be done, then the City *will* suffer.

'You two have done so much already, no one could ask you to do this task; it is dangerous and harder than you can imagine.'

Mal was a little apprehensive but Jasmine wanted to put things right, whether she would be the cause of the great suffering or not; she wanted to help all she could.

'Whatever the task is Anarlia, I want to help.'

Mal was spurred on by Jasmine's courage. 'I will help too; we will do the task together.'

A short while later Mal and Jasmine were stood with Anarlia in her study, they had had a chance to wash in a small bubbling fountain in a room nearby and have something to eat.

Their clothes were still very dirty and torn in some places but at least they had been able to have a little rest. The task before them would be more challenging and more difficult than their quest into the Catacombs.

As Anarlia explained what had to be done, Jasmine and Mal began to feel very anxious and scared, they had not realised how difficult their task was going to be.

The first thing they must do is return to the library and seek the council of Grancathai and make some quick preparations. Time was running out and there was a lot to be done.

'Farewell, Jasmine and Malmayorkia,' Anarlia said speaking slightly slower than usual. 'I will see you again soon. I must go to Zieen, and fulfil my part in all this.'

Mal and Jasmine thanked Anarlia for her kindness and help, and left through the Conveyance corridor.

'It is I who should be thanking you,' Anarlia said quietly under her breath as the conveyance corridor clicked closed.

CHAPTER 10

Crossing the Water

Kohrstan was still sat on the edge of the Catacombs' entrance; just as he said he would. Scattered around him were a few food remains and a couple of empty water bottles.

He turned around instantly as Mal and Jasmine approached. Kohrstan had good hearing and had spent the last few days listening intently to any sounds that could mean his friends were in trouble and needed help.

'You're back!' Kohrstan said cheerily, but his bright expression faded slightly, as he did not understand how his friends had come back into the City without going past him. 'I am so pleased so see you, but I am confused about how you got here.'

Mal smiled, he understood that it must be mystifying for Kohrstan to suddenly see his friends after waiting days for them to come up out of the vertical tunnel. 'We came back through the Outer City. Don't worry, we will explain everything; a lot of things have happened.'

Kohrstan stood and hugged his friends. 'What was it like in the Catacombs? Oh I am glad you are home; but you are hurt?'

Mal felt the grazes on his face. 'It is nothing serious. Where is Grancathai? We have a lot to tell both you.'

'He's in the library,' Kohrstan replied. 'He has started writing a new book to tell the story of your trip into the Catacombs.'

Kohrstan accompanied Mal and Jasmine through Grancathai's home room and into the library. The familiar musty smell was a pleasant reminder that they were now home.

Jasmine was beginning to fall in love with the City. The beautifully carved stonework, the light rooms, and the fresher air was all in stark contrast to the darker, colder, and more mysterious world below the City in the Catacombs.

Grancathai was sat at a table on the ground floor of the library; busily cutting pieces of paper and binding them together with string. He had been taught how to make books by his father and over the years had become exceptionally good at it. He did not have the tools or machinery to make hard covers or printed words; but the books he created were unique and well crafted.

'Jasmine, Malmayorkia!' he said loudly as they entered the room. 'You have been away for a long time, I was beginning to worry.'

'They didn't come up the iron rungs, they found another way back,' Kohrstan added excitedly.

Grancathai looked puzzled, 'I didn't believe there was any other way back. Please sit with me and tell me all about the Catacombs. Did you find the Tower of Light?'

The four people sat around the large polished table, and Mal and Jasmine explained what had happened to them since descending the iron rungs into the Catacombs. They found it an easier story to explain than when they had spoken to Zieen and Tantan in the Catacombs, and Anarlia in the Outer City as Kohrstan and Grancathai already knew so much.

Kohrstan in particular was concerned when Paluuka was mentioned and how he had deceived people and lied for his own personal gain.

'What does Anarlia expect us to do?' Grancathai asked as Jasmine finished off the story. 'Does she want us to go to Paluuka's Temple?'

Jasmine ran a hand through her hair; it was dirty and tangled. She was tired and in much need of a good wash, something to eat and a good nights sleep, but she knew she probably would not have time to do anything of the sort.

'Yes,' she said after a pause. 'Paluuka already knows what we have done to the Tower of Light and Anarlia thinks we should try and show Paluuka the effects he is having on the City. Mal and I have already discussed it, and are prepared to go to his Temple.'

Kohrstan looked sad. 'Why does it have to be you that goes? Surely there must be someone else that could help?'

Grancathai knew the answer to that, although people might be convinced to help their cause; it was highly unlikely that they would ever be convinced to actually go to Paluuka's Temple.

Mal put his hand on Kohrstan's shoulder. 'We set out to stop the Tamboli Rooms, and if we must go and see Paluuka; then that is what we must do. Jasmine and I have been through a lot together, we know what we have to do.'

Kohrstan did not really feel much better. He was scared and confused. He wanted to save his father from the Tamboli Room and help his friends with their endeavours but Paluuka was an evil man and no one had ever been to his Temple. 'My heart aches when I think about you going there, I feel I should be going but I don't think I would make it.'

'I'm sure if it came to it, you would be able to go with us, but this is something that Mal and I have to do. We were the ones who destroyed the Tower of Light and because of that Paluuka will rein terror upon the people of the Catacombs and the City; we must undo what we have done.'

The small group spoke for a long time. They discussed what options they had; but they were very few. Paluuka would be true to his word and make the people suffer because they went against him. More people than ever could become trapped in Tamboli Rooms, or endure something much worse.

Jasmine and Mal had already decided to go to Paluuka's Temple and confront him; they only needed to convince their friends that it was the right thing to do, and that they had a chance of achieving their goal. They were unsure what it would be like to actually meet Paluuka but they had become very strong willed and felt their friendship would help them to over come any difficulties.

They knew that Paluuka's Temple was at the edge of the cavern the City was built in, but there were no records of anyone ever going there. It would be difficult to know what the Temple was like or more importantly how to get in. Jasmine had asked

Grancathai about the library and if it contained any books that might help, but as she had suspected there was not any.

'How do we get to Paluuka's Temple?' Mal asked as he paced around the library. 'We can't swim across the lake!'

The important discussions had stopped briefly as Grancathai fetched something for them to drink. The air was dry in the library and people's throats quickly became parched, especially if they were talking a lot. Mal was concerned that the longer they waited the more difficult it could be to confront Paluuka, and so he wanted to restart their conversation as soon as possible. The quicker they got to Paluuka, the less chance there was of him doing anything to make the people suffer.

Grancathai had been checking over his books, looking for anything that might give even a small clue that could help them, but there was nothing. 'You mentioned that Paluuka frequently visited the Catacombs, could you not ask the people you met if they know how to get in. On the other hand, maybe Anarlia knows about a way in. She is even older than I am, and if her father was the last Principal Guardian she may know a lot about the City.'

Jasmine signed. 'Surely she would have told us if she knew anything. She mentioned his Temple and a small rocky beach in front of it where the lake water meets the land.

'What exactly did Anarlia say about going to his Temple?' Grancathai asked closing a book and returning it to its shelf. 'Did she say anything that could help?'

Mal and Jasmine thought back to the circular room where they had sat and talked to Anarlia. They carefully went through each part of the discussion and thought about the exact words she had said. Jasmine remembered that Anarlia had spoken in metaphors at times when she was speaking about Paluuka, but nothing pointed towards how to get to his Temple.

Mal remembered one fact that he thought might be useful. 'Anarlia was talking about Paluuka and said that his Temple was across the lake; which we already knew. However, she went on say that we must walk from the jetty on the waters edge along the causeway to an iron gate. It sounds like she expects us to arrive by the edge of the lake.'

'The jetty? Anarlia mentioned the Jetty?' Grancathai said; his eyes widening with a sudden realisation.

Mal nodded. 'She said the causeway leads from the jetty on the edge of the lake up to the Iron Gate, but how does that help? We still need to get to the jetty on the other side of the lake.'

'The jetty isn't at the other side of the lake,' Grancathai suddenly added. 'It's attached to the City!'

Jasmine was excited by this news. She did not really understand what Grancathai was talking about but he seemed to think that this information was helpful; perhaps they could use it to find a way across the lake. 'There's a jetty in the City? You mean we could take a boat across the water?'

Grancathai seemed to be thinking hard; trying to recall information he had been told a long time ago. 'No there aren't any boats, not any more, but the jetty will probably still be there.'

Jasmine and Mal were beginning to get confused, but patiently waited for Grancathai to explain what he was thinking about.

'Anarlia told you to take the causeway which starts at the jetty; I think she means the old Jetty at the edge of the Water Gallery. We assumed the Jetty was on the other side of the lake but it is right here, in the City.' Grancathai was talking to himself, or rather thinking aloud. 'If the causeway starts at the jetty and runs across the lake to the shore the other side, then everything makes sense.'

'What does that mean Grancathai?' Jasmine asked during a pause in the librarian's mumblings.

'I'm sorry, I was thinking to myself,' he replied turning towards his friends. 'There is an old wooden jetty near a place called the Water Gallery. I remember it from when I was a child. People used to take small rafts from the jetty to collect algae growing in the water around the City.

'If we could go to the Water Gallery and find the Jetty we may find that there is the causeway that leads across the lake.'

'You mean we could simply walk along this causeway and that would take us to the Temple?' Jasmine started smiling. It was the first clue that they had uncovered in a long time, and it could be a very important clue. 'You said you remember seeing the jetty when you were a child, can you take us there?'

Grancathai frowned and signed heavily. 'It was a very long time ago, and I don't remember it exactly. I'm not sure I could even find the Water Gallery.'

'What is the Water Gallery?' Mal asked, 'I haven't even heard of it.'

'The Water Gallery is a long corridor, similar to the Great Corridor where people used to have market stalls, selling things they had made. It was right near the bottom of the City and you could see the lake out of the windows. If only I could remember where it was.'

'I may be able to help with that. I know a man who lived near my father, he knows a lot about the City as it used to be; perhaps he knows how to get to the causeway.' Kohrstan seemed happy that he was joining in the conversation and helping. 'I can go to him and ask.'

Grancathai thought for a moment. 'If you think he may be able to help then you should speak to him, but don't mention too much about our plans. People were sceptical when you went to the Catacombs; they are likely to be very afraid if you say you want to go to Paluuka's Temple.'

Kohrstan nodded and walked out of the door. Mal thought about his friend for a while and realised how much like his father he was becoming. Gryss had always been good at knowing people and being able to find information or equipment whenever he needed.

Grancathai watched Kohrstan leave and then turned his attention back to Jasmine and Mal.

'Once we have found the way onto the causeway you can leave. Either Kohrstan or I will go to the Givings and fetch some more food and water to put in your bag, Jasmine. You can both rest here for the moment. It is a pity that you no longer have the oil lamp. The journey you now take will lead to somewhere darker than you can imagine. I must warn you that there will be bitter consequences at the end of the trip, what they will be I don't know but you cannot expect to go to a place like Paluuka's Temple and return the same people.'

Chills ran up Jasmine's spine and Mal drew in a sharp breath. Grancathai's words were haunting, but they knew he had to warn them about what they would expect on such a difficult journey.

The light shone gently through a glassless window; casting a long shadow of a man stood in front, looking outwards. It was difficult to make out exactly what he looked like with the light shining behind him, but he looked middle aged and wore dark trousers and shirt.

Kohrstan gestured to his friends to stay where they were and cautiously approached the man who turned his head slightly as if to show that he knew someone was behind him. Kohrstan drew closer and spoke quietly to the man.

Jasmine glanced around the small chamber, the conveyance corridor door shone brightly against the grey rock of the walls.

The last few hours had seemed a blur. They had waited in the library for Kohrstan to return with news of a way of getting onto the causeway.

He had been excited when he returned as the man he had gone to see said he could show them the way to the Water Gallery; the corridor that led to the jetty and the causeway.

'He said he will meet us outside his home room later on today, he can't help us now because he needs to get something that we will need,' Kohrstan said excitedly. 'I'm not sure what we need but he says we can't get there without it.'

'Thank you Kohrstan,' Mal said patting his friend on the shoulder. 'We couldn't have done it without you.'

Kohrstan knew that he had done only a very small task in the great scheme of things and could never dream of matching the hard work and effort that Jasmine and Mal had put in to their mission, but he was pleased with the sentiment.

The rest of the preparations had not taken long. There were no books or papers to read as they had done before their journey into the Catacombs. There was just the task of mentally preparing for the difficult road that lay ahead of them.

It was very late by the time they had finished packing and were ready to go. Mal desperately wanted to have one more trip to the Givings but he knew the stones would be rising soon, and it would be getting dark.

Kohrstan had led the way through a Conveyance corridor to the dark grey room they were now standing in. There was a tunnel leading off to the left and a narrow door on the right. Kohrstan had explained that the man, whose name he did not know, lived here and would take them to the Water Gallery.

A short time passed and the man was deep in conversation with Kohrstan although they never spoke above a whisper.

Finally, the man nodded his head and walked towards the tunnel on the left.

Kohrstan quickly returned to his friends, 'He says we should follow him down the tunnel, it leads to some stairs and they go to the Water Gallery.'

The man was walking fast down the tunnel and the ageing Grancathai struggled to keep up with the group as they hurried after him.

The tunnel opened into a small chamber with a wide tunnel leading to an archway. The man stopped near the tunnel entrance and picked up a long metal pole. He turned towards Kohrstan. He seemed slightly nervous about speaking to the others, especially Jasmine as he had heard that she wanted to speak to Paluuka.

'This is the Lowering Stick,' the man said holding the stick out to Kohrstan. 'There is a metal plate that will lower you down onto the Jetty. Put the pointed end of the stick into the slot on the metal plate and it will allow you to descend. Once the lift has gone down you will need to push the stick towards the end of the jetty and it will rise again. If you need to come back up and the lift is up, you must use the hooked end of the stick on a lever at the edge of the metal platform and pull it down.'

Kohrstan looked at both ends of the stick; it did not sound too complicated to work but he was unsure. 'Thank you for your help, but could you come to the platform with us?'

'I will not go any further than here,' the man said standing in the archway. 'No one has been through here in a long time and I will not be one of the first to walk through again. You must go alone. Use the lowering stick as I showed you.'

Kohrstan nodded and walked past the man and into the tunnel behind. Mal and Jasmine followed, both nodding in thanks to the man who had helped them.

The Water Gallery did have some resemblance to the Great Corridor, but it was certainly different in many ways. There were no doors on the inside wall, the floor was dirty and covered in loose rubble from the crumbing roof and the corridor actually looked curved. After seeing the Great Corridor many times it seemed strange to Jasmine to see, now, what it probably actually looked like. The strange effect of the Great Corridor looking straight was still bizarre in Jasmine's mind.

The opening at the side of the corridor was small and could easily have been missed had Kohrstan not been keeping an avid eye on the right hand wall.

The opening had been knocked through the outer wall in a very rough manner. Chips of stone stood jaggedly out from its roughly circular aperture. Beyond was simply darkness; the same as you would see out of any of the windows along the Great Corridor. Except here, if you were to look straight down, it was possible to make out a small wooden jetty about four metres long attached to the edge of the wall.

Kohrstan saw the metal platform at the edge of the wall. It was in its risen position and only just large enough for one person to stand on it at a time. Cautiously Kohrstan stepped on, unsure if it would take his weight, as it had not been used in a long time.

The metal platform did not move at all when he stepped on, but drifted silently downward as the lowering stick was pushed into the small opening on the side of the platform.

Jasmine was amazed, as there did not seem to be any workings, and the lift was silent; it just gracefully descended onto the wooden jetty below.

Kohrstan was now standing at the edge of the lake. The small wooden jetty had moved and creaked as he stepped onto it, but seemed to be holding.

The narrow walkway at the end did not seem inviting. It was submerged just below the water level and looked like it was covered in weeds or thick algae.

Kohrstan tapped the walkway with his lowering stick. It was stone, and should not be in as bad a state as the jetty.

Why did they build the causeway out of stone but the jetty out of simple bits of wood? It would have made more sense to build the whole thing out of stone, and then it would not begin to rot and become unsafe.

Kohrstan was satisfied it was safe for his friends to descend and placed the Lowering Stick back into the slot. Without standing on the platform he pulled the lever and the platform returned to the top.

Mal was next to descend, followed soon after by Jasmine. Grancathai stayed at the top as he could get a better view of the jetty and could just about see the top of the causeway beneath the dark water.

'It appears we must watch you depart again,' Grancathai said from the top of the lift. 'You go now to a dark place, you will return different, but I know you are strong and will return.'

The librarian's words had potent meanings and Jasmine and Mal shuddered slightly as they looked along the causeway. It was dark, but the stone causeway was only just below the water level and so should not be too difficult to traverse.

The quiet splashing of water around their feet was the only sound that Mal and Jasmine could hear as they began to walk along the causeway into the darkness.

Kohrstan stayed at the end of the jetty and watched until his friends disappeared into the distance, the occasional tear rolling down his cheeks. It was difficult to watch the people close to him going to a place that was terrifying and dangerous.

Mal was walking in front of Jasmine but had stopped occasionally to glance around and see the City slowly disappearing behind them, its high wall and numerous windows a curious sight, and something that Mal had never seen before; the outside of the City.

The causeway was straight and even, making walking across it easy and quick. It had not taken long for Mal and Jasmine to lose sight of the jetty and their friends that were staying behind.

There was nothing to see as they walked across the lake, just blackness in every direction, but slowly the blackness seemed to dull slightly and become a blurred grey.

It was a fine mist that hung in the air around the edge of the lake and it slowly became thicker and thicker as they walked, turning the darkness into a shrouded gloom.

It did not take long before the darkness to become totally obscured by the grey vapour, but Jasmine and Mal had to continue. Every step took them deeper into the mist and further away from their home.

The cold, grey tendrils soaked Mal and Jasmine's clothing and made the air feel bitterly cold. It was a strange feeling to be so cold and to be encased in mist.

Nothing could be seen beyond a few metres and Mal had to watch how fast he walked; he did not want to get too far ahead of Jasmine and for her to lose sight of him. Although there was only one route they could take, Mal wanted to ensure he was always close to his friend.

There was no way to tell how far they had walked, but they knew it had been a very long way as their legs began to feel tired and the skin on their feet began to rub against their wet shoes.

Rocks began appearing at the edge of the causeway, poking only a little way out of still, black water. They were covered in a thick layer of dark green algae and were difficult to see in the darkness.

Slowly, as Mal and Jasmine, progressed further along the

causeway, the rocks became larger and were resting further out of the water. The same green algae clung to them, in slimy fronds.

The lines of rocks down each side of the causeway were now closer together, some touching, and some out the water completely, simply resting on other rocks.

Eventually the line of rocks became a rocky beach, an end to the water. Jasmine suddenly remembered the beach she had been sat on the night that she had come into the City. This was a very different beach though.

The water was still and did not create waves to gently lap against the rocks. The air did not have the refreshing salty taste of the sea. It was stagnant and stunk of rotting algae. In the darkness, it was not possible to see how far the beach went. It could have simply been only a few metres and met a solid wall of rock, or it might have run the whole width of the cavern.

The causeway continued up the beach at a slight incline and Mal began to walk slowly up it. Jasmine paused shortly and looked behind her. In the distance was a faint glow that was the lights in the City. Although dimmed by the fog and murk, it was a place that the young woman was desperate to get back to. She was cold and frightened but knew she could not get back to the warm light of the City until she had completed her task.

Jasmine began to move again so not to lose sight of Mal, who was now a few paces ahead.

The causeway ended in a solid looking wall. It must be Paluuka's Temple, although the building was not how Jasmine had pictured it. It was incredibly old and had been slowly decaying over hundreds of years, but in a very different way to the City. The City seemed to be growing old gracefully, gently crumbling and fading. Paluuka's Temple was rotting. The surface of the walls were encrusted with minerals, coarse lichen and algae; as though it had been laid sunken on a seabed like an old ship.

The walkway continued along the edge of the building. Treading carefully to avoid holes and the dangerously slippery algae, the couple made their way silently along it. There were no windows in the wall, and the top, towering a hundred metres above, met the rocky ceiling of the cavern. Jasmine began to wonder how they would get into Paluuka's Temple. Even Grancathai knew nothing about this dark place, and could offer no advice on how to get past the huge wall and into the temple's interior.

Suddenly through the murk, Jasmine could see that the walkway ended at an Iron Gate, an entrance to the temple beyond. Jasmine could not tell if the huge granite blocks were part of an elaborate outer wall like a castle, or if it was in-fact, the outer wall of the temple itself.

The gate was made from six, wide, iron bars, hanging vertically in a solid iron frame. Small gaps, no wider than Jasmine's little finger shone with an eerie, green light. Jasmine held her hands up to the metal; it was ice cold and rough with rust and lichen.

'Jazz, look!' Mal pointed to a heavy metal chain on the side of the gate. It looked incredibly old and some parts had rusted through completely leaving two ends just dangling on the ground, rather than holding the gate secure. One end was still passed through a metal ring sunk into the wall and Mal lifted it to release the gate. It crumbled on the slightest touch, and fell to the ground in a pile of rust and metal fragments.

'Mal, I am frightened. What will we see in there?' Jasmine said taking the hand of her friend and holding it tightly in her own.

Mal wiped flakes of rust from his hand onto his jacket and looked into Jasmine's eyes. 'I wish I could say. No one from the City has ever been here; but whatever we find we will face together.'

The gate opened easier than both of them had expected; it swung open quietly on the first push to reveal a long flight of steps. Even with the green light inside, the top could not be seen.

'I hope this light continues throughout the Temple,' Jasmine said quietly. 'I don't fancy walking through the dark again.

The inside of Paluuka's Temple was very similar to the outside. The decaying surfaces of the walls were dripping with grime and there was a putrid smell of rotting algae.

Slowly and cautiously, they began to climb the treacherous steps. They were broken in many places and bits of rubble were littered across them. There were arches on either side cut into the rock with carvings of some kind, but they were too weathered to make out.

Both Mal and Jasmine began to recall the steps on their way to the City lookout, and hoped that these stairs would not be nearly as long.

Their hopes paid off, a single light appeared far head; it was bright green and flickering gently against the murky background.

Cautiously the two friends continued up the steps towards the light. It was difficult to see, as if it was shrouded in mist, but the mist seemed to have stopped at the Iron Gate at the entrance; too scared to enter.

As they got closer, the light seemed to illuminate the steps making them more visible and less treacherous, but suddenly the light went out.

Fumbling in the dark, Mal and Jasmine held each other's hands as they tried to walk further up the steps. It was extremely difficult; the steps were chipped and broken in many places.

It was pitch black, without the light shining from further up the steps; it was impossible to make out anything. It was times like this that Mal's lamp would have come in useful, but unfortunately, it was stuck forever more in the well of the Catacombs.

'Mal, I think I have found something,' Jasmine said feeling a gap in the wall. As they had trudged upwards through the gloom Jasmine had been gently running her fingers along the wall; trying to feel for anything that might be there. 'I think it's an opening. Hold my hand and I will guide us through it.'

Mal held Jasmine's hand tightly; he was not afraid of the dark but disliked it all the same. 'Jazz; are we not heading for the top of the stairs?'

'I think we are at the top, the wall curves slightly inwards and this opening is slightly to the side but more or less at the top.'

Beyond the opening, the steps disappeared and the walking

became easier. The ground was smooth and flat, and the walls on either side were close to each other making it easy for Jasmine to keep track of where they were going.

'Mal, I am going to walk in front of you so I can touch both sides of the tunnel with my hands, I want to know what is around so it will make it easier to come back. You can hold onto my shoulders.'

Mal did so, and Jasmine slowly walked ahead. Her fingers began to feel dirty and sticky as she rubbed them along the grime-covered walls.

The smell in the Temple seemed to be getting worse the further they went and they both began to feel a little sick at the pungent stench.

'Jazz can you see anything ahead?' Mal called from behind.

As hard as she tried, Jasmine could not see a single thing, the tunnel continued forward but there was no sign that the light would return. 'Nothing yet, I guess we just keep going. After all we must...'

Jasmine cut her sentence short as a light appearing in an entrance on her left suddenly startled her.

It was a wide archway of white marble. Although it was dirty and chipped it still seemed out of place in the darkness and gloom of the Temple; everything else was either black or dark grey in colour.

'Mal, I don't like this, it is almost as if someone knows we are here and is directing us to go this way,' Jasmine whispered quietly, not daring to speak any louder.

'I don't know if there are any other ways to go,' Mal said in reply. 'It would seem better to go somewhere that is light, rather than continuing in this darkness.'

Jasmine nodded and led the way through the marble archway and up another flight of steps. Although Mal's reasoning had seemed sound, neither of them really believed it; they were just grateful there was some light for them to see. If they had continued walking through complete darkness then they risked walking into walls or falling down holes. However unsettling it was to go this way, at least they could see the path in front of them.

The stairs were worn in the middle; they had been well used over the years, although it was not likely that many people had lived here. If Paluuka was as old as the City he could have walked up and down these stairs thousands or tens of thousands of time; wearing the stone into smooth gullies.

'Mal, do you remember what Anarlia told us about Paluuka?' Jasmine asked as they continued up the steps. 'She said that he had stones that could tell him what was happening around the City. So it is likely that he knows we are here.'

'I suppose so,' Mal agreed nervously. 'But maybe he wants to meet us and is showing us to where he is. This temple is huge, it would be nice if he was showing us the way or we could be here for days.'

The steps ended in a small room with rubble and plaster scattered on the floor from the ceiling above. It had once been an ornate ceiling; which was surprising in this temple with so much darkness and filth. It had been white with gold stars and gemstones to reflect the light from nearby candles and create sparkles across the room.

Paluuka had always been fascinated with light; its colours and its textures, and although most of his temple was dark he had created a few rooms where light was a prominent feature. Time, however, had taken its toll and the cold damp conditions had caused the plaster to crumble and fall to the ground. The gemstones and golden stars had been removed over the years and nothing remained of what was a small room of beauty in an otherwise dark temple.

There was only one exit from the room, it led towards a large chamber where a faint light glowed from crystals set into the walls.

The ceiling was high and supported by large stone pillars running down the centre. The tops of the pillars formed wide arches that disappeared into the dark ceiling. The row of arches seemed to separate the room into two sections.

Through the arches the floor sloped upwards, and created a raised platform on which were three tall dark chairs in a row.

Jasmine and Mal walked up the slope and stopped instantly

at the top; struck with horror at the sight of a figure sitting in the centre chair.

CHAPTER 11

Paluuka's Temple

The figure in the chair was immeasurably old. The small scraps of skin that appeared from beneath a heavy grey cloak were wrinkled and grey; a hood obscured most of its face. The figures whole appearance seemed colourless; a lifeless grey body shrouded in hatred and misery. His wooden chair, broken and stained, was covered in the same damp grime as the walls of the temple. The figure sat on the chair was Paluuka.

He seemed motionless for a long time, and then with great difficulty he raised his right hand, his palm facing towards Jasmine and Mal. His face twitched and his hand fell back down. Again, he was motionless, until his mouth opened slightly as if to speak, but no words came.

Jasmine took a step forward, but Mal grabbed her arm and pulled her back. 'No don't!' he whispered. 'We shouldn't go near him.'

'I am going to speak to him, and if I have to go right up to his face, then I will.' Jasmine had a determined look on her face and Mal knew there was nothing he could do to persuade her against what she wanted to do.

Turning their attention back to the figure in the chair the two people suddenly froze with shock. Paluuka was standing up on his feet. He was tall, much taller than Mal but his body was withered and diseased. His back was crooked and his legs wobbled under the weight of his body.

Paluuka's mouth opened again but this time there were words that came out in a deep booming voice. 'Why are you here?'

Jasmine and Mal stood motionless, Mal's hand still around Jasmine's arm.

Paluuka slowly moved his head side to side, looking carefully at the people in front of him. 'Why are you here?' he boomed again. 'You are fearful of me, but I require an answer.' His voice was powerful and authoritarian, Jasmine and Mal were too shocked to speak but too scared not to reply to the question.

Jasmine swallowed and took a deep breath. 'We are here to speak with you.'

'To speak with me? Why do you want to speak to me? It has been many years since anyone has come over here. I am not sure what you could possibly be after.'

Mal was puzzled by his response. Paluuka had used the word years. A term that Jasmine had used many times but in the first instance had had to explain to Mal, the only other people to use the term were from the Catacombs.

Jasmine took another deep breath, her heart was pounding, she knew she should speak but the words found themselves stuck in her throat. Paluuka's ageing, yet powerful presence made her fearful. Hate and anger seemed to flow from him, each of his words was like poison injected into the mind.

Paluuka spoke again. 'You come here expecting answers, I have none for you. Go back to the City, go back and live your lives there. Do not bother me with the trivial matters that bother you.'

Jasmine's heart felt like it had suddenly stopped, the life squeezed from her body. Something seemed to explode in her mind; thoughts of Mal's family, of Gryss and of all the people stuck in Tamboli rooms. She felt an unstoppable anger towards Paluuka; a man she did not even know, but knew was capable of great evil.

Now breathing heavily, the angry thoughts organised themselves into words. 'We have come here because of the fear that now grips the City, because people are losing their lives and being stuck in Tamboli rooms. The City is starting to fail, the people are starting to forget how to live properly and work together as a society. This is because of you! We have come here because you, you are stealing the life from the City, and we want you to give it back.'

Paluuka laughed a deep booming laugh that echoed around the stone hall. 'I have been stealing the life of the City? You are mistaken little girl, for one thousand five hundred and eight years I have lived underground and in that time I have devoted my life to running the City. Now I am accused killing it? Go back to the City, you have no place speaking to me, you don't even know the first thing about the City. You have lived your whole life in a city that I created and you don't even realise how important I am.'

'How can you think you are running the City if people are becoming trapped in Tamboli rooms?' Jasmine shouted in anger. 'You do nothing to help the people!'

'How dare you speak to me like that!' Paluuka trembled but even with his aged appearance, he was a dominant presence in the room. 'I created this City; you would be nothing without me. You tell me that I do nothing to help the people, when I have devoted my life to running the machines that give you water in your fountains, light over your heads and heat in the otherwise freezing cold conditions underground. You are but children, living in *my* world. You have no right to question me.'

'If that is true, why create the Tamboli rooms?'

'I must live, that is the most important thing. The only way for me to live this long is with the Tower of Light; it gives me life, but it has to take life from somewhere else in return. If a few people die to save me then it is a worthy sacrifice.' Paluuka returned to his seat. 'Get out of here; go back to your city!'

'Jasmine we should go; there is nothing we can do,' Mal whispered quietly in Jasmine's ear.

'No Mal, we came here to stop the Tamboli rooms and that is what we are going to do!' Jasmine's face seemed filled with anger and hatred. She despised Paluuka with every bone in her body. She had never felt like this before; the sickening filth of the Temple and Paluuka's poisonous words had changed her, not completely and not forever, but enough to give her the strength to confront Paluuka. 'Paluuka, we will not go from here until you have answered our questions.'

Paluuka let out a loud grunt. 'What further questions do you have? Do you still think I do nothing for the City?'

Jasmine walked closer to Paluuka and looked directly in his hazy grey eyes. 'You claim you care for the people in the City; then why not let the people run the machines, it doesn't have to be you.'

'None of you in the City has the faintest idea how to look after yourselves, let alone look after an entire city. Once, a long time ago they might have had a chance. I ruled over them and taught them what they needed to know, but then they sent me away. They didn't appreciate what I was doing for them, if only they would have done what I had told them to and accepted my rule; then everything would be different.

'Where I come from people don't like to be told how to live, they want to choose, and even if it is the wrong choice; it was their choice to make.'

Paluuka grunted again. 'Where you come from? It is my world you come from, and you should live by my rules. You would not be here if it wasn't for me, the first people here would have died long ago if I hadn't looked after them. Even now you refuse to realise that it was me who saved the people; you name your city after the madman Martin Blake.'

'I do not come from your world; I know more than you think. I am from England in the Outside World. That is a name you should remember, it was your home once.'

Paluuka seemed angrier now and stood from his chair again, leaning heavily on his staff. 'Lies, you nasty little girl, you speak nothing but lies. No one can enter from the Old World this is the only world that exists now.

'The world where you once lived still exists above our heads. The sky shines blue on hot summer days, birds sing in the trees, and the tides continue to go in and out. I'm sure things are probably different to when you were last outside but the world is still there.'

Paluuka walked towards a small door in the corner of the room, he appeared quite agitated. Could it be possible that after centuries of hatred Paluuka had remembered a little of the outside world? The details Jasmine had said triggering these memories and the normally powerful and evil face losing its potency for a moment. 'You will never understand what I have been through. I was banished from the City that I had built, and forced to live in the lower tunnels. The people there were easier to control but they too revolted against me. I had no alternative but to seek solitude here.

'I am not devoid of emotion, it pained me greatly when I was forced to leave the home I had built. I was already old when I left; I had seen many generations come and go, but then I was left to grow older on my own.

'Even in this situation, the cold darkness of this Temple, I still devote my life to the people of the cities. If only you could see that my survival is paramount to the cities survival. I would turn every room in the City into Tamboli if it meant I could survive.'

Jasmine calmed herself slightly and took a few deep breaths. 'No one should live that long, people die; that is the way of nature. You live, learn, and then pass on your knowledge to others. The people don't know anything because they have never been taught; they're not incapable they are just uneducated.'

Paluuka walked towards Jasmine, staring into her eyes. He breathed deeply and held his head as high as he could. 'I promise you, there is nothing you can do. I have calculated so much of what is to come. You can never destroy me and if you try; the people will suffer greatly.' In one quick movement, Paluuka swung out his staff in front on him. It struck Jasmine's legs and they flew out from under her, sending her crashing to the ground. 'Get out of my sight, you do not belong here.'

Mal moved to stand between Jasmine and her aggressor but Paluuka had already turned and was making for the door. He slammed it closed behind him. The sound echoed slightly around the high ceiling of the throne room.

'I'm alright Mal,' Jasmine said shakily as Mal crouched down next to his friend. 'It hurt, but I am not injured.'

Mal helped Jasmine to stand up, a large bruise was already appearing on her left leg. 'I am not sure I understand what Paluuka really is?' he said quietly.

Jasmine brushed off some of the grime that had stuck to her when she had landed on the dirty floor. 'He is a very bad man, but I wouldn't call him evil. He believes he is doing the right thing, but centuries of darkness and solitude has affected him. He doesn't really care about the City now, I think he did at one point but now he only cares about himself. As he said, he would turn the whole city to Tamboli as long as he could live. I don't think we could ever undo the years of madness to convince him of anything different.'

Mal took Jasmine's hand. 'We should go; there is no point in staying any longer if he won't speak to us.'

Jasmine was still shaking from her ordeal; the adrenaline that had been pumping around her body whilst she was speaking to Paluuka now gave her a sense of uncontrollable agitation. She was angry at how closed-minded Paluuka had been, and confused at the direction they should now take. She knew it would be impossible to reason with the Truth Slayer. He would never accept that he was causing more problems than he was solving.

The dark, putrid room around them seemed even more alien than before. The sound of water dripping from the walls and the stench of rotting algae was overpowering and confused the senses.

Jasmine started to sob, tears running down her face washing clean lines across the dirt. 'We have come so far Mal, we came and faced Paluuka, but it wasn't enough. We have failed.'

'We have done more than would be expected of us.' Mal mopped the tears from Jasmine cheeks. 'We have reached a point where we can progress no further.'

The two people stood in silence for a while; a silence broken only by dripping water and their heavy breathing.

'Does the waterfall still run with crystal water?'

Neither Mal nor Jasmine had spoken. A small quiet voice was coming from somewhere. 'It has been so long, I can't remember it.'

'Where are you?' Mal said looking around the darkness of the room. At first, he had thought he was hearing things, but soon realised Jasmine had also heard the voice.

'I remember the waterfall, it runs near the workshops where my father used to work, but that is all I can remember. Please can you describe it to me, I want to remember more,' the voice was difficult to make out and very quiet.

Jasmine drew a deep breath; she remembered the waterfall, it looked cool and inviting after the dryness of the zigzag tunnel and the Old City. 'The water falls from a hole in the ceiling. It cascades down creating a fine cooling mist. The water then bubbles over pebbles of every colour; the sound is relaxing and it is beautiful to see. The banks are filled with green; the blankets of moss grow thickly at the water's edge. The water flows gracefully over the pebbles and continues its course through a small tunnel at the end of the room.'

Mal listened intently as Jasmine spoke, she sounded poetic and the image of the water was calming and deeply rich with emotion. It was a strange request to ask someone to describe a simple waterfall, but in the cold darkness of the Temple, it was a small comfort.

The voice was silent for a moment as it began to remember more clearly the images it had once forgotten. 'When I was a boy I used to paddle along the stream to cool my feet after helping my father carry the heavy barrels in the workshops.'

'You are from the Catacombs?' Jasmine asked.

'A long time ago, a very long time ago,' the voice trailed off. A small face appeared from the shadows in the corner of the room. Its pale appearance dulled by layers of dirt.

It was a small boy, no older than ten or eleven years. He was thin and scrawny, and clothed in torn brown rags that barely covered him. His feet were bare and brown with dirt and dried blood from numerous cuts and grazes. Chains were strung between his ankles and the metal had rubbed the skin sore.

'I never thought I would see anyone again. When he took me and my brother from our home and forced us to work here; I thought I would spend my life alone.'

Jasmine's eyes again filled with tears. The boy standing before them looked so sad it was impossible to hold back emotions. Jasmine went to the boy and threw her arms around him. His tired arms held onto her tightly.

Jasmine did not know anything about this boy, but suspected he was one of the people what Paluuka had taken from the Catacombs. If that were true then this boy was older than she first thought. Tantan had said that no one had been taken from the City since his father was young. Perhaps Paluuka had also extended the life of the people who he took to work for him. It was a terrible possibility that this young boy was much older than he appeared and had been in service in this dark foreboding place for ages.

The young boy and Jasmine embraced each other for a long time, but finally relaxed.

'I heard you when you entered the gate and climbed the steps. I thought you would be seeking Paluuka, and I could see you might go the wrong way. I changed the lights so you would find the right path. I hope I did the right thing.'

Jasmine was slightly surprised by this information but in a way, it did make sense. They had had to walk through darkness but when they were directed through the opening made of marble; they came straight to Paluuka's throne room. 'Yes it was the right thing to do. Thank you.'

'I was worried I would have done the wrong thing.'

'What is your name?' Jasmine asked smiling at the boy.

The boy hung his head, looking at the floor. 'I left my name in the Catacombs when Paluuka came for me. I don't remember what it was.'

Jasmine's fears had proven right; Paluuka had taken this boy, and the shocking reality was worse than she could have imagined.

The boy and his brother had been playing along the stream near the workshops where their parents were working.

They were so busy splashing each other under the waterfall that they did not hear the people in the workshops leaving at the end of the day. Their parents had quickly looked in at them and decided to leave them to play for a little longer, and return to take them home later. They were good boys and would not have wandered off, or played with anything they should not have.

The boys' parents were devastated when they returned later to see they had disappeared, and rumours were spreading that Paluuka the Truth Slayer had been seen.

With their hands bound tightly behind their backs and gags across their mouths, Paluuka led the young boys through the long tunnel that led to his Temple.

They would never see their home or their family again, as Paluuka kept them locked in the Temple. At first, they were terribly afraid and cried for days. Paluuka gave them only small scraps to eat, just enough to keep them working.

They were locked in an empty room every time they spoke to each other, and had their food stopped if they ever did anything that Paluuka had not told them to do.

Slowly after time they grew accustomed to their life and almost forgot where they had come from. They worked hard, digging in a small mine Paluuka had built, or operating handles on large machines.

The boy, Jasmine and Mal were now looking at, had been alone for many years. His brother had become sick one day and Paluuka took him away to a small room in the Temple and was never seen again.

'I have to go soon,' the boy said scratching a scab on his arm. He felt very nervous and it had been a long time since he had spoken to anyone. 'I cannot be seen here with you, if Paluuka was to find out he would get angry.'

Jasmine felt so sorry for the boy and the life he was leading. 'Do you understand why we are here? We want to stop Paluuka from hurting people, stop everything he is doing.'

The boy shook his head. 'I don't understand, but I think you are good people.'

Mal knelt down next to the boy. 'Do you know where Paluuka had gone? Where does that door lead to?'

'The door leads to the dark stairs; that leads to a room with a single bright light. You cannot go down there because he always locks that door. If you want to follow him, you must take the ladders. If you come quickly I will show you.'

Jasmine looked at Mal, and without even speaking a word he knew that she was asking him if he wanted to continue. He thought for a moment but nodded his head in agreement.

The boy took them back down the corridor they had walked along towards the top of the stairs. One of the small entrances they had seen earlier led to a steep tunnel with wooden platforms built into the walls making ladder-like steps to help people climb down to the floor below.

The steps were slightly rotten and some were broken or missing, making it very difficult to descend the ladder. Mal had to assist Jasmine on many occasions by helping her down onto the next step. Considering the boy's small stature, he was very adept at climbing down the steps. Like a cat, he softly climbed from one rung to the next hardly pausing to look where he was going.

Paluuka had descended the dark steps to the machine room, and as the young boy had described to Mal and Jasmine; it contained a single bright light emanating from the far wall.

Along each side of the long room were pipes and cables joining large machines together at each end. To the untrained eye, it was a maze of complicated machinery with no practical purpose, but Paluuka had built each machine from scratch.

One had large dials on its front and numerous cogs whirring behind. It was a calendar clock; it counted seconds, hours, minutes, days, and even years. The dials had been counting the time since Paluuka had first moved to his Temple.

The machine on the opposite wall was more complex, it was linked via steam pipes to a larger machine protruding from the top of the Temple. It made the mist that shrouded the lake. Paluuka treasured his privacy and had made the mist to hide himself. It was also gratifying to know that he was feared because his Temple was hidden in mystery.

The machine at the end was particularly important. A light glowed brightly on top of a pillar of white crystal interspersed with diamonds. Below the crystal was a dome of gold and silver strips interwoven around thin metal tubes. This was the section of the Tower of light that had been missing from the machine in the Catacombs. Paluuka had used the immense power of this golden dome to prolong his life, to steal time from others in the underground world and direct it into his own body.

The effect of the Tower of Light had been experienced by all of the Truth Slayers, the original inhabitants of the Dayvene Laboratory, to varying degrees. They had all prospered in their extended lives but the machine, as it was, could only sustain them for so long, and slowly they died.

Their children were affected less by the machine, and it was not until Paluuka was exceptionally old he discovered a way of using the machine to concentrate its effects and use them solely for his own body.

To start with, his new machine worked well, and had enough power to keep Paluuka alive for over a thousand years, but after he had been expelled from the City and later expelled from the Catacombs, it had started to become less efficient.

The Golden Dome had been moved to its current position, and failed to give Paluuka the life he needed and so drastic measures were implemented. Adaptations to the machine made it much more powerful but at a price, it stole the time it needed from other rooms across the City.

Leading up from the Golden Dome machine was a wide gully and water came cascading down from a small lake at the top. The water was held back, partly, by stacks of stones that acted as a makeshift dam. As the water cascaded down the gully it turned a large water wheel which Paluuka had designed to generate the electricity he needed for his machines.

The giant stones hanging above the City moved to change between day and night, the fountains and the conveyance corridors all used natural energy from deep underground, but some of the Truth Slayer's machines needed energy from a difference source.

Paluuka began pulling a handle near the Golden Dome, and for a moment, the ground beneath his feet trembled slightly. A huge chunk of the sidewall began to slide out of position creating a doorway in front of downwardly spiralling steps.

Slowly the stone door inched open.

It had only been earlier that day that Paluuka has last opened this door and descended the stone steps behind it.

The steps led to a long tunnel, dripping with water that seeped through from the lake above. The tunnel had been built solely by Paluuka as an easy way of accessing the Catacombs. The causeway served as an entrance to the City and this tunnel was an entrance to the City below.

Paluuka had hobbled along the passageway, his staff thudding the rocky floor as he went, and his gargled breathing echoing along the corridor's length.

Paluuka had sensed something had happened to his machine. The small stones he carried, the Stones of the See-Smiths, were linked to everything in the City and someone of Paluuka's intellect could use them to find out what was happening there.

At the end of the tunnel was another large stone door, again with a lever to open it mechanically. Stone doors like those at either end of this tunnel could only be opened by machine; they were too heavy for any man to open with strength alone

The door opened into a small courtyard surrounded by white columns and blue discs sunk into the wall.

In the distance, the sound of bare feet upon the ground could be heard as the people of the Catacombs scurried away. They had been alerted to Paluuka's presence as the ground trembled whenever the stone door was opened.

Paluuka knew the people would run away, and it made no difference, as he was not there to find more people to work for him, only to find out what the people had done to his machine.

An archway and narrow passage led directly to the maze where Jasmine and Mal had been led earlier by Tantan.

It had taken Paluuka a long time to walk along the long tunnel from his Temple, and in that time Jasmine and Mal had departed the room of Shadows and were at that time, climbing the first few steps to the lookout.

Tantan was in mid conversation with Zieen as Paluuka entered the Room and Shadows and looked at his machine that was once bright with light.

As Paluuka opened the stone door again, he recalled Tantan and Zieen's expressions as they saw him entering the Room of Shadows; they had been so deep within the Catacombs that they had not heard the aged man approaching.

Paluuka would again return to the Catacombs and find the See-Smith known as Zieen. It must have been he who gave these people the knowledge to cross the causeway and enter the Temple. This time he would be even less forgiving.

Through years of calculation Paluuka knew this day would come, the people of the Catacombs would betray him, and allow strangers to question him in his own temple. Although he foretold the events, he would still punish the people for their betrayal.

Jasmine and Mal stopped at the edge of a large pool of water. The pool was filled by a stream, which poured from a dark channel on the left. On the right were piles of rocks and stones, held in place by wooden beams and ropes that formed a primitive dam. There were gaps between the piles of stones, allowing some of the water to flow out of the pool.

The young boy waded into the water and stood near the first pile of stones. The water was up to his waist and the pile of stones way above his head. He motioned for Mal and Jasmine to join him.

Mal was next into the water; it came just above his knees and was ice cold. As he waded over to the small boy he could see a bright light beyond. Jasmine soon arrived with them as they peered between the piles of the rocks. The water cascaded down a slope and disappeared under the floor of the room below.

They all instantly recognised the man who was standing in the room at the bottom, struggling with a wooden handle; it was Paluuka.

Jasmine glanced around the rest of the room and saw the bright lighting shining from the machine with the golden dome. 'I think that must be the other part of the Tower of Light,' she said quietly.

Mal looked towards the machine and wondered how they could get down to it without Paluuka seeing.

The boy nudged Jasmine gently in the ribs. 'Paluuka is trying to leave here, can you stop him? Or can you kill him?'

Although they had planned to stop Paluuka from harming the people of the City, they had not considered the possibility they would have to prevent him from running away or actually kill him.

Mal was particularly shocked. 'No, we can do nothing to harm him, if he truly is running the City then we must let him live.'

Jasmine totally disagreed. 'He is only needed to run the City because he forbids anyone from knowing how to run it themselves. I agree we cannot kill him, but we must do something.'

'What do you suggest?' Mal asked back scornfully.

'We must stop him from leaving here, and then we must stop him from creating Tamboli rooms. I do not know how to do that, yet, but we must find a way.'

'That door is opening quickly; it won't be long before he runs away. If you really think you can do something then you had better do it quickly, but you must think of the consequences; we may no longer have light in the City, or food, or water.'

'No Mal you are wrong,' Jasmine shouted back as loud as she could without the risk of being heard in the room below. The sound of the cascading water helped cover the sounds of their voices well, but they still had to be careful. 'The City will still run without him. I have an idea, no time to explain.'

Jasmine hurtled herself towards one of the wooden poles that helped to slow the water at the edge of the waterfall. With an almighty crash it moved, and acted as a lever; pushing over one of the piles of stones.

Paluuka heard the falling stones and stared up at Jasmine, now in full view. The water gushed like a torrent down the slope. The waterwheel, already damaged by the falling stones, began to spin at great speed then broke in two and was washed away with the water.

'Jasmine, this is not the way!' Mal screamed. 'Come back here.'

'No Mal, the water will not kill him.' Jasmine was still holding the wooden pole and it bobbed about at the edge of the waterfall. 'You can see; it has flooded the bottom of the room but nothing more.'

'You will stop whatever it is you think you are doing you stupid girl,' Paluuka boomed from below. 'What do you think you will achieve?'

'I will not stop until you stop making Tamboli rooms.'

Paluuka laughed and pulled on a rope hanging in the corner of the room. A series of pulleys were strung around the room leading to the dam that Jasmine was stood on. As the rope became tight, it lifted a wooden pole that was slightly submerged. Normally it would allow a little more water to flow down and turn the waterwheel, but this time it had a different effect. Jasmine was standing on the edge of a waterfall, with both feet on a now raising wooden pole. She lost her balance and tumbled over the edge.

Mal could see little from where he was and quickly moved across to the large opening Jasmine had created in the dam.

The water was flowing fast and creating spray that made seeing difficult, but Mal managed to look through the water and check he was not standing on any other pieces of wood that Paluuka could move.

Shaking with nerves, Mal looked over the edge, expecting to see Jasmine lying on the floor at the bottom of the waterfall, but she was not there. Paluuka was still standing in the room below, his feet soaked as the water overflowed from its channel onto the stone floor. The stone door had begun to close automatically. Paluuka would have to wait until it was fully closed before he could open it again.

'Mal!' To the side of the waterfall Jasmine clung frantically to an end of rope that was attached to the base of the dam. Mal was overwhelmed with relief to see his friend was still alive but panicking with what he could do to save her.

'Jasmine, try and climb up the rope. Use your hands and your feet. When you get higher I can pull you up.'

The door below had closed and Paluuka had pulled the wooden handle viciously to open it again. Even with his ageing strength, he managed to snap the wooden lever. Surprised, he held the wooden handle in his hands for a moment and then threw it with all his strength at the waterfall.

It hit Jasmine on the leg; the shock made her lose her grip for a moment and she slid further down the rope.

Mal was panicking more and looking around for some way to help. The young boy was standing near the water's edge as well and picked up a twig. Attached to it was a rope than ran away from the waterfall to a pulley at the far edge of the pool. It then ran back to the base of the dam.

'Here,' the boy shouted. 'If you can free this rope you can pull her up.'

Mal fumbled under the water. The rope was strung beneath the level of the water and had been looped around an angular rock holding it fast. To free the rope Mal had to duck his head under the water to see clearly how the rope was being held.

The water was deep at the centre of the pool and Mal found it difficult to stand upright as the water flowed but he knew he must do something to save his friend. He took a deep breath and went beneath the water.

The rope beyond the rock was obviously tight as Jasmine was holding the other end; it was difficult to free the loops that went round the angular rock. Frantically Mal pulled at the loops. One came free easily, the other was more difficult. It was tight and refusing to move. Mal had to put all his strength into pulling on the loop before it eventually came free.

The weight of Jasmine hanging on the other end pulled Mal forward and it took a little while for him to wedge his feet against the ground and stop himself from being pulled through the water.

Jasmine was sliding further down the waterfall, frantically kicking with her legs, trying to find a ledge that would support her weight.

Paluuka was again trying to open the stone door, struggling with the remains of the handle; the water that was now flooding the floor had flowed into the machinery and prevented it from working properly.

Mal was struggling to pull Jasmine up the waterfall; he could hold her weight but could not manoeuvre enough to pull on the rope.

'Mal!' Jasmine screamed frantically. 'I'm slipping.'

'Just keep holding on, don't let go and I will pull you up.'

'Hurry, I don't know if I can keep hold.' The water had made Jasmine's hands exceptionally cold and they were tired, making it difficult to keep a tight grip on the rope.

The young boy had been standing motionless; he was rigid with fear and unsure if he could do anything to help. The spray from the now huge waterfall made it difficult to see what was happening.

Desperate to save the life of his friend Mal tried to reposition his feet on the rocks in the pool. His arms were tired; it was now or never, he had to pull Jasmine up to safety.

Suddenly, without any warning, Mal flew backwards through the water, the rope snatched away from his hands. Terrifying thoughts ran through his mind; Jasmine must have fallen, or the rope had snapped. Something had made him move and lose his grip on the rope.

Mal looked around frantically, his heart pounding in his chest, and then the shocking reality of what had happened became clear.

Jasmine appeared at the top of the waterfall, clinging desperately onto a small rocky ledge. In less than a second Mal had waded over to her and pulled her up into the pool, she was safe, but lying motionless at the bottom of the room was a small figure.

The young boy that had helped them find Paluuka again, had realised how he could help even more and had given his own life in the process.

He had seen that Mal could not pull Jasmine up the waterfall and had watched the stick tied to the end of Mal's rope bob around in the water. Taking a deep breath, he had grabbed the stick and thrown himself over the edge of the waterfall as fast as he could. He was only small and light but the speed in which he dived over the edge had created enough force on the rope through a pulley to haul Jasmine up.

She had only risen a little way before the young boy had hit the rocks down the waterfall and his hands lost all grip on the rope, but it was enough for Jasmine to grab hold of a rocky outcrop and pull herself up.

Jasmine and Mal were shaking from head to toe; exhausted and deeply saddened by the sight of the small boy lying at the bottom of the waterfall.

There was no time to wait around, the cascading water had dislodged more rocks from the edge of the pool and they went tumbling over the edge. As each rock fell, the amount of water running down the edge increased, and each increase meant more force against the remaining parts of the dam. The sides of the cavern had already started to come crashing down.

In a huge shower of sparks the machine with the golden dome, the remainder of the Tower of Light exploded as it was hit by a powerful surge of water and falling rocks. The evil machine that had been stealing the time out of rooms in the City was shattered into a thousand pieces and swept away in the torrent of water.

Jasmine barely registered the explosion as she was looking for a way to get down to the boy, but it was useless; the rocks and huge gush of water made it impossible to even remain at the edge of the pool.

Mal grabbed Jasmine's arm and pulled her back towards the small tunnel they had entered through.

'No Mal, we have to help him,' Jasmine screamed and tried to pull away, but Mal was strong and held her arm firmly in his hands.

'It's too late, you can't help him,' Mal shouted in reply as he wrestled to keep hold of his friend's arm.

Reluctantly, Jasmine allowed herself to be pulled away from the water's edge and into the tunnel. Her last sight of the pool was one she would never forget for the rest of her life; the ceiling collapsed and another watercourse that ran above the chamber began to cascade down. A torrent of water and huge chunks of rock began to fall. The room filled rapidly, and it was not until Mal and Jasmine climbed to the top of the wooden ladders that they were finally safe.

The two people collapsed onto the hard stone floor. Tears were rolling down Jasmine's cheeks. 'He saved me, and we couldn't go back for him.'

Mal was also crying and looked desperately at Jasmine. 'There was nothing we could have done; we should not have come here in the first place.'

'But we have done what we came to do,' Jasmine said wearily. 'Did you see the explosion; we have stopped Paluuka and his machine.'

Shockingly, Mal shouted at Jasmine. He was so angry at everything that had happened. Angry that he was unable to pull Jasmine up when she was dangling so dangerously down the waterfall, and angry that they had caused the death of Paluuka and the small, frightened boy. 'We should never have come here; we should not have killed Paluuka.'

'What else could we have done?' Jasmine shouted back. 'We had to stop Paluuka!'

Floods of tears were rolling down their cheeks, they had never been so angry with each other, and in truth there was no reason to be, but Paluuka's Temple was a dark and hateful place. It had affected them, they had turned slightly towards the evil nature of Paluuka, and they knew it.

There was no point in continuing their argument; they knew it would not do any good; the events could not be undone.

Gradually they began to calm themselves slightly and slowly began to make their way out of the cold, dark and unpleasant temple.

CHAPTER 12

Time to Learn

Jasmine and Mal did not exchange a single word as they trudged, wet footed, back across the causeway. They both had sorrow and anger in their hearts, and it would be a long time before they could speak to each other as friends again.

Grancathai had said that going to Paluuka's Temple would be the hardest thing they would ever do in their lives, and he was right. However, to Jasmine it had not been the events inside the temple that had made the journey so difficult, and emotionally painful. Even the death of the small boy, however terrible, did not compare to her interaction with Mal, her best friend in the underground city. She had argued and shouted at him, and in the end had torn holes in their friendship. Jasmine hoped that the holes would repair, but she knew it would take a very long time. A painful reminder of what had happened in the dark and grimy temple of Paluuka.

In the end, Mal knew the right thing had been done, and would forgive Jasmine in time, but for now, he walked with her in silence unable to even exchange the simplest of words.

Slowly and carefully, the two people made their way back across the walkway, the lights of the City getting closer with every step.

As they approached the little wooden jetty, they were greeted by the beaming smiles of Kohrstan and Grancathai who were stood up on the ledge, and for a moment, their spirits lifted. The sight of their friends had made them briefly happy but then both Mal and Jasmine realised, almost simultaneously, that something might have happened to the City. Paluuka had warned them about meddling with his machines. The last part of the Tower of Light had been destroyed, but there were many more devices that could have been damaged by the massive cascade of water.

'We are glad you have returned Jasmine and Malmayorkia.' Grancathai spoke with his normal slow voice but something seemed to be troubling him and neither Jasmine nor Mal could work out what it was.

Kohrstan also seemed a little quiet as he held out the lowering stick to help pull his friends up from the Jetty.

Mal grabbed the lowering stick that Kohrstan passed down to him. Clipping it securely on the iron rung at the bottom of the wall, he ushered Jasmine onto the small metal plate. Jasmine tugged on the metal bar and the metal plate began to rise. Soon she was eye level with Grancathai and Kohrstan.

Jasmine unhooked the lowering stick from the iron rung and passed it back to Mal. It seemed to take less than five seconds for Mal to pull the metal plate back down to the ground and then use the stick again to bring him up to his awaiting friends.

'There are many things you need to know Malmayorkia.' Grancathai looked worried as he spoke. Mal had expected him to ask what they had seen and done in Paluuka's Temple, but it appeared there had been more taking place here in the City. 'You both must come with us to the Givings, but first we should stop by the meeting hall.'

Mal's heart jumped in his chest and he froze in mid step. 'So you mean the Tamboli Rooms are no more, my family is safe?'

Grancathai shook his head then stopped and just looked at Mal puzzled. 'Not exactly, it is difficult to explain. You are right that the Tamboli rooms no longer exist; now they are safe for everyone. But...'

Mal signed. 'But what about my parents, my sister and everyone that was in them?'

Kohrstan placed a hand on his friend's shoulder. 'They are all gone Mal. We do not know where, they just disappeared. I went to the Meeting Hall and looked into the entrance, as it looked as it always had, chairs and tables unmoved, but the people were not there.'

As Kohrstan finished speaking, Grancathai began. 'It is because of you that this has happened; you have made the rooms safe. The people who were in the rooms are resting now; you freed them from a life without time and allowed them to be at peace.'

Jasmine did not know what to feel any more, she was extremely exhausted and hungry, with cuts and bruisers all over her body. Mal was not much better off, he too was exhausted beyond belief, and his arms and legs were aching with every movement. It had been six days since Mal and Jasmine had first descended into the Catacombs on the start of their perilous journey to the bottom of the underground realm and then to the top of the Outer City and the Lookout before finally heading out to Paluuka's Temple on the far side of the lake.

As Grancathai's words began to sink in, Jasmine burst into tears. 'It's over, it's finally over, we can rest now Mal.'

Kohrstan looked oddly at Jasmine and then at Mal, something was up and Mal knew it. 'Kohrstan what are you not telling us?'

'Tell them Kohrstan, tell them about the Lessers,' Grancathai said with a sigh.

Kohrstan took a couple of deep breaths. 'We didn't know who they were at first; they came early, as soon as the stones had risen.'

'The Lessers are in the City?' Mal asked in a state of shock.

'Yes they are all up in the Givings. No one knows why they are here and everyone is scared.'

The group walked back along the lower gallery to the Conveyance corridor. Mal and Jasmine were happy to be home again although worried about what had been happening while they had been away. The clean, sweet smelling air was pleasant to breath, the well-lit tunnels and beautiful carved stones were a stark contrast to the dark, rancid Temple of Paluuka.

Grancathai led the way through the conveyance corridor and opened the door into the Givings. The warmth and the glorious green panorama of the Givings made Mal and Jasmine's hearts jump; they had not been here since the day they went into the Catacombs.

The view was somewhat different to what they were used to. Sitting on the grass and rocks, and under the trees were dozens of people, perhaps even hundreds. Mal and Jasmine recognised their clothes. They were all from the Catacombs, their long white robes shining brightly in the light from above.

Standing motionless around the Givings were the Tenders, nervously watching the people of the Catacombs in case they tried to do anything to damage the plants. The Tenders were totally dedicated to caring for the Givings, although none of them knew that one-day they would have to stand guard over it.

'When these people arrived they came straight here,' Grancathai announced turning to face his companions. 'One man was asking for you Jasmine, we could only believe he was one of the people you met when you had gone to the Catacombs.'

Jasmine felt a sudden excitement. 'Was his name Tantan?'

'He did not give us his name, just said he would wait with the others until you returned. Why are these people here Jasmine?'

Jasmine's excitement turned to apprehension; Tantan had once said that telling them about the handle to make the room of Shadows safe was punishable by death. She hoped that his fears were unfounded. 'I don't know why they are here; if I can speak to them I may be able to find out.'

A man sitting by a Night Stems tree stood and made his way over to the small group, still standing in the doorway of the conveyance corridor.

It was not Tantan, it was Zieen he looked older than before, tired and exhausted. He had spent a long time helping all of the people out of the Catacombs. It had been a difficult task, but as See-Smith, he was responsible for helping the people. There were children and old people who needed extra assistance in the long climb up the metal rungs to the opening just outside the library. Before they had left their homes they had discussed what route they should take to the City; the stairs to the lookout and the Outer City were very long and would have taken a very long time to climb. Climbing the metal rungs was very difficult too but was the easier option overall.

'Jasmine I am pleased you have got back safely.' The See-Smith bowed low as he approached, a custom normally reserved for See-Smiths and Halliers. Jasmine felt honoured for the gesture but was unsure if she deserved it. Once risen from his bow, he spoke in a calm, gentle voice. 'I understand you have been to Paluuka's Temple.'

Jasmine nodded. 'Yes, but it is difficult to talk about, I'm not sure we are ready to discuss the details. Paluuka and his machines won't hurt us again. Is Tantan here as well?'

'You do not need to give us any details just yet; we know much of what you have done.

'I have brought everyone from the Catacombs, but Tantan wasn't among them.' Zieen looked sad as he spoke. 'I am afraid that you did not kill Paluuka, he escaped the rock fall and went into the Catacombs. It was there that he met Tantan and I. He was angrier than you could ever imagine. He shouted and screamed at us for helping you. He hated us more than ever and went mad, throwing his cane around in a rage. Tantan tried to calm him and explain but Paluuka did not want to listen; unfortunately Tantan felt the true force of Paluuka's anger and is no longer with us.'

Mal and Jasmine were saddened by this information; they had been helped so much by Tantan. They had not known it at the time, but he had pointed them in the right direction; shown them the right way. They would not have done all the tasks they had if Tantan had not helped them. If Tantan had not moved the handle in the Room of Shadows, Jasmine would now be stuck in the dead room with no chance of release.

'He was a good man,' Mal added. 'I am sorry that we have caused so much trouble. This is all our fault. What will you do now?'

Zieen turned to Grancathai who was looking around at the people sat in the Givings. 'There are many of us, but there is space for us in the City. We have the skills to operate the machines in the City, we know how to find them and know how to keep them going. We are asking much of the people of the City but offer a lot in return. We cannot go home; Paluuka will not let us back into the Catacombs. He has other machines that he could use against us; powerful and dangerous machines, and he has an intelligence that we can't truly understand.'

'But we destroyed the machine that gave him life, the Tower of Light,' Jasmine interjected. 'How long will he live for?'

'That I don't know, but probably long enough to cause us great problems. There is something, however, we must do,' Zieen continued. 'Before your return, we spoke at length about Paluuka and the problems we now face. While the entrance to the Catacombs is open, we are in danger. We must seal the entrance near the Library and the stairs from the lookout. The rock fall you created has already sealed the tunnel from Paluuka's Temple into the lower tunnels.

'Paluuka, although powerful, is very old; he would not be able to find his way into the City if we seal the entrances.'

Mal was unsure of this plan. 'What would stop him from building another Tower of Light and creating Tamboli rooms again?'

'We have done some research and we believe the part of the Tower of Light that Paluuka had in his Temple was called the Golden Dome, and it was filled with diamonds. There are none to be found in the Catacombs, he cannot build another machine like that. As for other machines he could build, hopefully he will not live long enough to see them completed.'

Grancathai stepped forward. 'We must call a gathering in the meeting hall; the people of the Catacombs and the people of the City must unite and work together if we have any chance of stopping Paluuka. It won't be an easy task as there is distrust on both sides, but we must learn to trust each other.'

'Paluuka knew one day something like this would happen. He had hundreds of years to plan what he could do to stop anyone who tried to break his hold over the City. But there was one thing he failed to take into account.' Zieen turned to Jasmine. 'And that is you, Jasmine.'

'Me?' Jasmine was startled. 'Why do I make a difference?'

'Paluuka never thought someone from the Old World would ever be able to get into the City. You have the ability to unite the two peoples on this realm. If we weren't able to unite; we would not be able to beat Paluuka. The people of the Catacombs would never have escaped into the City if they thought they would not be able to join forces with the Tops. We would have stayed and continued to be his slaves, build his machines and we could have dug through any blockades that you made.

'Jasmine, I mean no disrespect to you, but you are an outsider. You are neither from the City or the Catacombs, you will be the one to mediate between our two peoples, tell the peoples they have nothing to fear from each other. You are the one thing Paluuka could never have foreseen.'

Jasmine did not know what to feel. She had set out to free the people from the Tamboli rooms. They had been freed, at least to the extent that they are now at rest and not stuck in a life of nothing. Now Jasmine was being told she could help unite the two peoples of the underground realm and it was a bit overwhelming. She remembered back to the evening she had sat on the beach and was thinking about what she would do with her life. Everything seemed complicated at the time but nothing to the life she was now leading.

When Jasmine first arrived in the City she was desperate to find a way home, but Mal had shown her such kindness that she had come to think of the City as her home. It now seemed she had more to do within the City, and however difficult it would be, she would face the tasks and do as much as she could. Now she had little interest in returning to the outside world. Her life had led her here, and here she would stay.

'I don't know what I can do, but I will try,' Jasmine said after thinking for a while. 'If you really think I am able to help.'

'Jasmine I know you have done so much for us already, but we must ask this of you. We are sure you will be able to help, you are strong and have a good heart.' Grancathai placed a hand on her shoulder. 'You have the ability, but we will always be with you to help.'

Mal again took Jasmine's hand in his own. 'Jazz are you sure this is what you want to do?'

Jasmine turned to her friend and looked him in the eyes. His kind face was filled with trust and understanding; he knew Jasmine well and would do anything for her. On the long walk back from Paluuka's Temple Jasmine thought it would take her and Mal a long time to be able to forgive each other and be able to continue their friendship. As it turned out they did not need time or effort to forgive each other; it came all by itself and they both knew it.

'I am sure Mal, whatever it takes. I am just glad I have you as a friend, you give me the strength I need.'

Grancathai did not want to interrupt this important moment for the two friends but there was an urgent matter pressing. 'We have very little time; we should go back to the library and talk for a while. We have plans to make.'

The group walked towards the conveyance corridor, Jasmine opened the door and walked through closely followed by Mal, with Grancathai, Kohrstan and Zieen closely behind.

Jasmine thought of the library as she walked along the corridor, knowing that it was there that the idea of stopping the Tamboli rooms had started. It was there she had first met Grancathai and learnt about the history of the City. It seemed right that they would now plan the city's future there.

At the end of the conveyance corridor Jasmine opened the door into the room with the tunnel that led to the Catacombs entrance and the library. Hearing the door closed behind her, Jasmine turned to check that everyone had come through, and saw Mal beaming with a huge smile.

'What are you smiling at?' Jasmine said jokingly.

Mal laughed. 'You, I am smiling at you. Think about how we got here.'

Jasmine did not know what Mal meant at first, but then suddenly realised that she had been first in the corridor; it had been her who had thought about the library and had directed the conveyance corridor there.

'Me? I used the conveyance corridor?' Jasmine smiled back at Mal. 'I didn't think I could, surely it was you who actually got us here?'

'No Jazz, it couldn't have been me. You were first through the corridor; it only works with the first person. You did it, you really did it!'

Jasmine was overjoyed by the news. She had learnt, finally, how to use the conveyance corridors. If she wanted, she could now travel to wherever she wanted in the City. This was the final boost in confidence that Jasmine needed; she now knew she would be able to unite the people of the City. In an otherwise nerve-racking situation, Jasmine felt happy as they continued towards the library.

Five men guarded the vertical tunnel with iron rungs that was the entrance to the Catacombs. They were dressed in the white robes that everyone from the Catacombs wore and bowed low as they saw Zieen the See-Smith walking past.

Sat around the large polished table on the bottom floor of the library; the group shared a jug of water, drunk from a set of fine crystal glasses Grancathai had kept securely in a chest in his home room. They were beautiful and delicate and he had never expected to have an event important enough in order to warrant using them.

The light from the luminescent stones in the ceiling made the glasses sparkle with every colour of the rainbow. Zieen thought it was a good symbol of differences combining, every colour combining in one drinking glass.

Jasmine and Mal felt a little awkward sitting in the grand splendour of the library still wearing the dirty and torn clothing they had worn to Paluuka's Temple. They both wished they had had time to change their clothes and bathe in the Pale Waters.

Zieen waited until everyone had finished drinking before he stood up to speak. 'I think we have already agreed that we must block the entrances to the City.'

The group of people sat around the table nodded in agreement.

'Then we must discuss how we are to do this. There are many of my people who are strong and can move stone and construct walls, but I fear it would not be enough manpower.'

Grancathai also stood. 'There are many more people here in the City, a few of them also possess the skills of building walls but it will be difficult to get them to do so.'

Zieen had returned to his seat as Grancathai spoke but stood to speak again. Jasmine had not seen this type of custom before in the City or the Catacombs, but it seemed appropriate as it gave each person the respect they deserved when they spoke, regardless of who they were.

'When we gather the people together in the meeting hall we must be prepared in what we are going to say to them,' Zieen said after the long silence. 'They will be confused and possibly even frightened.'

Grancathai knew a possible answer to this, but it would not be easy to do. 'We need to become the Circle, only then will we be able to properly speak to the people and get their co-operation in the difficult task.'

Zieen knew what the Circle was, Mal and Kohrstan had heard the term before but did not know what it meant, but Jasmine knew nothing about it.'

Zieen saw the blank look on Jasmine's face. 'Perhaps, Grancathai, you could explain to us all about the Circle. I'm sure it has been a long time since the Circle has sat.'

Grancathai nodded. 'The Circle is, or rather was, a group of people who were responsible for the organising of the people.'

'They were leaders?' Mal interjected.

'No, normally the power and leadership lied within the Council of Guardians and the Principal Guardians; like Chanchey who you said was Anarlia's father. The Circle was responsible for overseeing the election of the Council members, organising meetings and doing small tasks to assist the Council. Although they didn't really have much power over the City, they could elect the Council Guardians as long as the people of the City agree that they should, and if necessary, make some decisions during times that the Council was disbanded or awaiting election.'

'So the Circle only acted for the Council if the people believed that they should,' Zieen added. 'If we can get the people to recognise the Circle again we might be able to convince the people that what we are doing is the right thing. They might just follow the lead of the Circle.'

'The Circle was made up of five members, and there are five of us here,' Grancathai mentioned, again standing up. 'Already we are using the roles of the Circle; we are acting in absence of the Council Guardians.'

'I mean no disrespect to you Zieen, but I must say that the people may not respect the Circle, if there is someone from the Catacombs in it,' Mal said with a hesitation in his voice.

'You do not need to be so nervous when you speak Malmayorkia, you are correct. This is what we feared earlier, and it is for that reason that we must ask Jasmine to speak to both peoples, the Lessers and the Tops, and show them that unity is the way forward,' Zieen said eloquently, he had not been offended at all by Mal's statement and smiled at him to show this. Mal had in fact said what everyone else had been thinking.

Jasmine stood up slowly from her chair, which prompted Zieen to return, respectfully, to his. 'If we can show the people that the Circle can be made from Lessers and Tops, then the people may see that as a sign that they can be united too. I am worried that I will be unable to help, but I will do what I can.'

'Then we are agreed,' Zieen said standing again after Jasmine had finished speaking. 'We will call a gathering of the two peoples in the Meeting Hall and present ourselves as the Circle. Jasmine will speak to them and show them how we can all work together, and then we will explain to them how we are going to stop Paluuka from again entering the City. The dangerous threat we all face will certainly be a strong motivational force behind our decision to reform the Circle.'

'We can also tell them that once we have all worked together to protect the City, the Circle will elect a new Council of Guardians,' Grancathai added.

'Are we agreed?' Zieen asked without standing.

Everyone looked at each other for a moment, slowly glancing from one person to another trying to check what they were thinking. They all knew reforming the Circle was the best course of action. It would be difficult but they had to do something to be able to save the City from the imminent threat of Paluuka.

Slowly they all began to nod their heads at each other and turn their attention back to Zieen and Grancathai.

'We must get to work.' Zieen stood again and smiled. 'We must arrange the meeting as soon as we can; there is a lot to be done to stop Paluuka. Jasmine and Kohrstan, you will go with me to the Meeting Hall and prepare it to receive the people. Grancathai, if you and Mal can tell the people about the meeting, make sure they understand where they have to go; they will be confused.'

Grancathai nodded. 'We will ring the Meeting Bell and then go to the Great Corridor and speak to as many people as we can. News will soon travel to everyone, and hopefully the people will understand and go to the Meeting Hall. Perhaps you should speak to the Lessers; it would be easier for a See-Smith to tell them what to do.'

Zieen nodded. 'I will ensure they are ready.'

The five people of the Circle stood from their chairs and made their way out of the library.

Jasmine had a strange feeling in her stomach, like butterflies before a school exam, but much worse. She felt a little sick and very uneasy as she tried to decide what she would say to the people. How do you unite two groups of people who have lived in distrust and misunderstanding of each other for such a long time? Nothing in her life had prepared her for this, she was treading new ground and about to do something she had never done before, but this was so important; she had to do it and the future of the City rested squarely on her shoulders.

'I can take Malmayorkia to the bell; it is not far from a conveyance corridor, but I imagine it would be difficult to find unless you knew exactly where it was,' Grancathai said as they walked towards the conveyance corridor door. If they were to complete their plan then everything must be done as quickly as possible.

The conveyance corridor at the end of the small tunnel led to the Great Corridor. Mal had never heard of the bell room before, and he thought he had been to most places in the City. Surely, the bell could not be along the Great Corridor, but if it were not there, why would Grancathai have brought them here? Grancathai's actions confused Mal a little, but he trusted the aging librarian and followed him regardless.

Opposite the fountain, where Mal had been sitting when Jasmine had first spoken to him, was a plain door. Mal knew where it led; it went to a small complex of home rooms where about ten people lived.

'Grancathai?' Mal said as they walked to the end of a small corridor with openings on either side. 'I have been here before but have never seen the bell you described earlier.'

Grancathai chuckled to himself as he stopped at the corridor's end and turned to face Mal. 'Mal we are very near the bell, it's just below our feet.'

Mal looked down; the floor was made from large slabs of stone that neatly fitted together without mortar in-between. At first, the floor seemed like an ordinary floor but slowly an edge came into view. All of the stone slabs were different sizes and laid in a random order across the width of the tunnel, but at one point, they all lined up forming a straight edge. Next to the edge was a small metal ring embedded into the stone. It was covered with dust and difficult to see at first.

'Is it a trap door?' Mal asked after peering at the ground.

Again, Grancathai chuckled to himself but said nothing in reply. He leant down and pulled on the metal ring; with no effort at all, the trap door lifted open. It must have been counter-balanced or attached to pulleys or something to enable it to be raised so easily. The trap door was made from thick stones fastened together in a metal frame. The workmanship was so perfect that it was hidden in the ground to everyone unless you knew where to look. Many people had walked across it over the years, but none had looked down for more than a fraction of a second, and had seen nothing but solid floor.

Below the trapdoor was a wooden ladder that led to a strange triangular room. Grancathai and Mal were standing at the widest edge and the walls on either side tapered towards a point at the end where a single bell was hanging.

Jasmine had watched Mal and Grancathai as they left through the library door, knowing she would have to leave soon and go to the Meeting Hall. Kohrstan would be travelling with her, but she really wanted to try to use the conveyance corridor again; just to check it was not just luck last time, but actual skill.

'Do you want to go in first Jasmine?' Kohrstan asked cheerily.

'Yes please, I want to make sure I can properly use the corridors,' Jasmine said smiling and walking past Kohrstan into the brightly lit corridor.

Opening the door at the other end, Jasmine was excited to find that they were in the room near the balcony above the meeting room. It had been a long time since Mal had brought her here to explain what the Tamboli rooms were, but she remembered what it looked like and used the conveyance corridor to get them there.

'Well done Jasmine, you're an expert!' Kohrstan said with a big smile. 'It's easy once you have got the hang of it.'

Jasmine and Kohrstan descended the steps into the huge room below and looked around at the tables and chairs.

Grancathai had explained that the Circle should have a group of chairs one end facing outwards in a semicircle. When Grancathai was explaining what they needed to do, Jasmine had commented on the Circle only having half a circle of chairs. It seemed that Jasmine's humour was not always understood in the City of Martiblak.

As Jasmine and Kohrstan began to arrange the chairs and dust off the tables around the room, Zieen and a handful of people from the Catacombs arrived to help. Jasmine and Kohrstan were grateful for their assistance, it was a very big room with countless tables and chairs that had to be cleaned and organised into position.

The giant metal bell was hanging from strong ropes fixed to metal rings on the ceiling. The walls continued tapering behind it, and finally met at a sharp point. Along each wall were dark holes of all different shapes and sizes. Some were no bigger than Mal's fist; others were large enough for a person to crawl along easily. They probably ran to different parts of the City to allow the sound to travel a long way.

There was a wooden rack built into the right hand wall, numerous mallets and hammers were hanging there in rows. There were ten altogether; five metal hammers and five wooden mallets. They were hanging in size order.

Mal took the largest mallet off the rack, lifted it above his head and hurtled the end towards the bell. He was strong and the mallet hit with huge force.

A booming ringing sound erupted, causing the thick layer of dust to be thrown from the bell's surface and fill the room. Mal coughed and pulled his shirt up over his mouth and nose.

The sound of the bell echoed around the chamber as it reverberated to a high shrill. It was exceptionally loud. Mal and Grancathai were forced to cover their ears to dampen the otherwise deafening sound.

Throughout the City, the bell echoed, through every corridor and every room, from the Library on the level of the lake to the Givings over the top.

People stopped what they were doing and listened intently to the sound. Many people had been told about the bell, but very few people had actually ever heard it before. The people the same age as Grancathai, or older had heard the bell once or twice when they were young, but it was difficult to remember exactly what it had sounded like. The only bell they were used to hearing was the high pitched ringing that alerted them to the time the stones were rising. This bell was completely different, a deep booming sound.

Everyone stood silent, unsure what the ringing of the bell could mean for the City. Some people understood that the bell meant a gathering of the people, but the reason why a gathering was being called eluded everyone except for the small group of people that had met in the Library.

There were others in the population that knew nothing about the bell or what it stood for. They were more confused than the rest. The sound of the bell slowly dissipated and was lost into silence. The people were still motionless in wonder. Cautiously they turned to one another, and met blank looks and confused expressions. Slowly they began to speak to each other to try to understand why the bell had rung.

Mal placed the mallet back in its holder on the wall. He was sure it would be needed again and wanted to ensure it was kept in a safe place.

The dust that had erupted from the bell, when Mal had struck it, was still hanging thickly in the air. Slowly it began to settle on the two men's clothing and hair; turning them an odd shade of grey.

Looking back at the bell, Mal saw that it was now completely dust-less. The huge vibrations had shaken off the dust and sent it flying across the room. The metal now shone brightly with gold and silver and was a beautiful sight.

The bell was now silent but there was a gentle creaking as the bell rocked gently on the rope it was suspended by.

'Now Malmayorkia we must go back to the Great Corridor.' Grancathai moved towards the wooden steps. 'There are many people that will be confused, although I imagine some of them will understand the bell; others will know nothing about the meeting room, and that they should go there.'

Mal nodded and followed Grancathai up the steps. The stone trap door at the top closed as easily as it had been opened. A gentle push was all that was needed to send it silently back into position, and again it became almost invisible.

In the Great Corridor there were numerous people walking in both directions, and even a few people standing in small groups and talking. Normally at this time of the day, the corridor would be filled only with the Tenders as they made their way home from the Givings. Conveyance corridors would bring them in at different parts of the Great Corridor and they would have to walk to the doors that went to their home rooms. Today it was different; the Tenders were still at the Givings guarding the

Lessers from the Catacombs, whom had started to leave in small groups. The Tenders all knew the significance of the bell but would wait until every Lesser had gone before leaving and following them to the Meeting Hall. Zieen was stood by the conveyance corridors explaining to the people where to go. The Lessers seemed to have a greater ability of travelling through conveyance corridors on a simple explanation of where they were going. The people of the City could normally only go to places they had been to before.

'It is a time of great difficulty that has made us recreate the Circle and bring you all here in a gathering.' Zieen had been sat in the central chair in the Circle but had stood to address the people who had now filled the chairs in front of him. 'We must act now, or succumb to the rule of Paluuka, who even now is working to retake the City.'

There were some mumblings around the room as people took in this piece of information.

They had arrived a short time after hearing the bell. Grancathai and Mal had explained to a large number of people where they had to go, but some already knew what they had to do; the information passed down from their parents and grandparents who had been called to the Meeting Hall years before.

It had not taken long for the news of Jasmine's actions to spread amongst the people, she and Kohrstan had spoken to a number of them as they entered and took their seats around the tables in the Hall.

There was a degree of segregation amongst the people; the Lessers and the Tops did not mix around the tables. In fact, nearly all of the Lessers were sat on one side of the hall, and the Tops on the other. It was this problem of separation that Jasmine would have to solve in order to unite the people.

Grancathai had spoken first and explained to everyone the threat that was hanging over all of them, and explained exactly what Jasmine and Mal had done over the past few days by entering the Catacombs and going to Paluuka's Temple. It was a story that shocked many people who were unsure if the stories about the Truth Slayer were true.

Zieen continued his speech. 'I am a Lesser from the Catacombs, and I stand in front of you today, not as someone who has come here to create trouble in the City, but as someone who can help. We are homeless, we can no longer live in the Catacombs, Paluuka will have already seen to that, and we come here to form a union between our two peoples. There should never have been a divide amongst our people; the Truth Slayers that lived long ago separated us, but they are no longer among us and the old boundaries need no longer be in place.'

There were further mumblings around the hall; the people were not inclined to believe a Lesser, even if he was sat in the Circle among a group of Tops.

Zieen turned to Jasmine and nodded. It was this signal that made Jasmine feel even more nervous; it was her turn to speak.

Standing slowly, Jasmine took a deep breath and faced the people. 'I have lived among the people of the City and met people in the Catacombs and call them my friends. I have explored the Catacombs, climbed the stairs to the Lookout and the Old City, and I have been to Paluuka's Temple.

'I would not have been able to stop the Tamboli rooms if it wasn't for the help of both peoples, and as Grancathai has already explained to you, the Tamboli rooms are no more, and will never be again. I stand now before you, not as a Lesser or a Top, but simply as a person who lives in the Realm of Martiblak, and you are all the same, whether you are a Top or a Lesser you are the same.'

Jasmine motioned towards Zieen and Grancathai for them to stand and took their hands as they did, holding them high as a symbol of friendship.

'We cannot stop Paluuka if we are divided and he knows that, but together we can stop him. If we live in fear of each other then Paluuka will win, but united he cannot do anything to us at all.'

People began to turn to one another, some nodded their heads in agreement, and others looked blankly around the room;

unsure about the information they were getting.

Jasmine returned to her seat, she was shaking with nerves but pleased that she had managed to give a good speech. She had never been good at public speaking and had gone over in her head what she should say numerous times before she had spoken.

Zieen also returned to his seat and allowed Grancathai to address the people again. 'We are acting as the Circle and ask all of you to break down the boundaries between you and work together to stop Paluuka.

'If you agree that this needs to be done, then go now and get the tools of your trade and come back here. We need craftsmen of all different disciplines, builders, architects, rope makers, carpenters and blacksmiths. In addition, we need labourers, and people who know the City well and can find materials and tools.

'The people from the Catacombs have great skills but they were unable to bring any tools with them when they fled their homes so will need the help of the people of the City to give them the equipment they need.

'The Circle will remain here, and await your return.' Grancathai returned to his seat.

Slowly the people from the City began to leave their seats and head towards the doors. The people from the Catacombs remained where they were sat, as they did not have any equipment of their own that they could fetch. They would all work to save the City as they had nowhere else to go, but it was not known if anyone else would believe the stories that they had heard or simply return to their normal lives.

The small group of people waited patiently; sat on the Circle chairs. The people from the Catacombs sat around waiting at the nearby tables or pacing around chatting to one another. A few of them were beginning to make plans on how they could barricade the entrances to the Catacombs and prevent Paluuka from ever coming into the City.

A long time passed and none of the City folk had returned. Jasmine began to think that they were not coming back at all.

They had, for too long, ignored the life around them, and continued their own existence without concern for others.

The members of the Circle were preparing to leave when a man walked through the door and entered the meeting hall. He was carrying a large bundle of coloured ropes.

Close behind the rope maker; a woman walked in with metal hammers and chisels and a few lengths of timber that she had found.

It was such a relief to see people returning with tools and equipment. A long line of people began to enter carrying as much as they could. They were nervous to begin with, but soon started to talk to the people from the Catacombs.

It was a magical sight; they needed very little guidance, they just knew what had to be done and started to do it. The barriers of separation that had been between them had started to tumble in sight of their unified goal of protecting the City.

The craftsmen shared out their tools with the people from the Catacombs, ensuring that the right tools were given to the people with the right experience and skills. Some of them departed to other areas of the City where materials were given to them and almost instantly; plain blocks of stone were chipped into rectangular blocks, branches from trees were trimmed into planks and ropes were turned into straps in which to carry the materials easily.

There had not been an event like this for a very long time and for many people it felt good. They were facing an imminent and terrible danger but something inside made them feel that they could face anything. There were, of course, a large number of people from the City who still distrusted the Lessers but that would pass in time.

Grancathai and Zieen had been right about the Lessers and the Tops uniting; together it made them very strong.

CHAPTER 13

Walls of Stone

The construction had begun. All over the City, people were busy. Some gathered around the library entrance and awaited instruction from Grancathai, Zieen and a team of engineers who had taken up residency in the Library.

Jasmine has begun by assisting a woman named Jules to bundle together some large wooden poles and carry them to the top of the Catacombs entrance. A man named Cavrell from the Catacombs was there and was ready to use them as construction materials.

Mal had left Jasmine at the top of the Catacombs entrance and went to help guide people into the Outer City. Once they knew the rooms of the Outer City they could travel back and forwards on their own, but first; Mal had to take them through the conveyance corridor.

Kohrstan knew where there were stores of materials and spent a long time taking people to ancient storerooms that his father had found and stocked with a variety of equipment and resources.

There was an excited buzz around the City. People were scared, but more importantly they had hope in being able to protect the City from Paluuka.

Jasmine, as she worked, had many people stop and speak to her about what she had experienced in Paluuka's Temple. Everyone had great admiration for the young woman and enjoyed hearing stories of her travels, even if Jasmine herself did not enjoy telling them. She just wanted to work hard, and assist Cavrell in making a hoist to lower materials down to the small room below.

Cavrell had bound the tops of the wooden beams together with lengths of rope, and stood them over the vertical tunnel in the shape of a large tripod. In the centre, a pulley had been attached with a rope tied to a large bucket. Stones and other materials could be lowered down to the chamber below and then the bucket could be hoisted back up again.

The hoist was nearly finished; Cavrell was tying the last beams of wood between the bottoms of each leg of the tripod to keep them firmly in position.

Scores of people had already begun to arrive carrying the large blocks of stone that would form the protective wall. In addition to the larger stones, some people were carrying baskets filled with smaller stones or mortar to build the wall with.

As each person arrived, they stacked the materials they had brought against one of the sidewalls and left to get more. The engineers had said they would need to build a very thick and strong wall, and so a large amount of building materials was needed.

Jasmine was still assisting Cavrell, passing him pieces of rope and holding the beams in position as he lashed them securely together.

'Jasmine, I am ready to start lowering materials down the shaft,' Cavrell said as he had finished his last lashing and stood back to admire his work. 'It is time for the builders to go down, are they still waiting in the library?'

Jasmine nodded. 'Yes, I think they are just finalising their plans. I will go to see them and let them know you are ready.'

The library was a buzz with activity as Jasmine entered through the short tunnel onto the bottom floor.

Grancathai was busily looking along one of the shelves on the ground floor, looking for information that might help in building defences for the City.

Sat around the big table on the ground floor were five construction engineers from the Catacombs, looking over large paper diagrams and discussing different ideas.

Zieen and Anarlia were sat quietly reading in a corner. Although Anarlia had had a lot of contact with the people of the

Catacombs, she had never learnt to read the ancient language, that Jasmine and Zieen knew, but she could read the modern text that Grancathai's ancestors had developed.

Kohrstan was sat nearby having a short rest. He was a runner; taking important information from the engineers in the library to the workers all around the City.

'Zieen?' Jasmine said quietly, not really wanting to disturb the man as he read a book about mining. 'I am sorry to bother you, but Cavrell said he is ready for the engineers to go down the shaft.'

Zieen closed his book and returned it to its shelf. 'Thank you Jasmine. I will inform them.'

The five construction engineers were still busy discussing the various parts of their plan when Zieen came over. They stopped speaking immediately as their See-Smith arrived, and looked on attentively.

'It is time to begin,' Zieen said quietly, to which all the engineers nodded and walked towards the library door.

The engineers were all very intelligent people and had planned, with precise detail, how the passageways between the City and the Catacombs would be sealed. It was more complex than it seemed. Paluuka was somewhere in the Catacombs, confused that the people had fled their homes. He would have a hard time believing that they had gone to the City and united with the people there.

The engineers knew that Paluuka did not have any of his big machines or any physical strength in his body that could break through the barrier they would create, but during its construction; some of the Paluuka's smaller machines may prove damaging or dangerous.

'The first wall is to be made here,' Martan said as he examined the tunnel walls. 'But we must work very quickly.'

Two of the engineers, Martan and Elenora, had descended the iron rungs into the small chamber below and walked partway down the tunnel that Jasmine and Mal had walked down when they had first entered the Catacombs.

They had stopped just before the large cavern with the three exits. It had been here that Jasmine and Mal had started to think it was impossible to get any further into the Catacombs. That was until they found the small ledge around the well.

Jasmine had gone down the rungs with the engineers and looked on inquisitively as they chose sections of the tunnel in which to build.

Elenora was a little further back down the tunnel. 'And this section here will be the second wall.'

Jasmine was unsure what they were looking for; the walls all looked the same to her. 'Is there any sign that Paluuka has come up here yet?' She asked Martan who had walked into the large cavern.

He shook his head. 'Not yet, he is probably working on a plan or something. That gives us a little bit of time. I don't suppose he has thought about the prospect of us blocking him in or rather out.'

'Martan?' Elenora called from the tunnel. 'Are you ready? We must begin.'

'Yes. Signal the others to start bringing down the stones and send down the masons.'

Elenora called up the vertical tunnel to the people above and like a well-oiled machine; the people began to work.

The engineers' plan was in two parts. They knew it would take quite a long time to build the strong defensive wall so they needed a way to stop Paluuka getting to them before it was completed. Their solution was simple; they would build a mound of stones in a pile to the top of the tunnel. It would need to be a big pile of stones and as thick as possible to give them the time they needed to build the second wall.

Not long after Elenora had called up the shaft, a number of people had descended and large rough blocks of stone had already begun to be sent down using the bucket and rope.

The people spread themselves out down the tunnel and as each stone block arrived at the bottom, they passed it along the line. This was a very efficient method to move the countless number of blocks down the narrow tunnel.

Two more engineers had also descended and were examining the section of the wall that Elenora had picked out. They would need to cut deep groves into the sides of the tunnel in order to build the barrier into the existing sidewall; it would not be strong enough to simply build across it and just have it butting up against the wall. Luckily, there was just enough space to work on either side of the line of people carrying the stones.

Jasmine was not as strong as the other people carrying the stones were but helped position them as best she could in the pile.

A long time passed, and so many stones had been passed along the line that Jasmine had lost count. Her hands were sore and her muscles tired; it was an extremely physical job.

The tired young woman stood aside for a moment to rest. This was something that most people had done at one point or another; stepped out of the line for a few moments and let the other people move along slightly to fill the gap.

Although they had been working for a long time, the mound of stones was barely as high as Jasmine's knees. They were definitely going to need more people soon to replace those too tired to continue.

'Martan, are there more people waiting at the top to come down here?' Jasmine asked the engineer who was overseeing the work of the masons, who had made only slight progress through the dense stone. 'If there are, I think we should fetch them now; the people carrying the stones are much stronger than me but they too are starting to tire.'

Martan nodded and ran a hand through his dark hair. He too looked tired; his face was pale and his eyes distant. His white robe was dusty and looking grey rather than the brilliant white that it normally was. 'There should be some people up there, if there aren't enough then you should speak to Zieen.'

Jasmine agreed and carefully walked back along the tunnel and up the metal rungs. Her fingers were very sore and it was difficult to climb the shaft, but time was running out and everyone needed to work as fast as they could; sore fingers could not slow her down.

Back in the tunnel, Martan walked over to the people cutting the grooves into the wall. They had marked out lines across the floor, up both walls and across the ceiling, but had not got very far in cutting the grooves.

'The stone is very hard,' Elenora said putting down her chisel for a moment to dust off her clothes. Each time she hit the chisel against the wall with a hammer it created dust and small fragments that showered her clothes and hair. 'It will take longer than expected to cut the grooves deep enough.'

Martan examined the walls. The grooves were about as wide as Jasmine's shoulders but only a few centimetres deep at the moment. They had to be ten times deeper to make the wall strong enough.

Elenora and the two other stoneworkers had concentrated on the grooves on the walls and had not even started the floor or ceiling yet. It would be easier to do those after the blockade of stones was finished further down the tunnel and the line of people was no longer there.

'We will try and finish the first blockade as soon as possible and give you more room to work,' Martan said after a brief pause. 'If you need more people; speak to Jasmine and she will find people with the right skills. You are doing a good job; just keep working as fast as you can.'

Elenora was strong and determined, although she had a strange feeling in her heart because they were blocking off the entrance to what used to be her home, the Catacombs.

In the Outer City, work was moving a little slower but the tunnel they had to block was a lot narrower and lower than at the bottom of the shaft with metal rungs.

Kohrstan and Mal were working with Anarlia to organise the people who were also carrying stones and creating a similar two-stage barrier.

Just beyond the small entrance to the lookout, a mount of stones was being created on the steps. It was slightly more difficult to stack the stones on a surface that was stepped, but the engineers were very clever and carefully placed large stones on the lower steps to support the layers that went on top.

Mal often thought about Jasmine and wished he was with her, but agreed with her decision that they were needed in different places. The young man had never experienced these feelings before. He cared for Jasmine deeply, she was the closest friend he had ever had and would do anything for her and hoped that whatever she was doing at the moment was not bringing her too much pain or difficulty.

'Mal? What will happen if Paluuka comes up the stairs now?' Kohrstan asked quietly as they rested for a moment in Anarlia's study. 'The wall is not finished and won't protect us.'

Mal looked at his friend. 'I don't know. I'm not sure Grancathai or Zieen know what would happen either. He is only a man and could easily be killed, but he has a great intelligence and wouldn't risk coming up here if he thought he could so easily be stopped. Zieen said he has machines that do terrible things and can protect him.'

'You're not making me feel better,' Kohrstan said frowning.

'Your father taught us to always tell the exact truth and I am sure you wouldn't expect anything less from me.' Mal smiled and patted his friend on the back. 'I'm sure we will finish the wall in time.'

Time seemed to lose its meaning as the work continued. A Tamboli room would have taken away all the thoughts that you had, except the one you had when you became trapped. In some ways, the work they were doing made the people feel a little like that. They had one goal, one thought in their minds, and whatever job they were doing was all a part of that single purpose; stopping Paluuka from entering the City.

The piles of stones grew higher and the deep grooves being cut into the walls became deeper, but in achieving this, the people were becoming increasingly more exhausted. Amazingly, exhaustion was not preventing people from working. They would rest for a short time or quickly dash away to get food, but return as soon as they could and continue to work.

Jasmine had lost count of the amount of times she had climbed up and down the metal rungs to find certain people, or check where tools or equipment was and if they were ready to be brought down and used in the walls' construction.

Far below the City in a dark recess of the Catacombs, a withered grey figure stood quietly, arranging metal objects on a low table. His wrinkled hands moved slowly and carefully attaching the parts together and filling small containers with liquids and a very fine sand like material.

The man had spent a long time building something, and it was nearly finished. Every workshop, cupboard and storeroom throughout the Catacombs had been pillaged to get the precious materials that he needed. Only a little longer was needed and he could begin a journey upward towards the City.

Hate and anger was pouring from the man and darkness had penetrated deeper into his very soul. He was Paluuka, at least he was the body of Paluuka; the final act of defiance from the people of the City had made him lose all sense of being. He was now only a shell of a man with only a single thought brewing in his rapidly emptying mind- revenge!

In the library, Grancathai sat speaking to Zieen. They were trying to workout what should happen after they had completed the walls and made the City safe. The union between the Lessers and the Tops was strong now as they had a distinct goal before them. Once that no longer existed, it was uncertain whether they would continue to co-exist peacefully or if the distrust and fear they had endured for years would return.

'There is only one solution Zieen, and we both know what that is. The Council Guardians must be elected.'

'But the people of the Catacombs have never had a system like that; they are more used to having See-Smiths, Providers and Halliers to create order. Only the very old people in the City will remember the time of the Council and the role they played in running the City. I know it wasn't too long ago that the meeting hall was used for feasts but not as a council chamber; the council chairs don't even exist any more.'

Grancathai stood from the table and paced the room. 'I can see no other option. The Circle must elect a new Council to run the City.'

'If there is no other option then that is what me must do, but remember my friend, the Circle can only elect members of the Council if the people want them too. We must use the stones of Chan-chey.'

Grancathai nodded. 'Then it is agreed, we will ask the people if they want a new Council and then elect the members as is the old custom. Even if they choose against it, we cannot interfere, as it is not solely our choice to make. As members of the Circle we can only do what the people want.'

Jasmine wiped her arm across her forehead and then looked at her sleeve. It was soaked with sweat and thick grey dust and dirt had covered the once bright yellow colour. In front of the young women was a mound of stones and rocks that nearly reached the ceiling.

The stones had been carefully arranged allowing the last few stones to be pushed into place without dislodging any others.

Most of the people, who had been passing the large stones down the corridor, had left; only a few now remained.

The final stones that were to be placed at the top of the mount were stacked nearby and most of the stones for the strong wall had also been brought down and placed tidily in lines near the grooves.

'Jasmine?' Elenora called from back down the tunnel. 'How much longer will you be? We are nearly ready to start laying stones over here.'

'You can lay the first few stones if you need to,' Jasmine said turning. 'We can step over what you have built if it isn't too high...' Jasmine stopped abruptly she heard a strange noise behind her. Martan heard the noise as well and they both turned towards the mound of stones.

Two people were lifting one of the last few stones into place when suddenly a waft of boiling hot air came rushing through the gap. It hit them and they fell to the ground gasping for breath; their skin burnt red like the worst sunburn.

Smoke accompanied the raging heat and the sound of shattering stones on the other side of the mound. Jasmine helped the two people back down the tunnel, they were hurt but luckily, they had only felt the effects for a moment and would heal.

The temperature in the tunnel was increasing and the air was becoming thick and hard to breath. Most of the heat was still high up at the top of the tunnel but slowly it would increase and heat the air below it. They did not have much time until they would all be roasted alive.

'Paluuka is trying to break through the mound using something that generates heat,' Martan said coughing loudly. 'We must stay as low as we can to escape the fumes and the scorching hot air.'

'But how can we finish the wall if we have to stay crouching?' Jasmine asked covering her mouth with her sleeve.

'Smaller stones!' Elenora called out from further down the tunnel. 'We can throw loads of smaller stones up into the gap. It will take a long time and we probably wont fill the entire gap, but it will stop a lot of the heat and smoke from getting through.'

Martan turned to Jasmine. 'I need you to go back to the rungs and get someone to find as many small stones as you can, about the size of a fist should be the right size, hurry! Go as fast as you can, we haven't got long before it will be too hot to work in here.'

Jasmine turned and scurried off, keeping her body and knees bent to keep her away from the hottest air above.

'And bring back wet blankets and buckets of water to help us keep cool,' Elenora shouted as Jasmine reached the shaft.

The further away from the mound of stones Jasmine got the cooler the air became and when she arrived at the top of the rungs, the air felt fresh.

Out of breath after the long climb, she hurriedly explained to a group of people what they needed to get and they rushed off at full speed.

Martan had started to break some of the remaining large stones into smaller pieces and carefully threw them into the gap at the top of the mound. The heat was almost unbearable but they must find a way to give them enough time to finish the second wall.

Elenora had started placing the first few stones into the groove on the floor and fixing them in place with thick mortar, when suddenly she had an idea. She picked up the metal bucket filled with the brown mortar and ran towards the mound of stones. Feeling the intense heat, she hurtled the contents of the bucket at the gap at the top. Martan dived out of the way as the mortar sloshed into the gap, partly filling it. The heat dried the mortar within a couple of moments and it cracked but most of it stayed in place.

There was a noticeable drop in temperature as the smoke and heat had a much smaller gap to travel through, and the stone walls were good at absorbing the excess heat in the tunnel.

Martan continued throwing stones into, the now, much smaller gap in an attempt to plug it further.

Jasmine returned soon with five other people. Two were carrying cloth bags filled with pebbles and small stones, the others were carrying pales of water and sodden blankets.

The water was taken from the pails and thrown over Martan and Jasmine who were closest to the mound as they attempted to throw more stones into the gap. The blankets were nearby in case the heat increased any more.

The wall, Elenora and a few others were building, was very complex; it was built into the deep grooves all around the tunnel and was reinforced by thick metal bars in certain places. It was time-consuming work to fix each block in place with mortar and place each metal bar in exactly the right place, but the people worked as quickly as they could.

The engineers had expected it to take at least whole day to complete the strong wall but it was unlikely they had that much time. Luckily, there was one factor working in their favour; the temperature in the tunnel had increased dramatically and the air had become exceptionally dry making the mortar dry much faster. They no longer had to wait for so long for the mortar to dry before adding the next layer.

The wall was almost half way up when Jasmine and Martan, having almost filled the gap, left the mound and climbed over the strong wall. They could only hope that the mound would hold long enough to allow the wall to be finished.

The height of the wall increased; the mortar drying quickly and everyone helping by passing stones to Elenora and the other workers.

The sound of breaking stones in the mound was incredibly loud. Jasmine was concerned that Paluuka may be able to use the same device to break the stones in the second wall and break through, but Martan assured her that the second wall was made with a different type of stone, and even the mortar would withstand the heat; once it had been dried sufficiently. It was just imperative that the wall was finished quickly.

The heat was stifling and the work was back breaking. Everyone was working as hard as they could but they were all exhausted. The workers threw water over themselves in an endeavour to keep themselves cool, but nothing could stop the heat from attacking their skin and their lungs.

Occasionally there would be a big rumble and a section of stones in the mound would slide downwards, shaken from their position by whatever machine Paluuka was using. The gap at the top of the mound had also started to get bigger allowing more smoke through. It would not take long before the mound collapsed further allowing the ancient Truth Slayer and his terrible machines though.

It had seemed like it had taken an eternity, but all of a sudden, there were no more stones to place in the wall, it was at last finished. It stood proud and strong across the tunnel and would protect the City. It was only a wall, but it served as protection and as a symbol of what could be achieved when the two peoples of the underground realm worked together. The pale grey stones and the thick brown mortar was a glorious sight.

When the last stone was being carefully edged into position, Jasmine saw a couple of bright flashes as the top of the mound collapsed. She had expected to see Paluuka's face appearing through the large gap but there was only smoke and flame, and then it all disappeared behind the strong wall.

The group of workers stood back for a moment. They had been working for such a long time to build this wall and now it was complete it was almost difficult to understand that they had nothing left to do.

They did not bother to collect their tools; they just left the tunnel and climbed back up the shaft. Their limbs were tired; their skin sore and red from the heat and their fingers cut and bruised.

Martan was last to climb the metal rungs and as he did so, to carefully cut each rung below him; making it impossible for anyone else to climb up after him.

The top of the shaft was a buzz of activity and as Martan hauled himself off the last rung, a large wooded frame was lowered into place over the hole and then covered in large stone slabs.

The walls in the Outer City had also been completed and the door to the lookout stairs nailed shut and reinforced with thick wooden beams.

It was done; it was complete. No one would ever be entering the Catacombs again and Paluuka would never find his way into the City.

CHAPTER 14

A New Beginning for Old Things

The library was very quiet; the quietest it had been since they had started work on building the walls. Grancathai and Zieen were sitting around the large table on the ground floor of the library. The Catacombs' engineers had left to find somewhere to live in the City. Grancathai and Anarlia had carefully archived the plans they had drawn up, and all of the exhausted workers had eaten and drunk at the Givings and then returned to their home rooms to sleep.

'Today we are going to confirm that the people want to continue having the Circle, and to choose the members of the Council,' Zieen said sipping a glass of water. 'What will we do if the people choose *not* to have a circle anymore?'

Grancathai sighed. 'It is a possibility, but I would think they would be more inclined to keep the Circle and elect the Council rather than nothing. Surely they must see that we need leadership again.'

'That is true, something has to be better than nothing, but let us wait until the others arrive before we discuss this further.'

'Jasmine! You must wake up now,' Mal said softly, not wanting to disturb Jasmine's sleep too suddenly. 'It is time for the gathering, we must go.'

Jasmine's eyes slowly flickered open. She had slept less than three hours, and was very tired. Her body was drained; the events of the last few days had taken their toll on the young woman. Her mind was full of sorrow from Paluuka's Temple, her body aching and sore from building the walls.

Mal took Jasmine's hand in his own and squeezed it gently. 'It is another big day Jasmine, the Circle is meeting very soon in the library.'

Jasmine wondered how the people of the City knew what soon meant; how could they arrange a time and know it was soon if they had no clocks, watches or any means to tell the time?

Reluctantly Jasmine got out of bed, quickly had something to eat and put on some clean clothes.

When all the work, the day before, had been completed, Jasmine had gone to the Pale Water to relax in the warm water and later returned to Mal's home room to sleep. It was a strange feeling to wake up on a new day after such a difficult few days before. Somehow, they did not seem real, they felt like a dream, but then Jasmine looked at the cuts and bruises on her body and the painful memories came flooding back.

Mal had collected some food and drink for Jasmine and she ate heartily before they left to meet the other members of the Circle in the library.

They were all exhausted. The last two days had been exceptionally long; none of them had had more than a few hours rest in the whole time, and they had been doing a lot of physical work.

During the building of the protective walls between the City and the Catacombs, they had all spent many hours moving huge blocks of stone, mixing mortar or chopping logs. Most of them had small cuts on their hands and knees and all of them had bruising somewhere on their body.

The group sat quietly for a moment, their eyes looking all around but seeing little.

Today they would hold a gathering and ask the people to decide if they wanted to have a Council of Guardians. Neither Jasmine nor Mal knew what the Council of Guardians was but Grancathai explained it was a group of seven people chosen by the Circle who they believed had the skills and the knowledge to lead the people of the City. They acted as the government and were there to care for and protect the people as well as leading them. One of the members was known as the Principal Guardian and was responsible for organising the other six and taking overall control.

They sat and discussed a number of different names, carefully deciding who should be elected if the people agreed that the Council should be made again. It was not an easy discussion; there were so many people that had worked tirelessly in the construction of the walls, some had shown great leadership and compassion and others already held positions of respect such as a See-Smith or Hallier. Each name put forward had to be carefully considered.

'Seven names,' Zieen said when the group had finished their discussions. 'Seven names have been chosen for the new Council members. Now all we need is to ask the people a very important question.'

'How do we ask everyone?' Mal asked, worried they would have to go around and speak to everyone individually.

'There is an old custom,' Grancathai said in answer. 'There are bags of small stones, much smaller than felostones but are similar in shape and texture. They will be placed in a pile in the entrance room of the Meeting Hall. We will call a gathering later today and ask the people if they want the Circle to elect the Council Guardians and they will each receive a stone of Chen-Chey. When they leave the meeting hall, they must place the stone in one of the two bags. One bag will mean that they agree to have the Council and the other will mean that they disagree. We will count the stones and get our answer.'

The Circle all agreed with Grancathai to use the Stones of Chan-Chey and later that day Mal ringing the large bell called a gathering in the Great Hall.

The people came and listened to what the Circle had to say and each received their small white stone. Most of the people knew very little about the voting process, but Grancathai explained in detail what they had to do.

After the gathering, Grancathai and Zieen counted all of the stones that been placed into the two bags. There was a lot to count and it took them a long time to come up with the decision that the people had made.

The important questioned had been fairly answered by the people; they wanted the Council of Guardians to be voted in. Grancathai believed it was a good decision and would make the City a much better place to live. The City, again, would have direction and leadership.

When they had finished counting Zieen called one of the carpenters from the Catacombs to him and asked him to make something important. It was very special but he only had one night to make it. Zieen knew the carpenter well and trusted him to do a good job in the small amount of time that he had.

Jasmine and Mal sat in their home room for a long time after the stones had risen discussing what would happen the next day. In some ways, they were still recovering from their difficult journey into Paluuka's temple and, at last, had the opportunity to talk with each other about it. Although they were close, they found it difficult to talk about their feelings and thoughts from such a difficult time.

Eventually they fell asleep next to each other and both dreamt about what the City would be like in the future. There had been huge changes already, but more would come and they both hoped things would change for the better.

A loud thud echoed around the City as the stones fell to their daytime resting place, followed shortly after by a loud ringing of the bell, calling people to the Great Hall.

Jasmine and Mal had woken early and waited for the stones to fall so Mal could rush off to the bell, and Jasmine could make her way to the meeting hall to help finish the preparations there. She was amazed when she arrived and saw at the far end of the room, some brand new chairs and a large table. It had been these seats that Zieen had asked the carpenter to make, and they had been built for the new Council.

Grancathai and Zieen were already in the meeting hall and the carpenter and his assistants were just finishing packing away their tools.

The table and chairs for the Council members were incredibly beautiful. Jasmine was amazed at the ability of the artisans who could produce things of such beauty in such a short amount of time. The table was a dark oak colour, and polished to a high gleam. It had eight legs, which were thick and stout to hold the weight of the large tabletop. The council chairs had been neatly arranged in a row behind the table. There were seven in total with the Principal Guardian's chair featuring in the middle. The other six, grouped in threes, ran down each side of the middle chair.

All of the chairs were carved beautifully from a pale coloured wood. The backs were carved into the form of branches that interwove back and forth and joined at the top to form a single flower.

The Principal Guardian's chair was much higher than the others were and had a more uniform construction than the interweaving branches of the others. Its high back was simply two beams on either side rising to a point. Along the space between the side beams were four cross bars carved into a series of people in a line holding hands. The carpenters had designed this as a symbol of the Principal Guardian and their role in uniting and caring for all the people of the City.

Jasmine took her seat in the half circle of chairs they had used the day of the first union.

The room ahead of her was completely filled with people. The segregation that had been so apparent before was now almost non-existent. Lessers and Tops sat happily next to each other. The fear and uncertainty they held for each other was still present, but they were determined to work out their differences.

Every chair was filled, and even the walls were lined with people. Those who could not find a place to stand against the wall, or a chair to sit on had made their way to the front and sat on the floor; a few had climbed up to the far balcony and leant over the balustrade to get the best view they could.

As the last members of the circle took their seats, the entire room fell silent. All eyes turned towards the group of people in the Circle and waited expectantly for them to speak.

Grancathai stood and took a few deeps breaths. He had carried the white tiles of Chan-chey from the entrance room, and they were now lying out in front of him in wicker baskets.

'People of the City of Martiblak the Tiles of Chan-chey have been counted.' Grancathai spoke clearly although to Jasmine it seemed he had a slight nervousness in his voice. 'You have decided that the City needs a Council of Guardians to look after it and protect it. It is therefore a great honour to read out the names of the Council members. It will be the first Council there has been in three generations. By the placing of the tiles that you have all done, you agree that the Circle should nominate the Council members based on their strengths and abilities.

'The Council of Guardians and the Circle is an ancient way of ensuring that the City will always be a place of prosperity.

'When the Circle was originally created in the days of the Truth-Slayers, it was decided that they should have control over the people who sat in council chairs, as long as the tiles of Chan-chey agreed that they should. Once the Council has been chosen the circle will have no power to control their actions until it is agreed that a new Council should be elected.

'It is only with this fairness that we can truly learn to unite the two peoples of the realm of Martiblak. Once the Council have taken their seats, the circle will act as their advisors and nothing more.

'This is the decision you have made with the tiles of Chan-chey, a decision of fairness.'

Grancathai paused for a moment and took a strip of paper from his pocket.

'The Circle has nominated the following people to stand as the Council of Guardians. As is the ancient custom, if you are nominated you must freely choose if you want to sit at the council table, and may no one interfere with your decision.'

At the end of Grancathai's speech; Zieen stood and was handed the small strip of paper. It seemed only fair that a Lesser and a Top should share the calling of the Council members.

Zieen spoke with the same clarity as Grancathai but had an air of confidence about him. As a See-Smith in the Catacombs, he had a place of respect and responsibility, and was the leader of many people so was used to speaking as an important figurehead. 'The first to be nominated is Ortandarla. If you accept this responsibility please make your way to the council table.'

There was a slight murmur around the room as people looked around to see if the woman Zieen had mentioned would stand and walk to the council chairs.

After a few seconds, a tall blonde woman stood up from a table in the centre of the room. The room erupted with stamping feet and hands banging on tables in appreciation that she had accepted.

As she approached the table and sat down, Zieen spoke a little about her. 'Ortandarla is a talented craftswoman who makes rope and string. Her skills were vital in sealing the entrance to the Catacombs.'

When the room had returned to silence, Zieen called out the next name of the list. Again, the room erupted as a tall man named Lyon made his way to the council chairs. He was an engineer from the Catacombs and was an expert at building archways and stone walls.

The next two names that were called out were both Tenders, two brothers who had spent their lives caring for the plants and trees in the Givings.

An artist from the Catacombs was the second woman to be called and, like the others who had preceded her, had walked across the room and taken her seat at the council table amid sounds of stamping feet and table banging. The noise was a sign of approval for their new Council Guardians.

The last member of the Council Guardians to be called was a surprise to many people. As the name was called out a young girl, about thirteen years old stood from the floor in front of the Circle and made her way to the council chairs. She wore the customary white robes of the Catacombs. It seemed surprising that someone so young would be nominated as a Council

Guardian, and that she would have the courage to accept the responsibility. Zieen spoke about Fracey and the role she had played in helping the people escape from the Catacombs. Her strength and gymnastic abilities had proven helpful in helping the people climb the iron rungs into the City.

Sat at the council table was three men and three women; three of them were from the Catacombs and three were from the City. It seemed fair and just that they should choose people in equal amounts, but the equal group needed a spokes person. The Principal Guardian must be a person who could see both sides of every argument and who could guide and inspire the Council and all the other people in the City.

Jasmine recalled the night before when the Circle had sat in the library and discussed who they would nominate to be the Council Guardians and who would be the Principal Guardian and they could come to only one decision.

'Anarlia we ask you to sit as the Principal guardian,' Zieen said when the room had returned to complete silence. 'You have lived in the Outer City and had contact with both the people of the Catacombs and the people of the City. The circle decided you to be the only fair choice for this position.

Anarlia was sitting at a table just to the right of the Circle and as she stood the people cheered and stamped as loudly as they could. Calmly she walked towards the council table, but to everyone's surprise did not walk round the back and take her seat in the centre of the Council. Instead, she stood in front of the table, just behind the Circle, and raised her hands for quiet.

The people responded quickly and fell silent to wait for their Principal Guardian to speak.

'People of the Realm of Martiblak, I know you will agree with the Circle that I should take the place as Principal Guardian, and although I believe I could take on this responsibility; there is one other who is much better suited.

'I will sit as Principal Guardian if it is your wish, but first I wish to nominate another. I am not a member of the Circle and I have not yet taken my seat as Principal Guardian so I cannot officially make this nomination, but I feel it is important. I would like to ask the Circle to make the nomination for me, but the person I wish to nominate is in the Circle and therefore would not normally be open for nomination.

'This is a new Council, and a new way for us and I feel that Jasmine from the Old World should take her place as Principal Guardian. She came here from a different world but became our friend; she has travelled far through the catacombs and the outer City and journeyed to the dark Temple of Paluuka. She has worked tirelessly to rid our city of the threat of Tamboli and through courage and grace has united our two peoples. If you believe as I do, that Jasmine, a woman of strength and integrity, should be nominated, please now stand from your seats and thus cast your vote.'

Jasmine was struck by shock, her heart began pounding in her chest and her breathing quickened. It was unheard of for a member of the Circle to be nominated for such as position, and she was from the world above and not from the City or the Catacombs.

At first, there was silence around the room and not a soul made any move to stand up.

Anarlia started to look concerned, as soon as she had heard her nomination she had decided to concede the position to Jasmine, but only if the people agreed.

The room could have been turned into Tamboli as far as Jasmine was concerned; time was at a standstill, the room was silent and motionless.

Slowly Grancathai began to rise from his chair and spoke. 'Jasmine saved my life by being here to stop Paluuka. I stand to vote for her.'

Mal was quick to follow Grancathai's vote and also stood to speak. 'Jasmine is the kindest and most generous person I have ever met. I stand to vote for her.'

'It is not normal for a member of the Circle to take a place among the Council Guardians but this is a new time, and Jasmine's heart is pure and she has a strong mind.' Zieen spoke with his normal clarity, but it was obvious a lot of feeling was going into his voice.

Jasmine was shaking more with each comment but was suddenly overcome with emotions as everyone in the room began to stand up. There was not the normal cheering or foot stamping that came with the other nominations. A much deeper admiration was being given here; the complete silence that followed the speeches given by the members of the Circle was profoundly respectful.

After the initial influx of people of standing, it did not take long for everyone in the room to stand and thus cast their votes.

Nearly everyone in the City and in the Catacombs knew jasmine. Her determination to confront Paluuka was now almost legendary, even though it had been such a short time ago.

Once she had been considered an outsider, an unknown person who claimed to be from the Old World. People had whispered around her when they had seen her at the Givings or spotted her walking around the City. Mal had instantly seen the goodness in her heart and her actions had proved that to the rest of the people.

The atmosphere was almost overwhelming as Jasmine slowly stood from her seat in the Circle. She was shaking from head to toe but nobody seemed to notice. Quietly and with careful footsteps, she walked from her chair in the Circle to the council table and sat down in her place as Principal Guardian.

Jasmine looked at the people still standing in front of her. They looked pleased that she had accepted her role as their Principal Guardian. The life she had known had changed beyond any recognition, she had set out to save people from the Tamboli Rooms. It had seemed simple enough at the time, to find the Tower of Light and destroy it but Jasmine could never have imagined that she would have to face Paluuka, unite the peoples of the Catacombs and the City, and finally take her seat as the Principal Guardian.

Thoughts and emotions were whizzing through Jasmine's mind as she sat silently on her chair; the large wooden table spread out in front of her. She had accepted the responsibility. It had only been a few seconds ago that she was sitting in the Circle, but it seemed like a distant dream, or was she living the dream now? Jasmine remembered when she first entered the City that she believed she was dreaming, or unconscious in the cellar of Hillcroft House. That dream had faded into reality, and now back again into a dream.

Jasmine knew her life would continue to be full of interest and excitement, but for the moment, she was nervous and overcome with mixed emotion.

The people were expecting Jasmine to speak, and she knew that. What should she say? What could anyone say who was not expecting to be in this position?

Cautiously, Jasmine stood, her knees still shaking a little. The people responded by quietly sitting down. Anarlia returned to her seat over on the left of the Circle. She smiled at Jasmine and bowed her head slightly.

'I would like...' Jasmine began to felt a lump in her throat. She had spoken in front of all these people before when she convinced them that the people of the Catacombs and the people of the City could live together. Now things were different, she was no longer just a young woman telling people not to fear each other; she was now a leader and had even more important responsibility.

She would never have believed anyone who told her what would happen to her life when she entered Hillcroft House all that time ago, even dreams did not match the wonders she had seen or the difficulties she had faced.

She needed to say something, it should be something profound or important but Jasmine knew that it would be difficult to say very much at all.

'I came to this City as someone who was lost, and trying to get home. When I found all of you living here, and showing me so much kindness, I did not want to leave. I wanted to give something back to you and so I went with Malmayorkia to the temple across the lake and confronted Paluuka.

'I don't know what strength I have within me, but I will use all I have and be the best Principal Guardian I can be.

'I no longer think of this place, this City as just your home, but my home as well. Together we will make our home a place of happiness.' Jasmine stopped, her speech had come out better than she expected but did not want to continue in case she started to stumble or confuse her words.

What she had said was enough. The people smiled at her with admiration and love; a leader and figurehead that would help them remember the life they should have in the City and the golden age that had gone by; in recent times marred by Paluuka.

The gathering ended when Grancathai presented Jasmine with a small glass bell, which she held high and rang with all her might. The crystal sound echoed around the meeting hall amid cheers from the crowd.

The Council Guardians met in a small antechamber after the gathering and had their first official meeting. They had a lot to discuss but the first point of business was a feast to be held in ten days time. The meeting hall should be more than just a place that held official gatherings; it needed to be a place of fun and celebration as well.

The feast would give an opportunity for the Council members to wander around the people and speak more freely with them; identify how they wanted to the City to be, what skills the people had and how they could work together to make everything happen.

Jasmine was the last person to leave the antechamber but went straight to find Mal who was standing by the door to the entrance hall.

He smiled as she approached him. 'I know everything will be alright now you are in charge, but I hope you will still talk to me sometimes.'

Jasmine laughed; something she had not done for a long time. 'Thank you Mal and you know that we will always be friends. Best friends.'

Mal turned a little red and looked into Jasmine's eyes. 'Yes, we will always be, friends.'

There was a short pause as they looked into each other's eyes. Mal was first to break the silence. 'Do you want to go to the

Givings, I think we have a little while before the stones rise, and I am a little hungry.'

Mal seemed a little nervous when he spoke to Jasmine, possibly because she was now the Principal Guardian, but it seemed like another reason.

Jasmine led the way to the Givings. It was quiet there; the tenders had not worked today as they had been attending the gathering. A few people had gone to the small covered courtyard to fetch some food for the following day, or to have a quick snack before they went to sleep.

'Do you remember the first time I brought you here Jazz?' Mal asked as they walked towards a bush covered in bright red Bees. 'And I was teaching you how to pick these.'

'Yes I remember. It seems like a very long time ago.' Jasmine was now good at picking the fruit off the stems. 'This place was so different to what I was used to, but now it is home.'

Mal ate one of the berries and made further conversation. 'You said earlier that we would always be friends, and I would want nothing more than that, but...'

Jasmine sat down on the grass and Mal quickly followed and sat next to her. 'What is the matter Mal? I'm not sure what you are trying to say.'

Mal looked nervous again. 'I wanted to say that...well its not that I...maybe...'

The words that the young man wanted to say just would not come out and he stuttered, mixing up his words. Jasmine had an idea what he wanted to say, for she was thinking it too, and put a finger up to his lips. 'Perhaps there are no words to say.'

Slowly, with their hearts pounding in their chests, they leant forward. Their lips met and they kissed. It lasted only for a short moment, but in that time they realised the feelings they had towards each other was more than just friendship. They were deep and powerful feelings that had slowly grown from the moment they had first met. Through all the hardships they had been through; they had fallen in love and only now that the City was safe could they at last admit to themselves and to each other the love they felt.

They sat back from their kiss and smiled at each other. The kiss had been a nervous but electrifying moment, one they would never forget, and one that showed they both shared the same wonderful feelings for each other.

They hugged for a long time before lying down next to each other on the grass. It had been a long day and they were exhausted, it was nice just to lay in each other's company and rest.

The bell sounded, the stones began to rise, and Mal and Jasmine drifted off to sleep on the cool, green grass of the Givings. Tomorrow would be a new day, and new things would start to happen. Mal hoped the City would once again be full of happiness and joy and he knew Jasmine would never tire until their home was transformed back into the wonderful place it should be.

It had been hard work to convince the people that change could happen and it would be even harder for the changes to take place but there was a renewed and exciting sense of community amongst the people.

Change would happen, just as they wanted, it would just take time. Now, without the threat of Paluuka or Tamboli, and the Council of Guardians had been reinstated; they had all the time they needed, safe in their City under the world.

THE END